MW01068251

JOY AND JEALOUSY

An Isle of Man Ghostly Cozy

DIANA XARISSA

Text Copyright © 2019 DX Dunn, LLC
Cover Copyright © 2019 Linda Boulanger – Tell Tale Book Covers

ISBN: 978-1731446039

All Rights Reserved

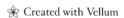 Created with Vellum

For everyone who loves the holiday season.

AUTHOR'S NOTE

Welcome to book ten in the Isle of Man Ghostly Cozy Series. I always suggest reading my series books in order (alphabetically), but each should be enjoyable on its own if you prefer not to do that. Fenella is getting ready for her first Christmas on the island, and I tried to incorporate some Manx and UK holiday traditions into the story.

As with all books in this series, I've primarily used American English except when British or Manx characters are speaking. I'm sure I've made a few mistakes throughout the story, and if you find any, please let me know. They are, fortunately, very easy to correct.

The Isle of Man, a UK crown dependency, is a unique and wonderful place, and I love having the opportunity to write about it and share it with readers. I hope you all enjoy visiting this special location with me through my stories.

This is a work of fiction. All of the characters are products of the author's imagination. Any resemblance to actual persons, living or dead, is entirely coincidental. The shops, restaurants, and businesses in this story are also fictional. The historical sites and other landmarks on the island are all real; however, the events that take place within them in this story are fictional.

My contact details are available in the back of the book. I'd love to hear from you if you have the time to get in touch. I have a monthly newsletter that can help keep you up to date on new releases. You can sign up for the newsletter on my website (dianaxarissa.com). Thank you for coming along on another adventure with Fenella and her friends.

PS The T-shirts and sweatshirts for the Tale and Tail mentioned in the story are actually available. There is a link to the shop on my website. (You can buy a coffee mug, too.)

❧ I ☙

"**T**he flat looks stunning," Shelly Quirk said as she turned in a slow circle in the middle of Fenella's living room.

"You don't think it's too much?" Fenella Woods asked her closest friend on the island.

Shelly shook her head. "I think it's just right."

"It's too much," Mona Kelly said from where she was sitting on one of the couches near the windows. "When all the fairy lights are on it's brighter than the sun in here."

Fenella looked at her aunt and then sighed. It was a good thing Shelly was there, because that kept her from having to reply to the woman. Mona was either a ghost or a figment of Fenella's imagination, which meant that Shelly couldn't see or hear her. "There are a lot of Christmas lights," she said slowly.

Shelly laughed. "That's what makes it so wonderful. It feels very festive. Mona did something very similar last Christmas."

"Did she?" Fenella asked, glaring at her aunt, who shrugged and then faded away.

"Did you use all of the decorations from her storage room?" Shelly wondered.

"Oh, no. All of this came from only three boxes. There are prob-

I

ably a dozen more boxes of Christmas things down there, but I thought I'd done enough."

"You've definitely done enough," Shelly agreed. "Now come and see what I've done in my flat."

Fenella didn't bother to lock her door before she followed her friend into the apartment next to hers. "It looks lovely," she exclaimed. "I love the tree."

"Thanks. It's a bit large for the space, but John and I bought it about ten years ago and it brings back a lot of good memories of Christmases past."

"I don't think it's too large at all."

Shelly's husband, John, had passed away unexpectedly over a year earlier. On her own for the first time in many years, Shelly had sold the house that she'd shared with John and taken early retirement from her teaching job. She insisted now that moving in next door to Fenella's Aunt Mona had been the smartest thing she'd ever done. Mona had helped the woman deal with the worst of her grief and encouraged her to embrace life fully.

When Mona passed away and Fenella moved in, she and Shelly quickly became good friends. Fenella only knew Shelly as the vibrant woman who wore bright colors and laughed often, but she knew that, in spite of outward appearances, Shelly still missed her husband and their former life together.

"What time do you need to leave for the airport?" Shelly asked.

Fenella sighed deeply and then glanced at her watch. "Probably now. Jack's flight is due to land in about an hour. The last time I checked it was on time."

"I wish I could go with you. I'm quite eager to meet Jack."

Fenella laughed. "I wish you could go and get him. I really don't want to see him again."

Fenella and Jack Dawson had been a couple for more than ten years, which was about ten years longer than they should have been together, at least as far as Fenella was concerned. It had been a comfortable relationship, so much so that Fenella had never found a good reason to end it, but once she'd inherited Mona's estate on the Isle of Man she'd finally had the motivation she'd needed to break up with Jack. She'd quit her job as a university professor in Buffalo, New York, sold her house and all of its furnishings, and moved everything else with her to the island.

Nine months later, she was happily living a very different life from the one she'd left behind, but Jack apparently didn't want to move on. He'd called in November and informed her that he was coming to visit for Christmas, and nothing Fenella said could persuade him to change his mind. That may have been because she'd struggled to speak with him once he'd announced him impending arrival. He never answered his telephone and he never called her, either. She'd been surprised when a card had turned up in her mail giving his flight details.

"You will meet my plane, won't you?" Jack had scrawled across the card.

It seemed too cruel to leave a negative reply on the man's answering machine. Fenella reluctantly called to confirm that she'd be there, but found that his answering machine wasn't turned on.

"He's probably turned it off so you can't refuse to meet him," Mona had said.

"Or maybe his electricity has been turned off because he forgot to pay the bill," Fenella had sighed as she'd put the phone down.

Jack was the epitome of an absent-minded professor. When they'd first begun dating, not long after Fenella began teaching in the same department as Jack, she'd found his inability to cope with the real world charming and amusing. After ten years of doing nearly everything for him, she'd no longer been charmed or amused. What had remained after her move was a sense of guilt that she'd left him to muddle through on his own. When she'd first arrived on the island he'd called her frequently with dozens of questions, but the calls had slowed some in the past few months. That he'd managed to get himself a passport and arrange for flights to the island suggested that he wasn't nearly as helpless as he often pretended.

"What are you going to do with him once he arrives?" Shelly asked.

"I'm hoping he'll be too jet-lagged to want to do anything more than get settled where he's staying."

"Which is where?"

"I have no idea. He told me that he'd met some man with a house on the island and that the man gave him the keys. I hope he also gave him the address."

"The whole thing sounds odd to me," Shelly said.

"It sounds odd to me, too, but I don't want Jack staying with me, so I really hope it works out."

"What if it doesn't?"

"Then I'll put him in the house on Poppy Drive, I suppose."

Fenella had inherited more than just a large apartment on the Douglas promenade from Mona. Much to Fenella's surprise, the woman had owned a great deal of property all over the island. Fenella's lawyer (or advocate to use the Manx term) Doncan Quayle, managed all the properties. A few months earlier, when one of her brothers had come to visit, Fenella had made use of one of the houses she owned in the Douglas suburbs. The house on Poppy Drive was large and comfortably furnished. As Fenella had yet to tell Doncan to rent it out again, it was available if Jack needed somewhere to stay.

"It's lucky you have that house," Shelly remarked. "Then Daniel can keep an eye on Jack for you, too."

Fenella flushed. The house in question was right across the street from Daniel Robinson's home. Daniel was an inspector with the island's police force, and he and Fenella had become quite good friends after they'd met over a dead body just after Fenella had arrived on the island. When Daniel had been sent to the UK for a lengthy course, both he and Fenella had dated other people. Now they were trying to work out where their relationship was going, although at the moment it seemed more like they were avoiding one another than anything else.

"I don't think that's likely to happen," Fenella muttered, "but I'd better get going." She made a face.

"I can ring Tim and cancel our plans if you want me to go with you," Shelly offered.

"No, you go and have fun with Tim. Jack is my problem. I have to deal with him."

Shelly had been dating Tim Blake for a few months. They were taking things slowly, and they seemed very happy together. Fenella didn't want to do anything to get in the way of their relationship.

"I'll ring you later to hear how it all went," Shelly replied.

"I hope to be back home before too long. Like I said, I'm hoping to just drop Jack off for tonight."

"Good luck."

Fenella went back into her apartment and quickly brushed her hair and touched up her lipstick. Her hazel eyes looked nervous as she brushed her shoulder-length brown hair. Just last week she'd had it trimmed and had the color touched up. She'd also had a few highlights added. She did want Jack to think she looked well, even if she didn't want him back.

"You don't intend to get back with him, do you?" Mona asked as she walked into Fenella's bedroom.

"Absolutely not."

"Good. He was all wrong for you."

"You've never met him."

"No, but I've heard enough about him to know that you were never happy with him. Remember that when he starts begging you to take him back."

Fenella shuddered. "I hope it won't come to that."

She grabbed her handbag and headed for the garage under the building. Mona's little red convertible was tempting, but Fenella opted to drive the much more sensible car that she'd purchased herself instead. It was the sort of car that Jack would be expecting her to be driving, which made her frown as she slid behind the steering wheel. As Jack was bound to have several suitcases, though, it made sense to take the larger car.

The drive to the airport didn't take as long as Fenella had hoped it might. She parked near the entrance and then walked inside. A quick look at the arrivals screen told her that Jack's plane was still expected on time. With half an hour to fill, she wandered around the terminal, looking through the small gift shop and then studying the menu in the café. Nothing was even the slightest bit tempting. Her stomach was in knots and she was dreading Jack's arrival more than she'd imagined she would. When she heard the announcement that Jack's flight had landed, she made her way back down to the arrivals area and took a seat.

Her heart skipped a beat when she spotted Jack's familiar figure.

While she was no longer interested in being romantically involved with him, Jack still held a place in her heart after their ten years together. They'd been more like brother or sister than lovers, especially after their first few months together, but she'd once cared very deeply for Jack and for a moment she was actually happy to see him.

He strode up to the baggage claim and waited patiently while the bags were unloaded onto it. Fenella watched as he gathered up three huge suitcases. She knew he was planning to stay for five weeks, but he seemed to have enough luggage for a much longer visit. She waited until he'd made it through the baggage claim exit and into the arrivals hall before she stood up and waved to him. He blinked at her and then began to shake his head.

"I hope I have everything," he said, sounding flustered as she joined him.

"How many suitcases did you bring?" she asked.

"Three."

"And you have three now, so you must have everything."

"I mean I hope I remembered to pack everything," he countered. "I made a list, but then I couldn't find it when I was actually doing my packing. I'm afraid I've forgotten important things."

"You have your medication?" Fenella asked. Jack was in good health, but needed tablets for his blood pressure and cholesterol every day.

"Yes, of course," he replied, "but I may have forgotten shampoo."

"You can buy shampoo here."

"But it won't be the same shampoo."

Fenella swallowed a sigh. "It might be, but if it isn't, I think you'll survive."

Jack frowned and then shook his head again. "But I was planning to greet you with a hug," he said. He took an awkward step toward her and then glanced down at his bags. "I don't want to get distracted, though. Someone might steal my bags."

"Let's just forget about the hug, then," Fenella suggested.

"Yes, but, well, I mean, I've missed you."

"And now you're here for a long visit. I don't know what you're going to do with yourself for five weeks."

"I thought I could spend them with you," Jack told her. "I brought my checkbook so you can help me balance it."

Fenella smiled tightly. "Great. Let's get out of here." That seemed preferable to starting to shout at him in public, anyway. She was Mona Kelly's niece and she had a certain reputation to uphold, after all. She turned and began to walk briskly out of the airport. Jack followed, struggling to drag all of his bags along with him. After a few paces, Fenella stopped.

"Let me help," she sighed.

"If you could take this one, I can manage the rest," Jack told her, handing her the largest of the bags.

"Why didn't you get luggage with wheels on it?" Fenella asked as she began to walk again.

"This was affordable."

"Of course it was."

The walk back to the car seemed to take forever. The bag Fenella was carrying was heavy, and Jack kept stopping every few feet to shift the bags he had from hand to hand. When they finally reached the car, Fenella was happy to finally put the heavy bag down.

"This is your car?" Jack asked.

"Yes, why?"

"I don't know. It isn't what I was expecting you to be driving."

As Fenella didn't know how to reply to that, she didn't bother. Instead, she loaded all of the bags into the trunk and then gestured to Jack. "Climb in."

He headed for the driver's door, which would have been the passenger door on an American car. Fenella smiled and then caught his arm. "Other side," she told him.

"I find that very peculiar," he told her as he opened the passenger door.

"I've gotten used to it."

"I suppose I will as well."

Fenella bit her tongue before she could reply. Hopefully he wouldn't be staying long enough to get used to anything, but it would be rude to say that to him.

"Where are we going?" she asked as they both fastened their seatbelts.

"What do you mean?"

"You told me you were staying at some man's house. What's the address?"

"Oh, yes, well, I just thought, that is, couldn't we just go to your apartment?" Jack asked. "I'm not sure about staying at Peter's house."

Fenella turned in her seat and looked at Jack. "What do you mean?"

"I just met the man at a party, you see," he said. "We only talked for a few minutes, mostly about women and what trouble they were. I told him all about you and how you'd moved away and broken my heart. When he heard where you were living now, he immediately offered me the use of his house for Christmas. At the time I was excited, but now that I think about it, it seems rather odd."

"It does," Fenella agreed. "What do you know about him?"

"His name is Peter Grady. Dr. Peter Grady. He teaches at a university in Liverpool but has a home here as well. He actually said that I'd be doing him a favor if I stayed at his house here, that I could keep an eye on things for him."

"I suppose that makes some sense."

"He said something about there being a lot of burglaries on the island in the last few months."

"There have been, actually," Fenella agreed.

"Right, so he said I could stay at his house, and then he gave me the keys and instructions on how to turn off the security system."

"If he has a security system why is he worried about burglars?" Fenella wondered.

"I don't know."

"Is Dr. Grady still in the US, then?"

Jack frowned. "I'm not sure where he is. He didn't actually say, or if he did, I don't remember. I'd had a few drinks, you see, and I'm sure he had, as well."

"Probably, if he gave his house keys to a total stranger."

"I wasn't a total stranger, exactly. We have mutual friends."

"Who?"

"Oh, well, I mean, he knew Hazel from some conference they'd both attended a few years back."

Hazel was another professor who had worked with both Jack and Fenella at the same university.

"So where does Dr. Grady live?" Fenella asked.

Jack shrugged. "Surely it would just be easier if I stayed with you."

"That isn't happening."

"What do you mean? We practically lived together for years."

"But we didn't. I always had my little house and you always had yours. We may have stayed with one another sometimes, but we never lived together."

"You're splitting hairs," Jack complained. "We were a couple for over ten years."

"We were, and then we broke up nearly a year ago. Staying together would not be appropriate."

"I'm sure a hotel for six weeks would be very expensive."

"I can probably find somewhere for you to stay," Fenella said slowly. "I have a friend who owns some rental properties. He may have somewhere you could stay." She didn't want Jack to know the extent of her fortune. Besides, if he knew that she owned the house on Poppy Drive, he might decide to stay even longer.

"That would probably be for the best, if you can arrange it."

"I'll need to make a few phone calls," Fenella said, "and you must be tired. Why don't I drop you off at Dr. Grady's house for a few hours? You can get some rest while I see what I can arrange."

Jack hesitated and then nodded. "I suppose that makes sense. I can check the place over for him, too, since he did ask me to look after it."

"Great, wonderful, let's go. Give me the address."

Jack pulled out his wallet and opened it. He read out an address that Fenella recognized. It seemed that Dr. Grady didn't live very far away from the house on Poppy Drive.

"That's a nice neighborhood," Fenella commented as she put the car into gear. "The houses are fairly new, too."

"Good. If it's really nice, maybe I'll just stay there."

We can hope, Fenella thought.

"There are palm trees," Jack said in surprise as they made their way out of the airport parking lot.

"Wave to the little people," Fenella told him a short while later.

Jack stared at her as she waved toward Fairy Bridge.

"You didn't wave," she said as they rounded the next corner.

"You're simply confusing me," Jack complained.

Fenella thought about explaining the little people to him, but then decided she couldn't be bothered. "Never mind," she sighed.

Jack was nearly asleep as she turned onto the road where Dr. Grady's house was located.

"What was the house number again?" she asked.

"What? Oh, er, thirty-two," he replied.

"This is it, then," Fenella said, pulling her car into the small driveway in front of the house.

"It isn't what I was expecting," Jack told her as he studied the house.

"Why not?"

"I don't know. Dr. Grady seemed like the type to live in something modern and fancy. This looks like an ordinary house."

"It's a large house for the island," Fenella told him as she climbed out of the car. The house was larger than the one she owned on Poppy Drive, which meant it probably had at least four bedrooms, maybe more.

Jack followed slowly behind her, looking nervous. "I'm not sure about this," he muttered as she reached the door.

"Do you want to ring the doorbell?" she asked him.

"Yes, let's do that first, just in case."

"Just in case what?"

"Maybe I have the address wrong or something."

Fenella didn't argue, she just rang the bell. The buzzer sounded loudly, making Jack jump. For several minutes they both stood and stared at the door.

"I don't think anyone is home," Fenella said eventually.

"It doesn't look like it."

"You have the key?"

"Yes, but, that is, I'm not sure about this."

"Jack, the man told you that you could stay here, right? He gave you the key and code for the security system, right? He even asked you to look after the house, right?"

Jack nodded slowly. "It all seemed perfectly reasonable at the time. It just feels odd now."

"As I said, I can try to work out other arrangements, but for now, I think you should just go inside and get some rest," Fenella said. She hoped it wasn't too obvious just how badly she wanted to get away. Seeing Jack again had brought back a bunch of feelings she really didn't want to analyze just then. If she could get away from him for a short while, she could try to work out what she was thinking.

"Of course. I'm sure it's fine," Jack said briskly. He pulled a key out of his pocket and inserted it into the door's lock. The door opened and then a loud beeping noise started. The control panel for the security system was right inside the door. Jack tapped in a four-digit code and the beeping stopped.

"So far, so good," Fenella said brightly. "I'll get your bags."

Jack nodded and then sank onto the low bench that was right inside the door. It took Fenella three trips to bring in all of the bags. Jack remained where he was, staring straight ahead.

"Are you okay?" she asked as she carried in the last bag and shut the door behind herself.

"I'm very tired," Jack admitted. "It was a long journey. I had to change planes four times."

Fenella thought about asking why he'd needed to change so many times, but decided that it really didn't matter. "Let's find a bedroom so you can get some sleep," she suggested.

"Yes, I think that would be for the best," Jack agreed.

The small foyer led into a large living room that was open to a spacious kitchen. There was a flight of stairs tucked away in one corner. Fenella climbed up the steps that led to a large landing.

"That will be the master, won't it?" Jack asked, pointing at a set of double doors near the top of the stairs.

"Probably."

"Let's try one of the other doors, then," Jack said. He opened the next door along and found a bathroom. "Ah, well, excuse me for a few minutes," he said, shutting himself into the room.

Fenella frowned at the door and then continued to explore the house. She found three large bedrooms, each furnished with a comfortable-looking bed, a wardrobe, and a chest of drawers. Two of the bedrooms also had their own attached bathrooms. Fenella was just about to peek into the master bedroom when Jack emerged.

"Right, then, which bedroom should I take?" he asked Fenella.

"This is the largest and it has its own bathroom," she told him, gesturing toward one of the rooms.

Jack nodded. "Peter told me that the guest rooms had their own bathrooms. He called them en-suites, but I was able to work out what he meant."

"I'll just bring up your bags, then," Fenella told him.

She carried the bags up the stairs one at a time. By the time she'd brought up the last bag, Jack was fast asleep in the room's large bed.

"Right, then, call me when you wake up," she muttered before she headed for the stairs.

She found a pad of paper in a kitchen drawer and wrote Jack a note with her telephone number on it. The middle of the kitchen table seemed the best place to leave it. Hopefully he would find it once he woke up.

After picking up her handbag from where she'd left it, she headed for the door. Someone knocked on it before she'd reached it. Frowning, she pulled out her mobile phone and pushed 999 before she opened it. If there was any problem, she only had to push the "talk" button to call the police.

"I knew it," the pretty thirty-something blonde on the front doorstep said triumphantly. "I knew Peter was back and I knew he had a woman with him. You're older than his usual women, but I suppose you're pretty enough."

Fenella flushed. "Gee, thanks," she replied. "But Dr. Grady isn't here. He told a friend of mine that he could use the house for a few weeks."

The woman laughed. "That sounds like Peter. I'll bet your friend is younger and prettier than you, and that Peter is planning on coming back and sharing her bed while she's here."

"My friend is a man in his sixties," Fenella replied. "He and Dr.

Grady met through work."

"Wow, I didn't think Peter ever did any favors for anyone other than beautiful women he wanted to shag. How interesting."

"As I've never met Dr. Grady, I couldn't possibly comment."

The other woman laughed again. "He'd like you, even if you are a bit too old for him. He's only forty-three, or so he claims, and he likes his women at least ten years younger than that, but I think he'd take you to bed if he stumbled across you, I really do."

"Am I supposed to be flattered to hear that?" Fenella asked.

"Oh, goodness, I meant it as a compliment, really, but I suppose it isn't much of one. Peter will sleep with just about anyone, if I'm honest. He's, well, he's just, I don't know, oversexed, maybe. He likes women, pretty much every single woman he meets, but he's only interested in fun. Try getting a little serious, maybe try to make plans for more than a day or two ahead, and he quickly runs the other way."

"He sounds charming," Fenella said dryly.

More laughter accompanied the reply. "He is, though, somehow. He's gorgeous, maybe that's it. I'm Carol Houston, by the way. Peter and I were together for a few weeks before he went away to the US for a lecture tour. Is that where your friend met him?"

"Yes, he met him Buffalo, New York."

Carol nodded. "He told me he was going to be going to universities all over the US. He also said he'd be back for Christmas. I've been driving past every day, waiting to see his car on the drive."

"And today you saw mine," Fenella guessed.

"Yep, and I assumed it belonged to whatever woman Peter was currently entertaining."

"Sorry to disappoint you."

"Oh, but I'm not disappointed. I'm delighted to find that you aren't Peter's latest, really."

"I suppose that makes sense," Fenella replied. "I'm Fenella Woods, and as I said, I've never met Peter."

"Fenella Woods? Mona's niece?"

"Yes, that's right."

Carol sighed. "She's my role model. She led a fabulous life."

Fenella nodded. She'd heard the same sentiment from a number of people, although many of the people she'd met had been more disapproving of Mona's lifestyle. Fenella had been surprised to learn about Mona's past. Her aunt had lived extravagantly thanks to the generous support of more than one very wealthy man. Maxwell Martin had been her primary benefactor. He'd given Mona the many properties that Fenella now owned. It was Max who'd had Mona's luxury apartment built for her when he'd turned the hotel he owned into expensive apartments. He'd paid for her fabulous wardrobe and bought her a fortune in jewelry as well.

"She did, indeed," Fenella replied.

"I'd love to live like that, being supported by fabulously wealthy men who adore me," Carol sighed. "Sadly, I haven't yet found a fabulously wealthy man to be my Maxwell Martin."

"Dr. Grady doesn't qualify?"

Carol laughed again. "He does okay, but he isn't rich and he doesn't adore anyone other than himself. Oh, he's bought me a few trinkets now and again, but nothing like the baubles that were showered on Mona."

Carol's words reminded Fenella that she still hadn't visited her aunt's safe-deposit boxes. No doubt they would be full of the baubles that Carol had mentioned.

"Well, good luck to you," Fenella said.

"Yeah, thanks," Carol replied. "I'll get out of your way, then."

"I was just leaving myself," Fenella told her. "My friend is jet-lagged and needs some sleep."

She let herself out of the house and then checked that the door had locked behind her. Since she didn't know the code, she hadn't been able to set the alarm, but Jack could sort that out when he woke up.

Carol waved as she climbed into a sporty little blue car and then roared away. Fenella followed at a more sedate pace, her mind racing as she tried to work out how she felt. She wasn't any closer to an answer when she reached home a short time later. The phone was ringing as she let herself into her apartment.

"Hello?"

"Maggie? Why did you leave me alone? What am I supposed to do with all these angry women?" Jack demanded.

❧ 2 ❧

Fenella could hear people shouting in the background. She sighed. "I'll come back," she said.

"Hurry," Jack told her.

She gave her kitten, Katie, a quick snack and then headed back to the house where she'd left Jack just a few minutes earlier. While she drove, she wondered why he always insisted on calling her Maggie. She'd gone by Margaret when she'd lived in the US, as it was easier than spelling Fenella a dozen times whenever she met someone new, but Jack was the only one who'd ever called her Maggie, and she'd always hated it. Maybe she'd never actually told him that, though, she thought as she pulled up to Dr. Grady's house. Maybe it was her own fault that Jack had kept calling her that because she'd not wanted to argue.

There were several cars parked every which way on the driveway in front of the house. Fenella left her car at the curb and headed for the door. She knocked loudly and then, when no one answered, tried the knob. The door opened under her hand. Once inside, she followed the sound of loud voices.

"Not another one," a brunette who looked no more than twenty-one snapped as Fenella walked into the kitchen.

"She's not one of Peter's conquests," an older redhead said dismissively. "She must be with the old man."

"I'm not old," Jack said crossly.

The woman looked at him and then shrugged. "Whatever."

"Do I want to know what's going on?" Fenella asked.

"We're the Dr. Peter Grady Appreciation Society," a strikingly beautiful brunette who was probably close to thirty drawled. "Sadly, Peter isn't here to be properly appreciated. I'm afraid we took your friend here by surprise when we all turned up."

"I was asleep," Jack said indignantly. "And then they started pounding on the front door."

"We thought Peter was here," the younger brunette said. "We're all eager to see him again."

"I'm going off the idea fast," the other brunette told her.

"Good," the younger girl shot back.

The redhead laughed. "You could both go off him and leave him to me," she suggested, winking at Fenella.

"Not likely," someone said.

"You'd like that, wouldn't you?" was another reply.

"Okay," Fenella said loudly. "Let's start with introductions. I'm Fenella Woods."

"It's a pleasure to meet you," the young brunette said. "I'm Bev Martin, and Peter and I were, well, just getting acquainted when he went away. He promised he'd be back to spend Christmas with me, though."

The other two women both laughed. The redhead turned to Fenella.

"I'm Hannah Lawson. Peter and I were very, very well acquainted before he went away, and I'm not naïve enough to have believed a word he said about when he'd be back. I just happened to be driving past and saw all of the cars on the drive. I was curious enough to stop to see what was going on, that's all."

The other brunette shrugged. "And I'm Diane Jenkins. Peter and I had some fun together, and he did say he'd be back before Christmas. Do you know when he'll actually get back?"

Fenella looked at Jack, who shook his head.

"He offered to let my friend use the house for December and January," Fenella told Diane. She gestured toward Jack. "He told Jack he wasn't going to be back until February."

"February?" Bev gasped. "But that's months away."

"Very good," Diane said, "and you didn't even count on your fingers."

Bev's cheeks turned bright red. "You don't have to be horrible to me," she said with tears in her eyes.

"Why shouldn't I be?" Diane asked. "We're all rivals for the same man, after all."

"It isn't like that," Bev told her. "Peter is in love with me. He just hasn't told anyone else about me yet. Once he gets back, he's going to end all of his other relationships and we're going to be together."

Diane and Hannah exchanged glances and then they both laughed.

"You poor thing," Hannah said. "I hope you don't really believe that."

"He promised," Bev said.

"I doubt that," Diane said. "Peter doesn't make promises. He's an expert at making vague statements that could be taken a dozen different ways. Then, when you challenge him later, he can point out how you totally misunderstood what he'd meant."

Bev flushed. "You're just trying to get in between me and Peter."

"We're just trying to warn you," Hannah said gently. "Peter is a lot of fun, but he can't be taken seriously."

"But I left my husband for him," Bev wailed.

"Oh, my goodness, you poor dear," Diane said. "What were you thinking?"

"Robert and I were having problems anyway," Bev told her. "Then I met Peter and it was, I don't know, magical."

"It isn't like Peter to get involved with a married woman," Hannah said.

Bev blushed again. "I may not have told him about Robert," she said softly.

Diane shook her head. "My dear girl, we need to talk," she said. "Come on, let's leave poor Jack on his own and go and get a drink somewhere."

"I don't know," Bev replied. "I mean, you weren't very nice to me earlier."

"That was before I realized just how, um, confused you are," Diane told her. "I know that Peter can't be trusted. It seems very much like you weren't aware of that little fact."

"I think I could do with a drink, too," Hannah said.

"You're more than welcome to join us," Diane told her. "Jack and Fenella can come, too, if they'd like."

Jack shook his head. "I'm tired. I just want to sleep."

"You'll come, won't you?" Diane asked Fenella. "You've never even met Peter, right?"

"No, I haven't," Fenella agreed.

"You probably don't need a drink, then," Hannah laughed, "but you're welcome to come with us. I'm sure you've had terrible relationships, even without Peter."

"Fenella and I had a wonderful relationship," Jack said angrily. "We were together for over ten years and would still be together if she hadn't decided to move to the Isle of Man."

Hannah looked at Jack and then raised her eyebrows at Fenella. "Let's get that drink," she suggested. "I can't wait to hear your side of the story."

"Jack, why don't you go back to bed," Fenella said. "I'll come back in a few hours, once you've had time to get some sleep."

"I'm hungry," Jack complained.

"We'll go for dinner when I get back," Fenella offered. "There's a pub nearby that does good food."

"I probably could do with some sleep," Jack said grudgingly.

"I'll be back before five," Fenella told him.

"Okay, then," Jack agreed. He turned and headed back toward the stairs.

Fenella watched him go before she smiled at the other three women. "Let's go and get that drink."

They agreed to meet at the pub that was only a short distance away. Fenella sat in her car and watched as the other women struggled to get their cars off the driveway without hitting one another. When they'd all managed it, she followed the last car down the road and around the corner. She didn't really want a drink, but she did want to keep the women from bothering Jack. He was difficult enough to get along with most of the time. When he was overtired, he was impossible. Dr. Peter Grady intrigued her, as well. She was looking forward to learning more about him from the others.

"Let's just get a bottle of wine," Hannah suggested once they were all seated together around a small table.

"I don't drink when I'm driving," Bev said primly.

"One glass of wine won't hurt," Diane told her. "Sip it slowly and you'll be fine."

Fenella didn't drink when she was driving, either, but she was happy to take a glass of wine and pretend to drink it for a short while.

"So, which of us met Peter first?" Diane asked after everyone had a drink.

"I met him about three months ago," Bev replied.

"I met him in May," Hannah said. "It was a beautiful spring day and I was at the park with some friends. He was playing tennis with some woman, but he left her to chase me down and get my number."

Diane laughed. "That would have been me," she said. "Or, at least, it could have been me. Peter and I often play tennis together at various parks around the island. I'm quite used to him dashing away for a short while, too. He always makes up an excuse, but I'm pretty sure he's usually just chasing after other women."

"Why do you let him treat you like that?" Fenella blurted out.

Diane shrugged. "There's just something irresistible about him," she sighed. "I've known him for years. At first I truly believed that we were meant for one another, but over time I've come to realize that Peter is never going to change. He simply doesn't do commitment, and I can live with that. We have fun together, more fun that I've ever had with anyone else."

"He's going to commit to me," Bev said fiercely. "He told me he's ready to settle down and maybe even get married and start a family."

Hannah laughed. "Is that what he said exactly? Because he told me that when he's with me he starts to think that maybe he's finally ready to settle down. The key word in the sentence is maybe, of course. That's the one he always reminds me of whenever I mention it."

"The other key phrase is the part about him feeling that way when he's with you," Diane added. "I truly believe that he really means it when he says such things, but then, as soon as he's with someone else, he starts to think the same way about her. He's sincere, but fickle."

Bev shook her head. "He truly means it with me. I'm sure of it. So sure that I left my husband for him."

"When was the last time you heard from him?" Diane asked.

Bev flushed. "He texts me once in a while."

"Yeah, he texts me once in a while, too," Hannah told her. "All about how much he misses me, but without ever telling me when he'll be back."

"He'd tell me if he knew," Bev said, "but he's traveling for work and they keep changing his plans on him. They keep sending him to more universities to lecture because he's proving very popular."

"He told me he'd be gone until February," Diane said. "Although he did say he might get to pop back to the island for a few days around Christmas. I haven't heard from him in a week or more, though. I assumed he'd found himself a nice American girl and she was keeping him busy for the moment."

"He wouldn't do that to me," Bev said firmly. She downed what was left of her wine and then refilled her glass.

"And yet you're sitting here with two other women who are also involved with him," Fenella pointed out.

"They aren't. Not anymore," Bev replied. "Like I said, Peter just hasn't told everyone about us yet."

"You can believe that if you choose, but it isn't true," Hannah said.

"Who stopped at the house first today?" Fenella asked as the question occurred to her.

"I did," Diane replied. "I have a friend who lives a few doors away. She rang me to tell me that she'd seen a car at Peter's house, so I thought I'd pop over and see what was going on."

"And then I saw Diane's car, although I didn't know it was hers at the time," Bev said. "That's why I stopped."

"When I saw two cars on the drive, well, I just had to stop," Hannah said, "but tell us about you and Jack. He said you were together for ten years?"

"Yes, but, well, we aren't together anymore," Fenella told her.

"Then why is he here?" Diane asked.

Fenella sighed. "He seems to think that we might get back together, but that isn't going to happen."

"He's too old and grumpy for you," Bev said. "What did you ever see in him?"

"He's a brilliant historian," Fenella replied. "We worked together at the same university. I'd had my heart badly broken some time before I met Jack. When we met, I thought he seemed perfect."

"Let me guess, he was nothing like the man who'd broken your heart," Hannah said.

"Nothing at all. That was part of his appeal, of course. When I decided to move to the island, I ended things with Jack, though," Fenella explained.

"And now he's followed you here. He wants you back, doesn't he?" Bev asked.

"Maybe, but that isn't going to happen," Fenella said firmly. She took a sip of her wine and then glanced at her watch. The three women seemed nice enough, but she really didn't feel like spending any more time with them.

"Is that the time?" Hannah gasped. "I'm meant to be on my lunch break. I'd better go."

"It was nice meeting you," Diane said. "We should start a club for women who are involved with Peter. Maybe it would help us keep better track of him."

Hannah laughed. "If you want to organize something, let me know. I'd be happy to meet up once in a while to compare notes."

"Put my number in your phone," Diane suggested.

Hannah dug through her handbag and then laughed. "I must have left my phone somewhere. I do that all the time."

Diane found a business card in her bag and handed it to Hannah. "Ring me," she suggested. "We aren't properly rivals for Peter, as he'll never commit to anyone."

"I will," Hannah agreed before she rushed out of the room.

"Don't expect Peter and me to invite you to the wedding," Bev said, taking another sip of her drink. "I won't want any of his former girl-friends there."

"What about your husband? Will you invite him?" Diane asked.

Two bright red spots appeared on Bev's cheeks. "That's just rude," she snapped.

"I'm sorry. I shouldn't tease you, should I? You've a nasty shock coming one of these days when you find out what Peter is really like. At least I can sleep easily at night knowing that I warned you."

Bev got to her feet. "Maybe I should invite you to the wedding," she said tightly. "I'd love to see your face as Peter promises to love and cherish me forever. Just because he never actually cared for you doesn't mean you should be horrible to me because he loves me."

Diane laughed. "There isn't going to be a wedding," she said softly. "You'd be better off going back to your husband."

"You'd like that, as it would get me away from Peter. You can't have him, though, he's mine." Bev picked up her bag and marched out of the pub with her head held high.

"That poor girl," Diane sighed. "It isn't like Peter to take up with someone so young and naïve."

"Maybe he really has fallen in love with her," Fenella suggested.

"You wouldn't say that if you knew Peter. He's loads of fun, but he's not capable of loving anyone other than himself. I'm afraid our friend Bev is going to get her heart badly broken once Peter gets back to the island."

Diane finished the bottle of wine while she and Fenella chatted about the weather and other innocuous subjects. They walked out of the pub together.

"Are you okay to drive?" Fenella asked.

"I'm going to leave my car here and walk over to my friend's house," Diane replied. "She'll listen to me rant about Peter and how badly he treats me and then make me some dinner. By the time her husband gets home from work, I'll be sober again and ready to go home."

Fenella insisted on giving Diane a ride to the house which was, as she had said, very near to Dr. Grady's home. She waited until Diane went inside and then drove herself back home.

"It's all something of a mess," she told Katie as she sank down into a chair.

"What is?" Mona asked.

Fenella jumped. "Where did you come from?"

"I was having a facial at the salon, but I rushed over when I saw that you were back because I thought you might need someone to talk with about Jack," Mona replied.

Was there really a salon for ghosts? Fenella didn't bother to question her aunt because she knew Mona wouldn't give her a straight answer. "Jack is less of a problem than Dr. Peter Grady seems to be," she said instead.

"Who is Dr. Peter Grady?" Mona asked.

"The man who's letting Jack stay at his home. He teaches in Liverpool, but has a house here, too. He told Jack he could stay there, but so far four different women have turned up looking for him."

"Four? And it's only been a few hours. This Dr. Grady must be something special. Tell me about the women."

Fenella told her aunt about the four women she'd met. "I feel sorry for Bev, and I don't understand why the other three put up with it," she concluded.

"You've been seeing several different men since you've been here. Why is this any different?"

"I don't know. It feels different."

Mona laughed. "I'm not sure that Donald or Daniel would agree."

"I didn't sleep with any of them," Fenella defended herself.

"Perhaps Dr. Grady isn't sleeping with any of the women you met, either."

"That wasn't the impression that I got."

Mona shrugged. "As long as everyone involved is fully aware of the situation, then I don't see a problem with it."

"I don't know that Bev was aware of the other women."

"From the way you've described her, it seems likely that Dr. Grady told her about them, but she simply chose to ignore that information. That she never told Dr. Grady about her husband makes me doubt everything she said."

Fenella nodded. "There is that. I suppose I should feel sorry for him, if I'm going to feel sorry for anyone."

"He may not deserve it, either, of course. He may be perfectly awful."

"I'm almost hoping that Dr. Grady will come home while Jack is staying there. I think I'd like to meet him."

"You'd only be disappointed if he didn't try to get you into bed and insulted if he did," Mona suggested.

Fenella made a face at the woman who knew her rather too well. "At least all of this is giving me something to think about other than Jack," she said.

"How is Jack?"

"Jet-lagged and grumpy."

"Wonderful. Don't bring him here."

"I've left him sleeping. I'm sure he'll be better when he wakes up."

"I've changed my mind. Do bring him here. I'm anxious to see him for myself."

"Why?"

"I'm still trying to understand you better, my dear niece. Getting to know the man to whom you devoted ten years of your life is part of that process."

"I can't imagine why I spent ten years with him."

"Inertia can be very powerful. It's often easier to simply keep doing the same things over and over again, even if they don't make us happy, as long as they aren't making us unhappy. Fear of change is also very real. Besides, you worked with him. Work would have been awkward between you if you'd ended your relationship."

Fenella nodded. "All of those things played a part. So did the fact that I did care about him."

"Of course you did. It's just a shame it was affection rather than proper love."

Feeling restless, Fenella took herself out for a walk on the promenade. It was crisp but not too cold as she walked briskly along. Christmas lights seemed to be sparkling everywhere as the sun set, and when she got closer to the shops in the town center she could hear the Christmas music they were playing to encourage shoppers.

Because she'd had to send nearly all of the gifts she'd bought to the US, Fenella had done her shopping early. Large boxes full of uniquely Manx items had been sent to her brothers and their families some weeks earlier. All that remained on the island were a few small gifts for Shelly. Fenella had also stockpiled bottles of wine and boxes of chocolates to give to anyone who unexpectedly turned up on her doorstep with a present.

She'd also bought a few small things for Jack, but she hadn't decided yet whether she was going to give them to him or not. Every year for the ten years they'd been together, she'd given him a bottle of the same aftershave, one that she loved and he was willing to wear. That brand wasn't available on the island, though, so she'd chosen something completely different. It wasn't a scent that she was particularly fond of, but it was one that she thought suited Jack. She'd kept the receipt in case she decided not to give it to him.

The only thing she hadn't worked out was whether she should be trying to find Mona a gift or not. It wasn't like she could actually give Mona something tangible, so she was busy trying to come up with a non-tangible present idea. So far, she was drawing a complete blank.

It was nearly five when she got back to her apartment. Aware that she needed to hurry, she crossed the road and then stopped as a large dog rushed toward her.

"Winston, it's good to see you," she exclaimed.

"Woof," he told her.

"And Fiona, there you are," she added to the much smaller dog who'd quickly joined them.

She was happily petting and scratching the two animals when their owner arrived a moment later. "They nearly took my arm off trying to get to you," Harvey Garus laughed as Fenella greeted him.

"I haven't seen them in a few days. We've missed each other," Fenella told him. She'd looked after both dogs on a couple of occasions, and she always loved getting to spend time with them. They were hard work on a day-to-day basis, but nothing but pure joy when she bumped into them by chance.

"They're getting all excited for Christmas," Harvey said. "You must stop over on the day. Winston and Fiona insisted on getting you a little something."

"Oh, you shouldn't have," she told the dogs, "but I'll make sure to visit and maybe, just maybe, bring you each a little something, too."

"No need. They're both spoiled rotten as it is," Harvey told her.

Fenella laughed and nodded as she made a mental note to go shopping for gifts for both the dogs and their elderly owner.

"But I'm afraid I have to run," she said a minute later. "I'm supposed to be somewhere at five."

"You're going to be late," Harvey chuckled as he glanced at his watch.

"Yes, well, I suppose it doesn't much matter," Fenella grinned. "It was worth it, anyway." She gave each dog one final pat and then headed inside her building. She had to brush her hair after being out in the wind. Touching up her makeup made her feel more ready to deal with Jack again. On her way to the door, she hesitated before she picked up her car keys. Unable to decide on whether she should be sensible or have fun, she closed her eyes and grabbed the first set of keys she touched.

"Yes!" she said happily when she opened her eyes and discovered the keys to Mona's convertible in her hand. Okay, she'd cheated a little bit and peeked at the keys as she'd reached for them, but no one had to know that.

In Mona's car, the drive back to Dr. Grady's house didn't seem to take any time at all. Fenella parked on the driveway and then made her way to the front door. She rang the bell and then waited for Jack to answer. After several minutes she rang again. While she waited for Jack, she idly turned the doorknob, and was shocked when it opened under her hand. As her heart raced, she tried to remember if she'd checked that it was properly locked when she'd left with the other women. Everything had been so confused that she simply couldn't recall what she'd done.

"Jack?" she called from the doorway. "Are you here?"

Somewhere in the house a clock was ticking, but that was all that Fenella could hear. A little voice in her head suggested that she should call the police, but she ignored it and stepped inside the house. "Jack?" she shouted, wincing at the hint of panic she could hear in her voice.

She shut the door behind herself and took a few deep breaths. Jack was just sleeping, she told herself firmly. He'd been exhausted. No doubt he was upstairs in the comfortable guest bedroom, fast asleep.

Feeling guilty for possibly neglecting to lock the door when she'd left earlier, Fenella walked further into the house. "Jack? Wake up and come down," she shouted.

When he didn't reply, she tried to decide what to do next. Calling the police seemed like an overreaction, even with her history of finding dead bodies. She really didn't want to go looking for Jack, but she'd told him she'd be back at five and it was already half past. Leaving him to sleep would probably only make him grumpier when he did wake up.

With her heart pounding and her mind racing, Fenella slowly climbed the stairs, calling Jack's name after each step. All of the bedroom doors were shut, and Fenella stood on the landing for a moment before heading to the guest room she thought Jack was using.

She knocked firmly and then shouted Jack's name again. "Are you awake?" she asked before slowly turning the door's knob. When she pushed the door open, she frowned at the empty bed. It looked as if it had been slept in, but it was definitely empty now.

"Jack?" she shouted from the doorway. "Are you here?" If he was in the bathroom, she didn't want to walk in on him.

"For heaven's sake, do stop shouting," a voice said from behind her.

Fenella screamed and spun around. Jack was standing in the doorway to one of the other bedrooms. His grey hair was a tangled mess and he looked tired and cross. "Jack," she gasped.

"Were you expecting someone else?" he asked.

After a shaky breath, Fenella shook her head. "No, but I couldn't find you. I was worried."

"And yet you keep telling me that you no longer care," Jack sighed. "But anyway, I'm here."

"I thought you were going to use this room," she said, nodding toward the guest room behind her.

"I was, but I changed my mind. The bed was too hard," Jack explained.

Fenella nodded. "Are you ready to go and get some dinner, then?"

"I'm not that hungry."

"Do you want me to go and get some bits and pieces for you to have a snack for tonight, then?" Fenella offered.

"No, let's go out somewhere," Jack replied. "After I've come all this way, you should buy me dinner, really."

Fenella swallowed a dozen retorts. "I'll just wait for you downstairs, then," she said tightly.

"What is the food like at this pub you mentioned? You know I don't like odd fancy foreign food."

"I've only been there once and I really don't recall, but I'm sure you'll be able to find something to keep you from starving. We can go grocery shopping tomorrow if you'd like. Then you can make your own meals while you're here."

"I thought maybe you'd cook for me," Jack said. "It would be just like old times."

Fenella counted to ten as slowly as she could and then added on another five before she could trust herself to reply. "No," was all that she said.

Jack frowned and then turned back around and shuffled back into the bedroom. "I'll just get ready," he said in a low voice.

Feeling mean, Fenalla headed back down the stairs. She'd only just reached the foyer when someone knocked on the door. Sighing deeply, Fenella opened the door and forced herself to smile at Bev Martin, who was standing on the doorstep.

"Oh, it's you," Bev said. "I saw the pretty red car and thought that Peter was back for sure."

"It's my car," Fenella told her.

"Really? I thought you were driving a blue car earlier."

"I was, but this one is mine, too."

Bev shrugged. "It doesn't look like your type of car."

"Would you like to see the registration documents?" Fenella asked dryly.

For a moment it seemed as if Bev was going to say yes, but then she shook her head and sighed. "I'm sorry, but I was sure Peter was back. He promised he'd be back for Christmas and it's already the nineteenth. Something awful must have happened to him."

"Maybe he's just busy with work," Fenella suggested.

"Can I come in for a minute?" Bev asked. "I need a second to pull myself together before I drive home."

"Sure," Fenella said, taking a step backward.

"Great," Bev exclaimed. She rushed over the threshold and then headed for the kitchen. "It isn't that I don't trust you," she called over her shoulder as she went. "But if you are involved with Peter, well, you'd lie to me about him. I just want to check for myself that he isn't here."

Fenella stood at the door and listened as Bev moved around the house's ground floor. Jack came down the stairs a short while later.

"What's going on?"

"Bev is searching the house. She thinks Dr. Grady is hiding here somewhere."

"I suppose we should wait until she's done to go out, then," Jack sighed. "I'm quite hungry now, you know."

"She should be about done with this floor. Hopefully it won't take her long to search the upstairs."

"I'll be quick," Bev promised as she dashed past a minute later. She bounded up the stairs, leaving Jack grumbling behind her.

"All things considered, I wouldn't blame Peter for hiding from that woman," he said to Fenella.

She didn't disagree as she listened to Bev opening and closing doors above them.

"She must be..." Jack began.

The sound of Bev screaming cut across his words and had Fenella running up the stairs.

3

Bev was standing in the doorway to the master bedroom with her hands over her mouth. That wasn't doing anything to mask the sound of the girl's shrieks. Fenella took one look into the bedroom and then grabbed Bev and dragged her back down the stairs. She had her mobile phone in her hand and was dialing 999 as they went.

"What is your emergency?" a cool voice asked.

"There's a dead man here," Fenella blurted out, trying to focus on what she was supposed to tell the woman, but unable to get rid of the horror of what she'd just seen.

"Take a deep breath," she was told. "Where are you?"

"Where are we?" Fenella asked Jack.

"What's going on?" he demanded.

"What's the address here?" Fenella asked him. "I can't remember it."

Jack dug through his pockets and pulled out the slip of paper with the house's address on it. Fenella read it to the police dispatcher.

"And what's your name?" was the next question.

"Fenella Woods," she replied, dreading what was going to come next.

"Really? I'll alert Inspector Robinson."

"Yeah, great," Fenella muttered.

"Did you say there was a dead man there?" the woman asked.

"Yes, and I'm pretty sure he was murdered."

Fenella didn't hear the reply through the receiver as Jack's loud gasp and Bev's screams drowned her out.

"It sounds as if there are quite a few people there with you," the dispatcher said after a moment.

"Just two others," Fenella replied, "but they're both upset."

"Understandably. A constable should be there within two minutes."

"That would be good."

Fenella opened the door and watched eagerly for a police car.

"I have to go," Bev said suddenly. She pushed past Fenella and out the door.

"You need to stay here until the police arrive," Fenella called after her.

"If I do that, then Robert will find out I was here," Bev replied. "I don't want that to happen."

"But you found the body," Fenella argued. "The police are going to want to talk to you."

"Don't tell them I was here," Bev begged. "Tell them you found the body."

"I'm still on the phone with them," Fenella pointed out. "They can hear this conversation."

Bev frowned and then dashed down the sidewalk to her car, which was parked at the curb. She jumped inside and started the engine. A dark-colored car pulled up next to Bev's and slid to a stop, blocking her in. She hit her car's horn and then threw the car into reverse. A police car, lights flashing and sirens blaring, slid into place right behind Bev, giving her nowhere to go.

"They've stopped her, haven't they?" the voice on the phone asked.

"Yes, and she's pretty unhappy about it," Fenella confirmed.

"As the police are there, I'm going to hang up now," the woman told her. "It's been interesting, anyway."

Fenella frowned at the phone and then switched it off and dropped it into her pocket.

"What is going on?" Jack asked again.

Fenella shook her head as she watched Constable Corlett climb out of the police car. He walked over to Bev's car and tapped on the window. The dark car was parked too close to her for her to climb out of her seat. When Daniel Robinson got out of the driver's seat of that car, Fenella wasn't surprised. He said a few words to the constable and to Bev before he crossed to Fenella.

"Good evening," he said. "I'm Inspector Robinson, Douglas CID," he told Jack.

"Dr. Jonathan Mathias Dawson," Jack replied. "I'm just visiting the island and I've no idea what's going on."

"Then I suppose I should start with Fenella," Daniel said.

"Fenella? Oh, you mean Maggie." Jack shrugged. "After all our years together, I don't think I could ever call her Fenella."

Daniel raised an eyebrow and then looked at Fenella. "Let's worry about that another time. I need you to tell me what's going on."

Daniel sent Jack out to sit in one of the other police cars that seemed to be arriving from all directions. Then Fenella led Daniel into the house.

"So that's Jack," Daniel said.

"I think I told you that he'd met a man who'd told him he could use his house for this visit," Fenella began. "This is the house. Since Jack arrived this morning, I've already met four different women who were in some sort of relationship with the house's owner, Dr. Peter Grady."

"Four? That seems a bit, well, anyway, go on."

"The girl who was trying to get away was one of them. She was here this afternoon, and then she came back tonight and asked if she could come in. Once she was inside, she decided to try to find Dr. Grady. She seemed convinced that he was hiding in the house somewhere."

"I'll save my questions for later," Daniel said when Fenella paused.

"Right, well, she checked down here and then went upstairs and started opening doors. When she started screaming, I went up and brought her back down here and called 999. There's a man in the bed in the master bedroom who appears to have been murdered."

Daniel studied her for a minute. "How do you keep getting mixed up in these things?" he muttered before he headed for the stairs. "Stay right there," he called over his shoulder as he went.

Fenella paced in a small circle as she waited. The image of the man on the bed seemed burned into her brain and nothing she could do seemed to help erase it. When Daniel came back down, he looked slightly shaken.

"There was a lot of blood," Fenella said softly.

"Please don't repeat that to anyone," Daniel told her. "I'll have to make sure to impress that upon Ms. Lawson as well."

"Ms. Lawson?"

"The girl in the car. I thought you knew her name."

"I do know her name, or at least the name she gave us earlier. It wasn't Lawson, though."

Daniel frowned. "I think you'd better take me through your whole day," he said with a sigh. "I'll have our friend in the car taken down to the station. She can wait there until I'm ready to speak to her."

Fenella nodded. "She may have been lying earlier."

"We'll see."

Daniel sent her to sit in one of the police cars while he waited for the crime scene team to arrive. Fenella watched as Bev was escorted out of her car and into the back of a police car that quickly whisked her away. Unsure of where Jack had gone, Fenella settled back in the seat and tried to think. She knew very little about how the human body worked, but the blood that had been everywhere in the master bedroom looked awfully fresh to her. That suggested that murder had happened recently, probably while Jack was sleeping in one of the guest rooms. Fenella felt sick as she remembered that she might have left the house's front door unlocked. Had she inadvertently given a murderer access to the victim?

But who was the victim? It seemed most likely that the dead man was Dr. Peter Grady. Of course, he would have had the keys to the house, so maybe he was the one who'd left the door unlocked. Perhaps he was expecting a visitor and had left the door open for his guest. She wondered if the dead man had even realized that Jack was there. A dozen different scenarios ran through Fenella's head. Maybe the victim had been there when she and Jack had first arrived. The question was, had he been dead or alive as they'd explored the house?

The question made Fenella feel sick, so she tried to think about other things instead. Four different women had turned up looking for Dr. Grady in a short space of time. Maybe their excuses about seeing cars and stopping were just that, excuses. It was possible, maybe even likely, that one of them had received a call or a message from Dr. Grady inviting her over. Since Bev was the one who'd come back and insisted that Peter had to be there, she seemed the most likely candidate.

"How are you?" Constable Corlett asked as he stuck his head into the car a short while later.

"Going slightly mad," Fenella replied.

The man nodded. "I'm sure it's odd, you being caught up in another murder investigation."

"It's awful," she told him. "Is Jack okay?"

"Is that Dr. Dawson? I think he's a bit overwhelmed by everything, but I'm sure he'll be fine."

Fenella could only hope that the constable was right. She could remember the first murder investigation she'd been involved with, so she knew how confused and upset Jack was probably feeling. The sooner Daniel could take their statements, the better.

"How's the baby?" she asked the constable, more to be polite and to change the subject than out of genuine interest.

"He's doing well. Jenny is excited for his first Christmas, but he won't remember it, of course."

"She'll never forget it, though."

"From what I can see, we'll be paying off the credit cards bills until Odin's at university," the constable sighed. "Jenny seems to have bought out an entire toy store for him."

Fenella laughed. "He's finally getting to an age where he can start to appreciate toys, though, right?"

"I suppose so, although mostly he just tries to eat everything."

Daniel's arrival provided a welcome interruption. "Okay, I'm ready for your statement," he told Fenella through the car's open window. "Would you mind terribly coming down to the station to give it? We don't have a space here we can use, and I hate trying to talk in the back of a police car."

"I can go wherever you like," Fenella assured him.

He spoke to the constable for a minute and then opened the door to the back of the police car. "Come on. You may as well ride in my car. It's more comfortable and you won't feel as if you're being arrested, either."

"What about my car?" Fenella asked, gesturing toward Mona's sports car.

"It's beautiful, and if I ever hit the lottery I'll buy one just like it," Daniel replied, "but for now, I'd rather you left it here. It'll be almost impossible to get it out at the moment."

Fenella looked around at the police cars, crime scene vans, and other vehicles that were parked all over the house's driveway and on the street. Daniel was right. Her car was well and truly blocked in.

"I'm going to have to move the car to give you room to climb in," Daniel told her as he opened his driver's door. "Give me a minute."

Fenella stood back and waited while Daniel reversed slowly. When she could, she opened the passenger door and got inside. The drive to the station was a short one. Daniel led her to his office.

"Have a seat. I need to find a constable to take notes. I'll be right back," he told her.

She sat in the uncomfortable visitor's chair and tried to look around discreetly. From what she could see, Daniel didn't have anything personal in the office at all. She only knew it was his office because of the nameplate on the desk.

"We're going to move to one of the interview rooms," he told her a moment later. "We need to keep everything official."

Fenella frowned, but she understood. The chairs in the interview rooms couldn't possibly be any worse than the one in Daniel's office, anyway, she thought as she followed him and a tall, thin constable down a short corridor.

It turned out she was wrong. The chairs in the interview room were worse, but she didn't bother to complain. Daniel made a face as he took a seat opposite her. The constable sat next to Daniel and put a pad of paper on the table in front of him.

"Constable Quayle is going to take notes," Daniel told her. "At some point I'll have a typed copy of your statement for you to sign, but it probably won't be today."

Fenella nodded.

"I'm going to take notes, too," Daniel continued. "Inspector Hammersmith may want to speak to you once we've finished."

She did her best not to make a face. Inspector Mark Hammersmith had investigated several cases that Fenella had been involved in while Daniel had been away on his course. He was good at his job, but Fenella had never warmed to him as a person. Why was he getting involved in this investigation, she wondered.

"Let's start with what Dr. Dawson told you about his visit to the island. He arranged to stay at Dr. Grady's house, correct?"

"Yes, Jack told me that he'd met Dr. Grady at a party or a bar. When they'd started talking, somehow the conversation turned to the Isle of Man, and at some point Dr. Grady offered Jack a place to stay when he visited."

"Repeat everything you can remember about that conversation," Daniel said.

Fenella did her best, but she knew she was forgetting things. It had been a while since the conversation had taken place, and she wasn't always very good at paying attention to Jack when he was talking, either.

"Take me through your day today, then," Daniel said when she'd finished. "Start with what time you woke up this morning."

Fenella nodded and then began to recount her day. She did her best to repeat everything that had been said about Dr. Peter Grady when she'd spoken to the four other women. Daniel listened closely and took a few notes as she talked.

"So the woman who found the body called herself Bev Martin when you first met her," he checked when she was done.

"Yes, that's right."

"And her husband is called Robert? Do you know if he's Robert Martin?"

Fenella shrugged. "I don't remember her saying his last name. She simply referred to him as Robert."

"Did anyone describe Peter Grady to you?"

"I remember someone saying that he was gorgeous, but I don't recall a proper description. Surely Bev can identify the body?"

"We'll see," was all that Daniel would say.

"As much as I hate to admit it, I'm a bit worried about Jack," Fenella said after a long silence spent watching Daniel making notes. "Is he okay?"

"He's being questioned by Inspector Hammersmith," Daniel told her. "As I said earlier, Mark will want to compare his statement with yours and may have some further questions for you."

"How long had the body been there? Jack only arrived on the island today."

"That's not for me to determine," Daniel replied. "For now, everyone is a suspect, including Jack and including you."

"Me? I'd never even met the man," Fenella argued.

Daniel shrugged. "I have to consider every possibility."

While Fenella wanted to argue with him, she didn't feel she could, not in front of the constable, anyway. Swallowing hard, she tried to think. "What next?" she asked eventually.

"We're tracking down the other three women you mentioned in your statement. Again, we're going to be comparing their statements with yours."

"Do I have to stay here until you've spoken to them, then?"

"No, not at all," Daniel replied. "I'll go and see how Mark is getting on. We may be able to get you out of here sooner rather than later."

"What about Jack?"

"He should be done soon, too."

"I was thinking more about the house where he's supposed to be staying," Fenella said. "It's now a crime scene. You aren't going to want him going back there, are you?"

"No, we aren't, not for several days, anyway."

"Dr. Grady's next of kin probably isn't going to be too excited about having a houseguest, anyway. I'll have to find somewhere else for Jack to stay."

"I'm sure Doncan can help you out there. Make sure you let us know where he'll be in case we need to get in touch with him."

Fenella nodded. The easiest solution would be to move Jack into the house on Poppy Drive, but that might be a little too close to Daniel for comfort. "What about his suitcases?" she asked.

"I'm sure we'll be able to sort something out," Daniel replied as he got to his feet. "I'm going to go and see how Mark is doing. I'll be back."

He walked out of the room. A minute later the constable got up and left as well, without saying a word. On her own in the tiny space, Fenella began to feel slightly claustrophobic. After struggling through a few of her times tables, she began to think about Anne Boleyn. When she'd first moved to the island, Fenella had planned to write a fictionalized autobiography of the former queen, but once she'd discovered the extent of her wealth, she'd mostly given up on the idea.

Now, feeling confined and slightly on edge, she began to consider how Anne must have felt after her arrest, when she was taken to the Tower of London. The poor woman must have been terrified, Fenella thought. Surely it wouldn't have taken her long to realize that Henry was going to get rid of her, even if he was going to have to create the evidence that would be used to bring about her death sentence. Fenella began to pace back and forth in small steps, letting her imagination run wild.

Anne would probably have thought that, while she'd been a faithful wife to Henry, perhaps she'd been too headstrong. Maybe she'd said too much and not deferred enough to her husband, the king. She had to know that her biggest fault was failing to produce a son, however. No doubt she worried about what might happen to the daughter that she had birthed. It was thought that Anne knew of Henry's affair with Jane Seymour. Would she have hated the other woman or felt sorry for her, knowing what Jane's future would entail? When the door swung open, Fenella stared at Mark Hammersmith.

"Hello," he said brightly. "I was hoping I'd never have to see you again."

Fenella blinked and then struggled to pull her thoughts back to the present. "Thanks," she said dryly.

Mark laughed and then sat down at the table. "Sit," he suggested.

She dropped back into her chair and then sighed. "Sorry, I was lost in thought. Hello."

"How are you?" Mark asked.

Fenella shrugged. "Not happy to be caught up in another murder investigation. Not thrilled that Jack is here."

"How did his visit come about?"

"He called me and told me he was coming."

"You didn't invite him?"

"No, quite the opposite. I told him not to come. We split up nearly a year ago. As far as I'm concerned, we've no reason to see one another again."

"You weren't considering getting back together with Dr. Dawson?"

"No, never, not under any circumstances."

"That sounds very definite."

"I am very definite on the subject."

"Would it surprise you if I told you that Dr. Dawson has a different opinion?"

Fenella sighed. "Jack seems to think that if he nags me enough I'll agree to move back to Buffalo or maybe agree to his moving here. He ignores my objections."

"Interesting," Mark said, making a note on his phone. "What did Dr. Dawson tell you about the man who'd offered to let him stay at his house?"

Fenella swallowed another sigh and then repeated everything she'd just told Daniel. Mark tapped notes into his phone as she spoke. When she was finished, he scrolled through a few screens.

"When you left with the women to go for a drink, did the door lock behind you?" he asked eventually.

Fenella shrugged. "I told Daniel that I simply can't remember if I checked it or not. I know I checked it when I left the first time, but with everything else going on, I don't know if I checked it or not after that second visit."

"Perhaps you simply assumed it would lock because it had the first time," Mark suggested.

"I may have," Fenella agreed. "Door locks are different here from the US. I know how mine works, but I didn't pay that much attention to the one at Dr. Grady's house. Jack had the key and the alarm code. I probably should have told him to lock up behind me."

"What order did the women leave the pub?" was the next question.

Fenella answered and then waited to see what he would ask next.

"What time did you leave the pub?"

"I wasn't paying that much attention, but it was probably around three," Fenella told him. "I had time to go home and then for a walk on the promenade before I went back to the house."

"Did you see anyone while you were home or during your walk?"

Mark was specifically asking for her alibi, Fenella thought. He couldn't possibly think that she had anything to do with Peter Grady's murder. "I ran into Harvey Garus when I got back to my building," she replied. "That was right around five. Other than that, I only saw Katie."

"Your cat?"

"Yes."

Mark nodded and then typed a few more notes into his phone. "No phone calls while you were home?"

"No, sorry." She had had a long conversation with Mona, of course, but there was no way she was going to tell the police inspector about that.

"Which of the four women seemed the most upset about the others?" he asked after a moment.

The question was unexpected and it took Fenella a moment to answer. "Carol didn't meet the others," she said eventually. "Of the other three, Bev seemed the most surprised and upset, I suppose. Hannah and Diane both seemed to know that they weren't Dr. Grady's only, um, friends."

Mark chuckled. "So Bev got something of a shock?"

"I suppose so. I wasn't there when they all first arrived, of course. You'd have to ask Jack what happened at that point."

"I have," Mark told her. "Considering she hadn't known about the other women, it surprises me that Bev was willing to join you all for a drink."

"Diane was very persuasive. Actually, she was just very friendly, and it seemed that Bev needed a friend at that point. Both Diane and Hannah seemed to want to help Bev understand the situation."

"And the situation was that Dr. Grady was sleeping with all three, or make that four, of them?"

"I've no idea the extent of any of the relationships," Fenella replied, knowing that she was blushing. "Hannah said something that seemed to imply an intimate relationship, but the topic was never actually discussed."

Mark nodded. Fenella took a few deep breaths as he typed into his phone with an annoying tapping noise that made Fenella want to snap at him.

"Right, I think that's all I have for you right now," he said after what felt like hours. "I'll be in touch, or Inspector Robinson will be. I'm sure we'll have more questions."

"I'll be happy to help if I can," Fenella replied, hoping it would be Daniel who would be doing any subsequent questioning.

"Just wait here for a minute, please," the inspector said as he left the room.

Fenella glanced at her watch. No doubt she'd be waiting a good deal longer than a minute. It was closer to ten minutes before the door opened again.

"Sorry to keep you waiting," Daniel said. "Your car is still at Dr. Grady's house, isn't it?"

"Yes," Fenella replied. Daniel knew that. He was the one who'd told her to leave it there.

"I'll give you a ride back there, then," he said. "There are still quite a few people working at the house, but there should be fewer cars blocking up the drive now."

"Great. What about Jack?"

"Mark has a few more questions for him. I'm sure Jack will ring you as soon as Mark is finished with him."

"And while I'm waiting, I can find him a place to stay."

Daniel nodded. "Have you rented out the house near mine yet?" he asked.

"No, not yet," Fenella sighed. "It's probably the best option."

"But you don't want to let Jack stay there?"

"I don't want to do anything that suggests to Jack that I'm trying to help him," Fenella replied. "He doesn't need any encouragement. He still seems to think that we're going to get back together."

"And you don't think that?"

"Not even if he were the last man on earth."

A huge smile flashed over Daniel's face for a moment before he returned to a more serious look. "I can't imagine all of the hotels on the island are booked at the moment."

"It seems mean to force Jack to pay for a hotel when I have a large house sitting empty, though," Fenella replied. "After all our years together, I felt that letting him stay in the house is the least I can do."

"It's up to you, of course."

"And whatever I decide, I'll probably regret it," Fenella muttered under her breath.

Daniel led her back through the station to his car. They were both silent on the drive back to Dr. Grady's house. A single police car was parked next to Mona's convertible in front of the house.

"I'll probably ring you later," Daniel told her as she got out of the car. "I'll want to know where Jack is staying, once you've worked that out."

Fenella nodded and then crossed to the little red car. She slid behind the steering wheel and took a long, deep breath. In spite of everything, just being in the car made her smile. As she slowly reversed onto the road and began to drive away, she wondered what Jack would do if she simply disappeared for a few days. She could drive to the south of the island and check herself into a hotel. He'd never be able to track her down, and she could enjoy some peace and quiet away from him, and the murder investigation as well.

While the idea was tempting, she settled for taking the long way back to her apartment, relishing a bit of extra time behind the wheel of the racy little car.

"What's going on now?" Mona demanded as soon as Fenella unlocked her door. "There are all sorts of disturbances all over the ghost world."

"What does that mean?"

"I couldn't possibly explain. It would take ages and you wouldn't understand anyway. Just tell me what happened."

"One of the women from earlier came back to the house when I went to pick up Jack," Fenella told her. "She insisted on searching for Dr. Grady, but what she found was a dead man in the bed in the master bedroom."

"Dr. Grady?"

"I've no idea, but that would be my best guess."

"So he was in the bedroom, dead, all while Jack was sleeping?"

"I don't know. When I glanced into the room, well, the blood looked awfully fresh," Fenella said with a shiver.

"You think he was murdered while Jack was in the house? How could Jack sleep through something like that?"

"He was jet-lagged and exhausted. He slept through me knocking on the door and shouting his name. I've no idea what happened, though, and I don't even want to think about it, really."

"I do," Mona said excitedly. "You said Bev insisted on searching the house? She must have known that Dr. Grady was back on the island. I wonder if he got in touch with her or if she found out some other way."

"I've no idea. I do know that she gave the police a fake name when they stopped her as she tried to get away from the house, though."

"Oh, that is interesting," Mona said. "Tell me more."

Fenella shrugged. "Apparently she told the police she was Hannah Lawson."

"One of the other women from this afternoon. How interesting. Lying to the police is never a good idea, of course. I wonder what she was thinking."

"From what I could see, she wasn't thinking at all. She wanted to get away before the police arrived because she didn't want her husband to know that she'd been at Dr. Grady's house."

Mona nodded. "All of this puts both Bev and her husband at the top of my list of suspects."

"There must be many others on the list, though. The other three women, for example, should be there."

"Of course, and any of their husbands if they have them."

"Oh, goodness, I hope none of them are married, not if they were involved with Dr. Grady."

"This is going to be interesting," Mona said happily. "The first thing we need to do is find out everything we can about the four women."

"We need to leave the investigation to Daniel and Mark Hammersmith," Fenella told her firmly. "I have enough to worry about with Jack."

The phone cut across Mona's reply.

"Maggie? Where are you? I need you," Jack whined when Fenella answered the call.

4

Feeling cross with the world, Fenella picked up the keys to her boring, sensible car and headed for the door.

"Meerrooww," Katie grumbled.

"Sorry, darling," Fenella said as she stopped and turned around. Katie had walked into the apartment within days of Fenella's arrival, and the tiny kitten had quickly made herself at home. Having never considered getting a pet before, Fenella now found it impossible to imagine life without her tiny furry friend.

In the kitchen, she filled Katie's food and water bowls and then gave her a handful of treats. "I have to go and get Jack and take him somewhere," she told the animal. "But I won't be bringing him back here, not tonight. He's far too grumpy tonight."

"Meerrew," Katie agreed.

"I'm going to have to bring him here eventually, though," Fenella sighed. "If I were you, I'd just hide somewhere while he's around."

Katie stopped eating long enough to nod before going back to her meal. Feeling slightly guilty about the delay, Fenella headed for the door again.

"He can wait," Mona told her. "He's hasn't any choice, really."

"Yes, but he's already upset. The longer he has to wait, the more upset he'll be when I finally get there."

"Why do you care?"

Fenella opened her mouth to reply and then stopped herself. Why did she care? Yes, she still had a soft spot in her heart for Jack, but that didn't mean that she had to rush to his side when he was upset. The man was nearly sixty and should have been more than capable of looking after himself. It had been his decision to come to the island. She hadn't invited him. Maybe she should simply leave him to find his own way out of the mess in which he found himself.

When the phone began to ring again, Fenella sighed. "That will be Jack again," she predicted. She listened to her answering machine message and then waited to hear Jack's voice.

"Maggie? I just wanted to check that you are coming for me. I'm sorry about all of this," he said in a low voice.

"He knows exactly how to get you to do what he wants," Mona observed.

Fenella didn't bother to reply. She knew that Mona was right, but that didn't stop her from feeling sorry for Jack. After shutting the door behind her, she made sure that it was locked and then headed back down to the garage under the building. It had been a long day and it wasn't over yet.

"Where are we going?" Jack asked as soon as he'd climbed into Fenella's car.

"I don't know," Fenella replied. She pulled the car over to the side of the road and looked at him. "Any ideas?"

"I suppose I could stay in a hotel for a few days, but didn't you say something about another place I could stay?"

Fenella nodded. "Like I said, I have a friend who has some rental properties. I just don't know if he'll be around tonight." She pulled out her mobile phone and found Doncan Quayle in her contact list. No one answered when she tried his office number. Hanging up on the machine, she frowned at the phone. The next number on the list was the man's home number, but calling him there seemed intrusive.

"I could just stay in your apartment for tonight," Jack suggested in a pitiful voice.

That was all the encouragement Fenella needed. She tapped in Doncan's home number and waited for the call to connect.

"Hello?" a woman's voice said after a handful of rings.

"I'm trying to reach Doncan Quayle. It's Fenella Woods calling," she replied.

"Ah, Ms. Woods, Doncan was just talking about ringing you. Let me get him for you."

Doncan's deep, calming voice sounded in her ear a moment later. "Fenella, are you okay?" he asked.

"I'm fine."

"I understand you needed to ring the police earlier. Can you talk about it?"

"Now probably isn't the best time," she replied, glancing at Jack, who was clearly listening to her every word. "I was just calling to see if you had any rental properties that were empty at the moment. My friend, Jack, is visiting from the US and the house he was going to stay in is suddenly no longer available."

Ah, and you don't want your friend to realize that you own the property we're discussing," Doncan guessed.

"Yes, that's it exactly."

"The house on Poppy Drive is still empty," Doncan told her, "but you know that, don't you?"

"Yes, but I thought it would be best to check."

"Is that too close to home? Would you like me to see if you have anything else available?"

"If you could, it might be better," Fenella agreed.

"Can I ring you back in five minutes?" he asked. "I'll need to ring the letting agent and check the computers."

"That's fine." Fenella ended the call and then looked at Jack. "He's going to see what's available."

"I hope he has something suitable," Jack told her. "I'd prefer a family home to an apartment, and I'd like something in a quiet neighborhood."

"Beggars can't be choosers," Fenella said dryly. "You'll be happy with a roof over your head, right?"

"Yes, I suppose so," Jack sighed.

The pair sat in silence by the side of the road, waiting for Fenella's phone to ring. True to his word, Doncan called back almost exactly five minutes later.

"I'm sorry, but the house on Poppy Drive is the only one that's empty at the moment," he said when Fenella answered. "It's nearly Christmas. No one wants to move at Christmas."

Fenella nodded. "Yes, of course," she said quickly when she remembered that Doncan couldn't see her. "I still have the keys to Poppy Drive, so I'll take Jack there. Thank you so much."

"You're very welcome. How long is he planning on staying?"

"Until the middle of January, I believe."

"There is a flat in Ramsey that is being vacated at the end of the year. I can give you more information if you want it."

"I'll call you back about that. For now we'll be happy with Poppy Drive."

"Let me know if you need anything else," he told her. "Ring me anytime."

"Thank you," Fenella said before she ended the call and dropped the phone back into her handbag.

"You have found me something, haven't you?" Jack asked as Fenella pulled back onto the road.

"Yes, I have. It's the same house that James used when he was here."

"James?"

"My brother."

"Oh, that James," Jack laughed nervously. "I just wasn't sure whom you meant."

And you couldn't name all four of my brothers if you had to, Fenella added to herself. It didn't really matter at this point, though. They weren't together any longer, she reminded herself as she drove.

Fenella couldn't stop herself from noticing the lights on in Daniel's house as she pulled into the driveway at the house on Poppy Drive.

"It's small," Jack complained.

"It's larger than your house in Buffalo, and it's fully furnished. If you don't like it, I can take you to a hotel and you can pay for a room for the next five weeks."

Jack sighed deeply. "I'm sure it will do," he said peevishly.

For a moment Fenella was tempted to take him straight to the most expensive hotel in Douglas, but she took a deep breath and then dug the keys to the house out of the bottom of her bag.

"Why do you have the keys?" Jack asked.

"I told you, James stayed here when he visited. I haven't seen Doncan since to give them back and he hasn't needed them."

"So no one wants to live here?"

Fenella didn't bother to reply. She simply got out of the car and walked up to the door. After a moment Jack followed. Once inside, she sat in the living room while Jack took a look around.

"It's adequate," he conceded when he joined her a short while later.

"Gosh, are you sure? I could ring around and try to find you a castle, or at the very least a mansion, if you'd rather," Fenella snapped.

Jack immediately looked contrite. "I'm sorry," he said quickly. "I'm tired and upset and I'm taking it out on you. I shouldn't be. This day hasn't exactly gone the way I'd hoped, but that isn't totally your fault."

"I would hope none of it is my fault."

Jack shrugged. "I did hope that you'd be a bit happier to see me. If you would have agreed to let me stay with you, we never would have been at Dr. Grady's house, either."

"You were the one who befriended the man and accepted his offer of a place to stay," Fenella reminded him.

"Yes, but I obviously never expected that he'd be dead in one of the bedrooms when I arrived."

Fenella bit her tongue. She wasn't sure that the victim had been dead when Jack arrived, but he didn't need to know that, at least not yet.

"We can't change the situation, so we'll just have to make the best of it," she said after a moment. "I hope you'll be comfortable here."

"It's very nice, really," Jack said unconvincingly. "I'm terribly tired, but I'm not sure I'll be able to sleep."

"You should try. The sooner you can get your body clock adjusted to Manx time the better."

"Yes, I suppose so. The police gave me my medication, but they wouldn't let me have anything else from my suitcases. I don't suppose you could go and get me some pajamas?"

Fenella counted slowly to ten before she replied. "I can't imagine where I'd find an open shop at this hour."

Jack looked at the clock. "It's only ten o'clock. Surely they have shops that are open all hours."

"No they don't," Fenella replied, "but I may be able to find you something." There was a collection of men's pajamas in the wardrobe in the guest room at Fenella's apartment. She wasn't exactly sure why Mona had needed them, and she'd never worked up the nerve to ask her aunt. "Are you hungry?"

"Starving, actually. The inspector gave me a sandwich, but that was hours ago."

"I didn't get a sandwich," Fenella muttered. "Okay, I'm going to go and get some pajamas and some food. You get settled in here."

"Until I get my suitcases, I'm hardly going to be able to get settled," Jack told her. "Are there any books in the house?"

"Why don't you look around and see what you can find," she suggested. "I'll be back as quickly as I can."

"Bring books," he told her. "As I planned the trip at the last minute, I didn't have time to learn anything about the island's history. Bring me all of your books on the subject, if you don't mind."

"I'll see what I can find."

Jack wandered away, heading for the stairs again. As Fenella let herself out, she tried to remember if she'd seen any books in the house. It seemed unlikely that there would be any in a rental property. She'd have to bring a few titles back for him.

Back at home, she rushed through her apartment, grabbing a small suitcase and quickly dumping in two pairs of pajamas in two different sizes. When they'd been together she'd done nearly all of Jack's shopping for him, but he looked as if he'd lost a bit of weight since she'd seen him last. Not wanting to have to make another trip back, she found pajamas in the size she'd always purchased for him and also one size smaller. She added a few pairs of boxer shorts that were also in the drawer before heading for the bathroom.

A spare toothbrush and a tube of toothpaste got added to the case.

She found a disposable razor and an unopened bottle of mouthwash and threw them on top. In the months she'd been on the island she'd assembled a small collection of books about the island's history. While she hated lending books to anyone, she knew Jack was going to need reading material. Selecting some of her least favorite titles, she tucked them into the bag. Before she headed back to the car, she called the closest pizza place and ordered a large pizza and some garlic bread. The order was ready by the time she got to the restaurant. She added a few bottles of soda to the order before heading for Poppy Drive.

"I'm back," she shouted as she let herself back into the house, balancing the food in one hand and the bag in the other.

"Excellent. I hope you brought lots of books," Jack called as he walked down the stairs.

"A few," she replied, "and food."

She headed straight to the kitchen. By the time Jack joined her she'd already pulled down plates and opened the food boxes.

"Pizza?" Jack asked, wrinkling his nose.

"Don't have any if you don't want it," Fenella told him. She filled a plate and then poured herself a glass of soda. Ignoring Jack, who was still standing in the kitchen's doorway, she sat down and started to eat. After a minute, Jack picked up a plate and hesitantly took a slice of pizza. He filled a glass with water from the tap and then sat down opposite Fenella.

She was on her third slice of pizza before he finished his first.

"It's good," he said.

"Try the garlic bread," she suggested.

"Oh, yes, of course."

Half an hour later, Fenella had eaten over half the pizza and most of the garlic bread. Jack had eaten a bit and was yawning over his glass of water.

"I think I should go and let you get some sleep," Fenella said. "It's been a very long day for you."

"I did have a nap, but I'm exhausted."

"You traveled a long way and then had to deal with a lot of upset. Tomorrow will be a better day."

"What are we doing tomorrow?"

Fenella frowned. "What did you want to do while you were here?"

"Spend time with you, really. That's why I came."

"We can spend time together, but you must remember that we aren't a couple anymore," Fenella said firmly. "I'll show you around the island as your friend."

"I'll take whatever I can get, but you can't blame me for hoping I might change your mind before my visit is over."

"I'm not going to change my mind. I have other men in my life now."

"I want to meet them."

Fenella shook her head. "We aren't even going to discuss them. They aren't your concern. What sights do you want to see?"

"I don't even know what there is to see."

"I've brought you a few books on the history of the island. Why don't you have a look through them in the morning and then decide what you want to see? Castle Rushen isn't open during the day at the moment, but I have tickets for Christmas at the Castle later this week."

"What's Christmas at the Castle?"

"It's a big fundraising event for Manx National Heritage and other island charities. Each charity decorates a room in the castle for Christmas and then they sell tickets to people to come and see the results. They also auction off the decorations and other donated items."

"It doesn't sound like my sort of thing."

"You don't have to come with me," Fenella said quickly. "I won't mind."

"If it's important to you, then of course I'll come."

Where was that attitude when we were dating, Fenella wondered. "I'm not actually sure which historical sites are open at the moment, but I'll see what I can find out before I come back tomorrow. Maybe the Manx Museum would be the best place to start. I know it's open all year."

"You know I don't really like museums," Jack replied.

Fenella didn't bother to reply. "What time do you think you'll get up tomorrow?" she asked instead.

"I'm always up at seven. I have been for years. You should remember that."

"You aren't usually jet-lagged," she reminded him. "I'll plan to be here around nine. I'll bring something for breakfast."

"I'd like two poached eggs, bacon, whole wheat toast, and orange juice."

"You'll get a pastry in a bag," Fenella told him, "and maybe a cup of coffee."

Jack pressed his lips together and then frowned at her. "This isn't at all what I was expecting."

"So maybe we should skip the sightseeing tomorrow in favor of grocery shopping. Then you can make yourself whatever you want for breakfast."

"It would be good to have some food in the house," Jack replied. "Maybe you could cook for me a few times. I always loved your cooking."

"We'll see," was all that Fenella was prepared to say.

"You're leaving, then?"

"I'm going home to bed. It's been a long day."

Jack nodded and then reached across the table and took her hands. "What did you see in that bedroom?" he asked in a whisper.

"I can't tell you, not during the police investigation," she replied.

"Was it Dr. Grady?"

"As I never met Dr. Grady, I have no idea."

"Oh, that's right. I forgot that you never met him," Jack frowned. "It must have been Dr. Grady. That's the only thing that makes sense. I can't believe that I was sleeping in that house for all those hours with a dead man."

"It's probably best if you try not to think about it."

"I'm not sure that's possible. Do you think one of those women killed him?"

"I've no idea who killed him. Maybe he had a heart attack or something." Fenella was positive the victim had been murdered, but she wasn't going to share that with Jack.

"I hadn't thought of that. The police seemed to think it was murder, though, didn't they?"

"I don't know what they thought. Whatever happened, it's their problem, not mine." You're my problem, she added to herself, and that was quite enough for her to worry about for now.

"I was surprised that he had three different girlfriends, although he did seem very popular with women the night I met him."

"Four," Fenella corrected him. "I met one women on my way out the first time."

"Four? My goodness, how did he have time for four women?"

"I've no idea, and I don't care. I'm going home to bed."

"That woman who searched the house, the young one, must have known something. Otherwise, why would she have searched the house?"

"I don't know. Let's let the police worry about that, shall we?"

Jack nodded. "Of course, but aren't you the least little bit curious? I've never been involved in a murder investigation before. It's fascinating, like something off the television."

"I've been involved in several before and I've hated every minute of every one of them. Let's just hope you don't become a suspect."

"How could I possibly be a suspect? Whoever the dead man was, he'd been dead for ages, right?"

Fenella shrugged. "That's up to the police to determine, not me."

Jack sat back in his seat, his face pale. "You aren't suggesting that the murder might have taken place while I was in the house, are you?"

"I'm not suggesting anything. As I said, the police will work it all out."

"He wasn't in the house when we arrived. He would have come out and said hello."

"Did you go into the master bedroom after I left?"

"No, of course not. The doors were shut and it was obvious that bedroom was the master. I didn't have any reason to go in there, and doing so would have felt, well, intrusive."

Fenella nodded. "So we don't know if the body was there or not when you arrived. Let's hope the police can quickly figure out exactly what happened."

"Yes, let's," Jack murmured. He glanced around the room. "Does this house have a security system?"

"No."

"I'm not sure I'll feel safe here. What if the killer comes after me?"

"Why would he or she do that?"

"I don't know, but now that you've said that Peter might have been killed while I was in the house, I'm not sure what to think."

"I think you need sleep."

"You'll be sorry tomorrow if I get murdered in my sleep like Peter Grady."

"What makes you think he was murdered in his sleep?"

"In his sleep or in his bed, it's the same thing," Jack said. "I'm sure I won't sleep a wink tonight."

"You're worried for nothing. Even if the killer did want to kill you, he or she doesn't know where you are."

Jack thought about that for a minute and then nodded slowly. "I hadn't thought of that."

"Lock me out and then go and get some sleep. There are pajamas and some boxers in the bag I brought. There are also a few books. I'll be back around nine tomorrow, then we'll talk about what you want to do next."

Jack nodded. "Go home, maybe," he muttered.

"Back to Buffalo?"

"No, of course not," he said quickly. "I'm just tired and a bit anxious about everything that's happened today. I'm sure I'll feel better tomorrow."

"Yes, of course you will," Fenella agreed.

She got to her feet and spent a minute putting all of the leftover food and drinks into the refrigerator. There was no doubt in her mind that such a thing would never have occurred to Jack. When the kitchen was tidied, she had him follow her to the door.

"Here's the key to the front door," she said, handing him a key ring. "I have another one, but I won't let myself in while you're here. I'll ring the doorbell and wait for you to answer."

She showed him how to lock the door and then waited on the doorstep for him to lock the door behind her.

"Good night," she called through the door.

"Good night," he replied.

A wave of exhaustion washed over her as she headed for her car. She was climbing in when she heard her name being called.

"Fenella?"

She straightened and then smiled at Daniel as he crossed the street. "Hello."

"Hi," he said, grinning at her. "I thought you were going to let me know where Jack ended up tonight."

"I forgot," she said honestly. "He's staying here, but I really just got him settled. I had to find him some pajamas and things since you still have his suitcases."

Daniel nodded. "Sorry about that. We should be able to release them back to him tomorrow."

"I'm sure Jack will appreciate that."

"I'd invite you in for a drink, but you look tired."

"I'm exhausted. Dealing with Jack is bad enough. Getting tangled up in a murder investigation hasn't helped."

"It was definitely murder," Daniel told her. "Although I'm sure you knew that already."

"There was so much blood," Fenella replied, shuddering.

"The body has been identified, as well. It was Dr. Peter Grady. We're going to have a lot more questions for Jack," he warned her. "Make sure you keep me informed as to where to find him."

"He'll be here for the foreseeable future. It's the only property that I have that's empty."

"You have a spare bedroom in your flat."

"And Jack definitely won't be using it."

Daniel nodded. "I probably don't have to tell you this, but we're going to have to keep things between us strictly professional until the case is solved. Technically Mark is heading up the investigation, anyway, because I have a personal connection to the case."

"You do?"

"The chief constable is aware that you and I are good friends," Daniel told her. "Since the case involves not only you but your former partner, he thought it was best to put Mark in charge."

"I'm sorry."

"It isn't your fault," Daniel shrugged. "It's just uncanny how you keep finding yourself caught up in these things."

"This one doesn't have anything to do with me. This is all Jack's fault."

Daniel chuckled. "I suppose I can't argue with that."

"And now he's worried that the killer might come after him," Fenella added.

"That's one reason why I want to know exactly where Jack is," Daniel surprised her by saying.

"You think he might be a target for the killer?"

"We aren't sure when Dr. Grady died, but it's possible it was while Jack was in the house. If that's the case, the killer might start to wonder if Jack might have witnessed anything."

"If he had, he would have told you about it."

"Unless he doesn't realize what he saw."

Fenella thought about that for a minute and then shook her head. "Maybe I'm just too tired to work it out, but I can't imagine what Jack could have seen."

"I don't think he saw anything. I think he was fast asleep when Dr. Grady died, but the killer might believe otherwise."

"Great, now I have to worry about Jack getting himself murdered while he's here," Fenella sighed.

"We'll be keeping a close eye on him," Daniel assured her. "What are your plans for tomorrow?"

"I'm going to come back over around nine to discuss that with Jack. We were talking about doing some sightseeing and maybe some grocery shopping."

"Both of those things should be perfectly safe. Ring me and let me know exactly where you're going before you leave the house, though, okay?"

Fenella frowned at him. "You're serious, aren't you? Do you really think the killer is going to go after Jack?"

"No, I don't, but I'd rather take extra precautions than deal with another murder investigation."

Fenella nodded, but she didn't feel reassured. "Maybe Jack should just go home," she said softly.

"Does he want to go home?"

"I don't think so. It was just something he mentioned in passing."

"We'd like him to stay on the island for the moment. Right now I still have his passport, anyway."

"He didn't mention that, but maybe he forgot."

"It was in a drawer in the bedroom he was using. We've locked it up at the station for safekeeping."

"And you'll keep it until you have Dr. Grady's killer behind bars," Fenella guessed.

"Maybe not that long, but certainly for a short while."

"I won't mention it to him. The less he has to worry about, the better."

"That's probably for the best."

Fenella stared at Daniel for a moment, feeling an irrational urge to pull him close. Something in his eyes suggested that he feeling the same thing. After an awkward pause, he took a step backward.

"I should let you get home, then," he said. "You're tired."

"I am," she agreed.

"Good night," he told her, taking another step away.

She got into the car and settled herself behind the wheel. It took her a minute to focus her attention on driving. Daniel was still standing on the sidewalk as she slowly backed out onto the road. She waved and then drove away, forcing herself to pay close attention to what she was doing. She hadn't been driving on the island long enough to drive back to her apartment without thinking. Just staying on the correct side of the road took concentration when she was tired.

Feeling relieved that she'd reached home safely, she parked her car next to Mona's and then took the elevator to the sixth floor. Her apartment felt oddly empty as she let herself in.

"Katie?" she called.

The kitten didn't reply. It only took Fenella a minute to find her, curled up in the center of Fenella's king-sized bed. Mona was nowhere to be seen. No doubt she was at a party or off having dinner with royalty or something, Fenella thought as she washed her face and brushed her teeth. Mona didn't have to worry about murder investigations, difficult former boyfriends, or awkward potential ones, either.

From everything she'd said, Mona still had Maxwell Martin for company. According to Mona, he spent most of his time, now that he was dead, in what had once been the grand ballroom of the hotel. It was now offices for the apartment building, but apparently Max didn't see it that way.

Sighing deeply, Fenella crawled into bed and plumped up her pillow. "You could at least give me a few minutes of cuddle time when I come home," she told Katie.

The kitten didn't even open her eyes. Fenella tossed and turned for a few minutes before she fell into a restless sleep. It didn't seem more than a few minutes later when Katie began to tap gently on her nose.

"Can't you sleep until nine or even ten?" Fenella asked, as she opened one eye to squint at the clock. It was seven, which was the same time Katie woke her almost every day.

"Meeroow," Katie told her.

"I had a late night. It wasn't my fault, though. It was Jack's fault, well, his and Daniel's."

"Yow," Katie replied.

"Yes, okay," Fenella sighed. She got out of bed and got Katie her breakfast before she took a long and very hot shower. It was too early to leave for the house on Poppy Drive, so she made herself a nice breakfast and washed it down with most of a pot of coffee. At quarter to nine she headed to the nearest café and got Jack a cup of coffee and a croissant. Then she pointed her car back toward Poppy Drive.

$\mathscr{S}$ he'd been knocking for several minutes when Daniel crossed the road. "He isn't answering?"

"No. I hope he just overslept," Fenella replied.

Daniel frowned. "Do you have a key?"

"Yes, but I told him I wouldn't use it. I don't want to invade his privacy."

"Under the circumstances, I'm not overly worried about his privacy," Daniel told her. "If you don't want to go in, I will."

Fenella hesitated and then sighed. "It might be best if you do it. I'll open the door for you and then stay out of the way."

"I have no reason to believe that there's anything wrong," Daniel said. He waited until Fenella was looking at him before he continued. "I really do believe that Jack has simply overslept."

Fenella nodded and tried to ignore the sick feeling in the pit of her stomach. She'd never forgive herself if something terrible had happened to Jack. She could have taken him back to her apartment where there was security in the lobby. If Jack was just sleeping, he wasn't going to be happy to wake up to a police inspector, either. Sighing, Fenella dug out the key and unlocked the door.

Daniel started to open it and then frowned. "There's something blocking the door," he said.

"What sort of something?" Fenella asked worriedly.

"I think it's a table," Daniel replied as he pushed the door open a few inches.

Fenella looked through the gap. "Jack must have moved the coffee table from the living room over in front of the door," she guessed.

Daniel pushed harder on the door and the table slid back a few more inches. A loud crashing noise made him stop.

"What was that?" Fenella asked.

"It looks as if there were glasses and plates piled on the table," Daniel told her. "When I moved it, some of them fell off and shattered."

"I suppose, as burglar alarms go, it's better than nothing."

"It would be, if it actually woke up the person in the house."

Fenella shook her head. She found it hard to believe that Jack had slept through all of the noise they were making. She and Daniel waited for a minute to see if Jack would materialize before Daniel tried pushing on the door again.

"It won't move any further," he sighed. "I think the table is jammed against the back wall. Do you have a key for the back door?"

"I think it's the same key," Fenella replied. "I hope it's the same key, anyway."

Daniel pulled the door shut and then the pair made their way around the side of the house.

"I can't wait to see what Jack did back here," Fenella muttered as they opened the side gate and approached the house's rear door. She slid the key into the lock and smiled when it turned easily. Once the door was unlocked, she took a step back.

"Good luck," she told Daniel.

He pushed open the door and then glanced around the inside of the house. "I don't see anything out of the ordinary back here."

"Maybe Jack didn't realize there was a back door."

"Jack? Dr. Dawson? It's Inspector Robinson. I'm coming into the house now," Daniel called. He stepped inside and then looked at Fenella. "Why don't you come in and wait back here," he suggested.

Fenella stepped into the small utility room into which the back door opened and then stopped. While Daniel headed for the front of the house, still shouting Jack's name, Fenella shut and locked the back door behind them. Worry about Jack made her jumpy, and when she heard a door open somewhere in the house she shrieked.

"What's going on?" Jack's voice carried through the entire house. "Who's there?"

"It's Inspector Robinson from the police. You didn't answer the door to Fenella when she knocked," Daniel called.

Fenella made her way to the front of the house as Jack stomped down the stairs in his borrowed pajamas.

"What time is it?" he demanded, looking from Fenella to Daniel and back again.

"Quarter past nine," Daniel told him.

"It can't be," Jack replied. "I never sleep late."

"Well, you have today. Of course, your body clock is still recovering from your transatlantic journey. It's understandable," Daniel said.

"Are you quite certain of the time?" Jack asked.

"Yes, quite," Daniel replied, chuckling.

Jack flushed and looked at Fenella. "I can't believe you called the police when I didn't answer the door," he said grumpily.

"She didn't call me," Daniel answered for Fenella. "I was just leaving for work and noticed her pounding on the door. In light of what happened yesterday, it seemed like a good idea to investigate."

"You should be investigating Peter's murder," Jack retorted. "I can't see why I'm of any interest to you at all."

"You're an important witness in our investigation. I'd hate for anything to happen to you," Daniel told him.

Jack frowned and then shook his head. "I'm so tired that I can't think straight," he said. "I need coffee and breakfast."

"Here," Fenella said, handing him the coffee that she was still holding. She dug into her handbag and then handed him the bag with the croissant in it as well.

Jack took a sip of the drink and made a face. Fenella braced herself for his complaint, but he didn't say anything.

"I'd better get to work, then," Daniel said. "Maybe I should go out the back way."

Jack glanced toward the door, where the table was still jammed into the wall, and then shrugged. "I thought it made sense to block access somehow. That was the best idea I could come up with last night."

"If you're that worried, I can find a safe house for you," Daniel offered. "We have one in Liverpool that could accommodate you today."

"Liverpool? I don't want to go to Liverpool."

"I might be able to find you a place on the island, but if I do, you'll have to stay there, and Fenella won't be able to visit," Daniel replied.

"Thank you, but I think I'm better off here," Jack said. "The killer shouldn't have the first clue where to look for me, after all."

"That's true," Daniel agreed. "We're keeping an eye on the place for you, too."

"Thank you. I'll just let you out, then, shall I?" Jack asked. He slid the table back into the living room and then took a step toward the door. "Ouch!" he shouted as Fenella heard glass crunching under his bare feet.

"Are you okay? Fenella asked.

"I think I've cut my foot."

"And ruined all of the glasses and plates in the cupboards," Fenella added as she took a better look at the mess Jack's makeshift alarm had made.

"Surely that's better than my getting murdered in my sleep," he snapped.

"As long as you're willing to pay for replacements," she shot back.

Jack pressed his lips together and then sat down on the couch. "I think I'm bleeding," he complained as he studied his feet.

"I'll let you out," Fenella told Daniel, who was watching the scene with an amused expression on his face.

She stepped as carefully as she could around as much of the glass as possible, feeling fortunate that she was wearing sneakers with thick soles. Daniel's black shoes were similarly well equipped for dealing with the mess.

"Do you need to borrow a vacuum cleaner?" he asked her at the door.

"There's one in the utility room," she replied. "I used it to clean up after James. It should be able to handle this mess."

She locked the door behind Daniel and then turned to look at Jack. He was still sitting on the couch, inspecting his feet.

"Are you okay?" she asked after a minute.

"There are a few cuts, but nothing serious."

Fenella didn't argue, even though she could see no sign of any blood anywhere. "Why don't you go and take a shower and get dressed," she suggested. "I'll clean up down here."

"I don't have clean clothes to put on," Jack grumbled. "The police still have everything."

"Just put on your clothes from yesterday. I did bring you clean underwear, at least. Hopefully you'll get your bags back later today."

"You should have asked that police inspector about them. Why wasn't he already at work, anyway? It's after nine. What sort of short hours do the police keep over here?"

"No doubt he worked late last night. I'm sure the police here work very hard indeed."

Jack frowned and then stood up and headed for the stairs. "I'll go and get ready."

"Excellent."

Fenella started by picking up the largest of the pieces of broken glass and crockery. Then she vacuumed the floor several times to try to get every last tiny sliver. When she'd finished, she ran a handful of wet paper towels over the floor.

"That's as good as it gets," she said eventually. "No doubt Jack will manage to find the one little bit I missed, probably with one of his feet."

A quick check in the kitchen confirmed that Jack had piled nearly every glass, cup, and plate that had been in the cupboards onto the table. Only a very few had managed to survive when Daniel had pushed the table into the wall. Feeling as if she really ought to make Jack pay for the damages, Fenella put the vacuum away and then paced around the kitchen while she waited for Jack.

"I'm sorry about the broken glasses and things," Jack said when he found her in the kitchen a short while later. "After you left last night, I went straight to bed, but I couldn't sleep. I kept thinking about how Peter had been murdered in his bed, you see, and I started to get really worried about my own safety. I finally got back up and moved the table in front of the door. Once I'd done that, I decided that I needed some sort of alarm as well. I thought the breaking glass would wake me."

"But it didn't," Fenella sighed, "and now I'll have to pay for replacements."

"How long will it take to get them?"

"I've no idea," Fenella replied to the unexpected question.

"It's just that I'll need them for tonight, to reset the alarm, you see."

"You are not breaking any more dishes or glasses," Fenella said firmly. "You can use cans of soup or something like that, whatever you want to buy when we go to the store later."

"I'm not sure that cans would be loud enough."

"The glasses and plates weren't loud enough. My pounding on the door wasn't loud enough, either."

"Perhaps it would be best, therefore, if you stayed here with me," Jack suggested. "I'm sure all of that noise would have woken you."

"I'm not staying here with you, but if you really don't feel safe here, you should take Daniel, er, Inspector Robinson up on his offer and let him find somewhere for you to stay."

"I came to spend time with you. If I can't do that, I may as well just go back to Buffalo."

"Maybe you should talk to the police about that. It would definitely be safer, anyway."

"I'm not going anywhere yet," Jack told her. "Not until I've won back your heart."

"That isn't going to happen."

"You keep saying that, but I keep seeing signs that you still care for me. It won't be long before you find yourself falling back in love with me. I'm sure of it."

Fenella shook her head. "Please stop thinking like that. I'm not going to fall back in love with you and I really don't want to hurt you. Maybe it would be best if you went back to Buffalo now."

"What are we going to do today, then?" Jack asked.

"How about a visit to the Manx Museum?" Fenella asked, swallowing a sigh and letting the difficult subject drop.

"What's at the Manx Museum?"

"It gives a good, basic history of the island. Some of the exhibits are excellent."

"Okay, then, let's start there."

"I know I need to take you grocery shopping, too," Fenella said as she headed for the door. "But we can do that later."

Fenella drove them the short distance to the museum and parked in its small parking lot.

"At one time this was the island's hospital," she told Jack as she led him to the building's main entrance.

"How nice," he replied, clearly uninterested.

She frowned. Jack was an expert in American military history. She'd never realized how narrow his focus was, though. He'd never shown any interest in her research, but it seemed he didn't care about the island's history, either.

Fenella spent an hour dragging Jack around the museum. He showed a passing interest in a few of the displays that centered on the First and Second World Wars, but beyond that he was clearly bored. She tried to get him interested in the Civil War period, but once he found out that no actual fighting had taken place on the island he lost interest.

"Do you want to get lunch in the café?" she asked as they walked through the gift shop.

"Is the food good?"

"It's just soups and sandwiches, but it's good."

"I think I'd rather just go to the store and buy my own sandwich ingredients," Jack said, "and maybe a few cans of soup, too."

Fenella thought about arguing, but didn't bother. Jack had never liked eating in restaurants. She'd learned that early in their relationship. There was no reason to think that he'd changed since she'd moved to the island.

"You were going to get the ingredients to make some of my favorite things," Jack said as Fenella drove them to the closest grocery store. "I'm really looking forward to having your cooking again."

"I never agreed to that," Fenella sighed. "I assumed, since you're on vacation, that you'd want to try all of the different restaurants the island has to offer."

Jack made a face. "Restaurants always put all sorts of odd things into their meals," he complained. "You know I like plain things."

Fenella swallowed another sigh. "Then you'll have to get whatever you need to cook your own meals. I'll cook Christmas dinner, but beyond that you're on your own."

Jack reached over and took Fenella's hand. "I don't mean to make more work for you," he said softly. "I just thought it would be nice to have some quiet dinners at home together. Your cooking skills are one of the things I love best about you, and I always thought you enjoyed cooking for us both."

"You were wrong," Fenella replied, pulling her hand away. "I never liked cooking, and since I've been on the island I've done very little of it, aside from simple things. As I said, I'll make Christmas dinner, as we'd struggle to find a restaurant open on Christmas Day, but you aren't going to sweet-talk me into anything more than that."

"What are we having for Christmas dinner?"

"Turkey, as that's traditional over here. I thought I'd just do all of the usual trimmings."

"I just had turkey for Thanksgiving. We always had ham for Christmas in Buffalo."

"Yes, well, this year I'm making turkey. If you want ham, you'll have to buy one and cook it yourself."

Jack sighed. "I feel like we're arguing all the time," he said plaintively. "I don't want to argue with you, I really don't. I'm not sure you appreciate how difficult this has been for me."

Fenella bit back a dozen flippant replies. Jack was right. She hadn't given much thought to how her leaving affected him.

"I thought we were happy together," he said after a while when she didn't reply. "I thought we loved one another and that we might even get married one day. Then you announced that you were leaving me and leaving the country. I was devastated."

"Jack, we talked about all of this before I left," she reminded him. "I told you then that I was sorry, but I had to take advantage of the opportunity I was being given to start a whole new life."

"Was your old life that bad?" Jack asked sadly.

"It wasn't bad," Fenella tried to explain. "I was fairly content with my little house, teaching all day and grading papers all night. But it wasn't exciting or even very interesting. I spent all of my time planning what I wanted to do when I retired and had time to chase my dreams. And then I was given a chance to take early retirement and start chasing them immediately. I couldn't turn it down."

"You could have brought me with you."

I didn't love you enough, Fenella thought but didn't say. "You were happy where you were," she said instead. "I had no idea what I was getting myself into over here. I couldn't have asked you to give up everything you knew, not when I wasn't sure what I was going to find here."

"I miss you every single day."

"I miss you, too, but I've moved on with my life. I don't want to try again. I'm sorry if that hurts you."

"It hurts me very badly," he sighed. "You don't seem to be the same person I loved so much back in Buffalo. My Maggie would have cooked for me while I was here."

"I'm not your Maggie anymore," she said softly. She pulled the car into the first parking space she saw at the grocery store, switched off the engine, and then turned to Jack. "I really hope you enjoy your visit to the island, but I think it's probably best if we don't see each other again after you leave."

"I'm here for five weeks. I'm still hoping I can change your mind."

Fenella sighed. "That isn't going to happen."

"We'll see. Let's do some shopping for now."

Feeling as if everything she'd just said was being completely ignored, Fenella climbed out of the car and followed Jack into the grocery store. You are not cooking for him, she reminded herself sternly as she went.

An hour later, they were heading back to the house on Poppy Drive. The car's trunk was full of simple things that Jack could throw together for meals. It also contained the ingredients for Fenella's favorite meatloaf. After some discussion, she'd agreed to cook for herself and Jack that evening.

"I don't intend to cook for you again," she warned him.

"I'm going to take notes while you cook," he replied. "I want to be able to make your meatloaf for myself, but I don't have the recipe."

Fenella loved meatloaf and she very rarely made it for just herself. It would be nice to prepare it to share with someone who would truly appreciate it, even if that someone was Jack.

"It's too early to start cooking," she said after they'd put away all of the groceries. "Let's go for a walk around the neighborhood."

Jack shrugged. "If you'd like."

"It's cool, but not cold. Nothing like Buffalo winters. I would think you'd want to enjoy the better weather."

"I don't mind Buffalo winters. I have someone come to plow my driveway, and if the roads aren't plowed, I simply stay home."

Fenella had had someone to plow her driveway, too, but she had still needed to shovel the path to her front door and dig out around her mailbox so the mailman could deliver. While she wondered how Christmas would feel this year without any snow, she didn't really miss it, at least not yet.

They walked in silence for several minutes. Jack seemed to be studying his surroundings as they went.

"What would a house like that cost?" he asked after a while. He gestured toward a tiny single-story house that sat on a small lot.

Fenella gave Jack her best guess, converted into dollars, and then hid a smile as he gasped and then shook his head.

"I don't believe it," he replied. "That's far more than that house is worth."

"Houses on the island are expensive, especially compared to house prices in Buffalo. There are a limited number of properties and demand is fairly steady."

"I don't know that I could afford a house here, then."

"You can't simply move here, anyway. You'd need some sort of visa."

"I could get one if we got married, though, right?"

"Maybe, but we aren't going to get married. We've been all through this."

Jack sighed. "I don't understand why you're being so difficult. We're perfect together. Why can't you see that?"

Fenella swallowed a dozen replies. In some ways she did still care deeply for Jack, but it was a friendly affection rather than romantic love. They'd spent a considerable amount of time together since his arrival and he hadn't done so much as try to hold her hand. If she hadn't dated a few other men since she'd left Buffalo, she might have believed that she was too old to feel physical chemistry, but she knew better now. "We aren't perfect together, and once you meet the right woman you'll find that I'm right," she said eventually.

"What if I never meet her? I don't want to be alone."

"That isn't a good reason to stay with someone who isn't right for you," Fenella told him. "Anyway, being alone isn't bad. I'm enjoying it."

They walked back to the house, and once Fenella had the meatloaf in the oven, she sat down with Jack's checkbook and tried to make it balance.

"You haven't written any amounts next to the checks you've written," she said after a few minutes.

"I'm sure I can remember the amounts. Which checks?"

"Let's start with number 3271."

"To whom was that written?"

"You didn't write that down either."

Jack sighed. "Maybe I'd better take the whole thing to the bank and let them help me."

Fenella tried for a few minutes longer, but in the end she had to give up. "You have to keep track of everything," she told him. "The bank is going to charge you for their time if they have to sort it all out."

"Maybe I need to find an accountant."

Fenella peeled and chopped potatoes and then put them into a pan on the stove. "I got broccoli and cauliflower to go with the meatloaf. Do you like one more that the other?"

"I'm not a fan of either. You should know that."

Fenella shrugged. "I thought maybe you'd learned to eat more healthily since I've been gone."

They ate at the kitchen table off plates that didn't match, thanks to Jack's burglar alarm system. When they were done, Fenella insisted that Jack wash the dishes.

"Really? You know I'm not very good at household chores," he argued.

"I cooked. You can clean up," Fenella replied. She sat at the table sipping coffee while Jack clattered plates and pots and pans together ineptly. He managed to break one plate and somehow snapped the handle off one of the pots. Fenella just watched, feeling amused for the most part.

"Now I have one less plate for my meals while I'm here," Jack complained when he was done.

"It's a good thing I don't plan on eating here again," Fenella said calmly. "Now that dinner is over, I'm going to go home. What do you want to do tomorrow?"

"What can we do?"

"There are lots more sights to see. Douglas town center has some interesting shops. There's a wildlife park. Didn't you look into what the island had to offer before you came?"

"No, not at all. I came to spend time with you."

"So you just want to sit around the house with me?"

Jack shrugged. "That's what we did in Buffalo."

Fenella laughed. "And that's why we aren't together anymore," she muttered under her breath. "Let's go to the wildlife park," she said. "It might be cold, but you're used to cold weather. If it rains, maybe we'll reconsider."

"If that's what you want to do."

It wasn't really what Fenella wanted to do, but she didn't feel right leaving Jack to his own devices. He'd come a long way to see her. The least she could do was spend some time with him. Clearly, working out what to do with that time was going to be her job, which was unfortunate but hardly surprising, knowing Jack.

"Maybe we'll go to Peel on Thursday," she said. "The House of Manannan is a totally different sort of museum."

"Another museum? I mean, if that's what you really want to do."

"We'll see. We can take it one day at a time," Fenella told him. "For now I think we both could do with an early night. Yesterday was a long day."

"Yes, I suppose so."

Fenella was heading for the door when someone knocked. "Are you expecting anyone?" she asked Jack, mostly teasing.

"Of course not," he told her. "I don't even know anyone on the island."

Fenella opened the door to Daniel Robinson. "Good evening," she said brightly. "What brings you here?"

He smiled at her. "I thought I recognized your car. I have a few more questions for Dr. Dawson, and then I'd like to talk to you, too."

"You know I'm always happy to help in any way I can."

He nodded. "But I need to speak to Dr. Dawson first."

"I was just leaving. Do you want to talk to me at my apartment once you've finished with Jack?"

"That would work," he told her. "I'll be there as soon as I can."

"Great." Fenella glanced back at Jack. "I'll be back around nine tomorrow," she told him. "If it isn't raining, we'll head out to the wildlife park."

"Sure," he replied unenthusiastically.

Daniel raised an eyebrow at Fenella, but didn't say anything.

"Bye," she said to Jack before she walked away, leaving Daniel to ask his questions. She drove back to her apartment building and parked her car next to Mona's.

"I thought for sure you'd bring Jack here today," Mona said as Fenella let herself into the apartment.

"I'm not even certain I'm going to bring him here. I'm not sure I want him here."

"But I want to meet him."

"We'll see. I'm trying to spend as little time as possible with him. He still doesn't seem to have accepted that we aren't a couple any longer."

"But let's talk about the murder investigation. How is it going?" Mona asked.

"I've no idea. Jack and I went to the Manx Museum and then grocery shopping. I haven't heard any news about the case at all."

"Ring Daniel," Mona suggested. "We don't even know if the dead man was Peter Grady yet."

"I'm not going to call Daniel." Mona made a face and opened her mouth to argue. Fenella held up a hand. "He came to the house to talk to Jack just before I left. He's going to come here when he'd done talking to Jack. The dead man was Peter Grady. He told me that last night, actually."

"Excellent. Now you must get Daniel to tell you more about those four women. If one of them didn't kill Dr. Grady, I'm sure one of them knows who did."

"That's just wild speculation. Everything I've heard about Peter Grady suggests that he might have been involved with quite a few more women than just those four. Daniel will have a job tracking them all down, I'm sure."

"But those four all turned up at the house yesterday. That means that they knew Dr. Grady was going to be there."

Fenella frowned. "None of them mentioned knowing any such thing. In fact, they all questioned Jack and me about what we knew of Dr. Grady's plans. It was only Bev, when she came the second time, who seemed convinced that he was back on the island."

"Which makes her my number-one suspect," Mona said. "Either her or her husband. You need to track him down and ask him some questions. That's your first job for tomorrow."

"I've no idea where to find him and I've no interest in getting involved in the investigation. I've enough on my plate keeping Jack entertained. Which reminds me, he's out of plates."

"Out of plates?"

Fenella explained about Jack's attempt to alarm the house's front door and the subsequent damage that had occurred. "I think I'll buy him a package of paper plates to use while he's here," she concluded. "I can buy more proper plates for the house after he's gone home, before I let Doncan rent it out again."

"There are boxes and boxes of plates and kitchen things in my storage room," Mona told her. "Don't buy anything, just help yourself."

"I don't remember seeing any plates when I was looking through the Christmas decorations," Fenella replied.

"But you weren't looking for plates then. If you go looking, I can assure you you'll find more plates than you'll ever need."

Fenella didn't bother to argue with Mona. In the months that she'd known her, Mona had never been wrong. It was infuriating in many ways.

"I'm sure Daniel will tell you where to find Robert Martin, assuming that is his surname," Mona said. "Ask Daniel about the other women, too. Some of them probably have boyfriends or husbands they didn't bother to mention to you."

"I'm not asking Daniel anything. He's coming to ask me questions. My job is to answer them."

"They won't let Jack leave until the case is solved," Mona told her. "Think about that for a few minutes."

"They can't keep Jack here forever," Fenella said, shuddering at the very idea. "I'm sure Daniel will let Jack go when it's time for his flight home, no matter what's happening with the murder investigation."

"Maybe we could find a way to implicate Jack in Dr. Grady's death," Mona said speculatively. "Of course, if he were thrown into prison here, you'd probably feel the need to visit him regularly."

The ringing doorbell kept Fenella from having to reply.

6

"I rang you twice last night, but you never answered," Shelly said when Fenella opened the door. "I wasn't expecting you to stay out late with Jack on his first night."

Fenella sighed. "I wasn't staying out late with Jack. I was being interviewed by the police."

"Don't tell me that Jack made you so mad in a single day that you killed him," Shelly gasped.

Chuckling, Fenella shook her head and then stepped back to let her friend into the apartment. "Jack's fine, or at least he was an hour ago. It's the man whose house he was staying in that got himself murdered."

Shelly gasped again and then sat down on the nearest chair. "Not another murder!" she exclaimed. "I heard something on the radio about a body discovered in a house in Douglas. That was the house where Jack was staying?"

"It was, at least until the body was found."

"Where is he now?" Shelly asked, glancing toward Fenella's guest bedroom.

"The house on Poppy Drive. There's no way I'd let him stay here."

"Tell me everything," Shelly demanded.

Fenella set a pot of coffee brewing and then told Shelly everything that had happened since Jack arrived. Mona listened closely to every word.

"My goodness, so one of his girlfriends must have killed him, don't you think?" Shelly asked when Fenella was finished.

"I've no idea," Fenella replied. "For all I know, he had a dozen other women in his life."

"You said the girl who found the body was married. If I were Daniel, I'd be taking a really good look at her husband," Shelly said thoughtfully. "I wonder if any of the other women are married."

"None of them mentioned husbands or even boyfriends," Fenella told her.

"From what you said, none of them were surprised to find out about the others, aside from the married one, Bev, wasn't it?"

"That was the name she gave me when we met, but she gave the police a different name after she'd found the body."

"Which is highly suspicious," Shelly suggested.

"Maybe, but if she'd killed him, surely the last thing she'd want to do is find the body. It seems like the longer the body stayed hidden the better it would be for the killer," Fenella replied.

"I wonder how she knew Dr. Grady was back on the island," Shelly said. "She wouldn't have searched the house that way if she hadn't been sure."

"I'd guess that Dr. Grady called or texted her or maybe he even invited her over."

"Where were Jack's bags?" Mona asked.

"In his room," Fenella replied.

"What was in whose room?" Shelly wondered, looking confused.

Fenella blushed. She'd forgotten that Shelly couldn't see or hear Mona. "Jack's bags were in his room," she explained. "I was just thinking about where Jack had put his things."

"I was wondering why Dr. Grady didn't wake Jack to greet him," Mona explained. "If the bags were in the room with Jack, though, maybe Dr. Grady didn't know Jack was there."

Fenella nodded and then got up and poured herself another cup of coffee. Responding to Mona twice in only a few minutes clearly showed that she wasn't alert enough. "I wonder if Dr. Grady even realized that Jack was there," Fenella said after her first sip.

"I wonder if the killer knew that Jack was there," Shelly said.

"If the killer was one of the women we'd met earlier, then she knew about Jack. That suggests to me that the killer was someone else," Fenella told her.

"Like Bev's husband," Shelly replied. "If I were Daniel, he'd be on the top of my list."

"I'm not sure if Daniel is making a list or if he's leaving that up to Mark Hammersmith," Fenella told her. "Apparently the chief constable is aware that Daniel and I are friends. Daniel said something about the case being turned over to Mark."

"That's unfortunate," Mona sighed. "Mark isn't nearly as forthcoming with the details."

Fenella managed to bite her tongue before she could accidentally reply again.

"I'm fascinated by the idea that he was seeing four different women at the same time," Shelly said after a moment. "How did he find the time?"

"He didn't even live or work on the island," Fenella said. "His home here was just a vacation home, or at least that's what Jack told me. He worked in Liverpool and had a house there, too."

"Maybe he was married," Mona suggested. "Maybe he kept his wife in Liverpool, and she found out about all of the women here and came across and killed him."

Fenella thought that seemed like a nice and tidy solution. "I'm sure one of the women told me Dr. Grady was single," she said, trying to address Mona's words without answering them directly, since Shelly hadn't heard them.

"She could have been wrong," Mona shot back. "He probably told her he was single, but he could have been living a totally different life in Liverpool."

The knock on the door was a welcome interruption. Fenella let Daniel in and quickly poured him a cup of coffee.

"I hope Jack was cooperative," she said as he took a sip.

"He was," Daniel replied. "I'm sure he wants the case solved as much as anyone."

"He's afraid the killer might come after him next," Fenella told Shelly.

"If the killer didn't realize Jack was in the house when he or she murdered Dr. Grady, then I can understand Jack's concerns," Shelly replied. "If the killer finds out that Jack was there, he or she might be worried about what Jack might know."

"I don't think Jack knows anything," Daniel sighed. "We're doing our best to keep Jack's existence quiet, but the four women who visited the house before the murder all know about him, so that may not be possible."

"Does that suggest that none of them killed Dr. Grady, then?" Fenella asked.

"I'm not going to speculate about that," Daniel told her. "Technically, the case is Mark's to investigate. I'm doing what I can to help, but only in an unofficial capacity."

"But you have questions for me?" Fenella asked.

"I was just wondering what you did today," he replied.

Fenella frowned. "Today? Did something else happen today?"

"Not at all. You don't have to answer if you don't want to," he said.

"Jack and I went to the Manx Museum and then I took him grocery shopping. I made meatloaf for both of us for dinner and then I came home."

"You cooked for him at the house on Poppy Drive?" Daniel checked.

"Yes, that's right. He managed to break another plate, too. I think he's down to two now."

"You'll have to buy more before you cook for him again," Daniel suggested.

"I've no intention of cooking for him again," Fenella replied. "I felt sorry for him tonight, since he came all this way to see me and all, but I don't plan to repeat the experience."

Daniel nodded and then shrugged. "That's between you and Dr. Dawson, of course. Did anything unusual happen during the day?"

"Unusual? What do you mean?" Fenella demanded.

"Did anyone speak to Dr. Dawson? Did you see any of the women whom you'd met at Dr. Grady's house?" he replied.

"No one spoke to him except me, and I only spoke when I had to," Fenella said dryly. "As for Dr. Grady's women, no, I didn't see any of them today."

"I think we all need a trip to the pub," Shelly announced.

Daniel frowned and then shook his head. "I don't think so," he said hesitantly.

"Why not?" Shelly asked. "You aren't even officially investigating, right? The chief constable knows you and Fenella are friends anyway. Come and have a drink with us."

"One drink," Daniel replied. "I really want an early night tonight."

Fenella headed to her bathroom to comb her hair and touch up her lipstick. She really wanted several drinks, enough to make her forget all about Jack and Dr. Grady, but she knew she had to be sensible. Still, a trip to the pub was always enjoyable, especially with Shelly.

Shelly had gone back to her own apartment to get herself ready. She was back by the time Fenella found shoes and checked that she had everything she needed in her handbag.

"Don't talk about the case," Mona said sternly. "I don't want to miss hearing about that."

Fenella rolled her eyes at the woman. It wasn't her fault that Mona couldn't come along to the pub. If they talked about the case, she'd repeat everything to Mona eventually, anyway, and Mona knew that.

"Ready to go?" Daniel asked after Fenella had given Katie a few treats and refilled her water bowl.

"Yes," Fenella nodded happily.

The nearest pub was in the building right next to their apartment building, but Shelly and Fenella much preferred the Tale and Tail, which was only a few doors further away. The pub had once been the library of a huge seaside mansion. New owners had converted the mansion into a luxury hotel. The library had remained largely intact. The owners had added a bar in the middle of the ground floor and then scattered a number of cat beds around the place to make for a unique pub experience. Thousands of books still filled the shelves, and they were all available to be borrowed by customers. A dozen or more cats called the pub home, and if they weren't lounging in their beds, they were probably curled up on customers' laps enjoying being fussed over.

As always, Fenella walked into the building and then stopped and sighed with delight. A large black cat, one she'd not seen before, raced over and greeted her with a long vocal demand.

"I think you've made a new friend," Shelly laughed.

"I'm not sure if he likes me or hates me," Fenella replied.

"I'm sure you'll find out once we sit down," Daniel told her.

He insisted on going to the bar and getting the drinks while the women found seats on the upper level. Tables with chairs and couches around them were liberally scattered around the space. Once they'd climbed the winding staircase, Fenella and Shelly found an empty table and settled in together on a couch. The black cat had followed them up the stairs. As soon as Fenella was seated, he jumped into her lap and made himself at home.

"It's a good thing Katie isn't here. She'd be awfully jealous," Shelly said.

"We mustn't tell her," Fenella laughed.

"She'll probably be able to tell, though. Don't be surprised if she's mad at you when you get home."

Daniel arrived with the drinks a moment later. "It's busy tonight," he remarked as he passed around the glasses.

"It's nearly Christmas" Shelly replied. "Everyone is out celebrating."

"Ah, yes, Christmas," Daniel sighed.

"What are you doing for Christmas?" Shelly asked him.

"Working," he replied.

"Oh, dear, how awful," Shelly said. As soon as the words were out of her mouth, she blushed. "I didn't mean for that to come out that way," she added quickly. "But it's Christmas, after all. You should be celebrating with family and friends."

"The constabulary asked for volunteers," he explained. "Police stations need to be manned all year round, even on Christmas, after all. I offered to work since I don't have any family on the island. One of the inspectors has twin three-year-old girls. If I work, he can be home with them."

"That's very good of you," Shelly said. "I hope he appreciates it."

"Oh, he's very grateful," Daniel assured her. "It will be the first Christmas that he's been off since the girls were born. His wife is even happier than he is, I think."

"What are you doing?" Fenella asked Shelly.

She shrugged. "I told Tim I'd cook dinner, but I think I'd rather go out if we can find anywhere that's open. I always cooked for John and me. It will feel odd to cook for someone else."

"I told Jack I'd make Christmas dinner," Fenella said. "You and Tim are welcome to join us. I'd rather not be alone with him any day, but especially not on Christmas."

Shelly laughed. "What if he proposes?"

Fenella shuddered. "I hope he knows better than that," she sighed. "Daniel, you can come for dinner, too, if you'd like. I can plan it for whatever time your shift finishes."

"That's very kind of you," he said, smiling at her, "but I can't promise what time I'll be done working."

"What time are you supposed to finish?" she asked.

"On paper, around five."

"So I'll plan dinner for five-thirty. If you aren't there, we'll sit down without you and you can have leftovers when you turn up," Fenella said.

"That would be great, if you're sure," he told her.

"Of course I'm sure. Like I said, I don't want to be alone with Jack any more than I have to be. It's going to be difficult enough finding ways to entertain him during his stay, but at least we can go sightseeing and shopping. Nothing will be open on Christmas."

"I'll talk to Tim and see what he wants to do," Shelly said. "As long as he doesn't have to cook, I can't see him complaining, though."

"Good. I'd love it if you guys could come over before Jack arrives and stay until he's gone home," Fenella told her. "Although I suppose I'll have to pick him up and take him home again."

"I can probably take him home after dinner," Daniel said.

"That would help," Fenella sighed. "I'm sorry to be dragging you both into all of this. I didn't want Jack to visit, and now that he's here, all I can think about is avoiding him. He deserves better, really."

"Except he invited himself, right? And you split up with him before you moved here, didn't you? And every time he rings you, you remind him that you aren't together anymore, don't you?" Shelly asked.

Fenella nodded. "I know, but he was an important part of life for a long time. I feel like I should be treating him better."

"Which would just encourage him," Shelly told her. "You really don't want to do that."

Fenella sipped her drink and tried to work out how she really felt about Jack. He'd come into her life after she'd been badly hurt by another man. Jack had been kind and patient and had helped her recover from her heartbreak. She'd always be grateful to him for showing her how to trust again.

"Are you okay?" Daniel asked after several minutes.

"I'm fine," she replied. "I just wish I could get Jack to see that we're better off apart without having to be horrible to him."

"He'll come around eventually," Daniel said, patting her hand. "He isn't stupid, just stubborn. He doesn't like change, but he'll come to accept it, given time."

"I hope you're right," Fenella sighed.

"What about another round?" Shelly asked as they finished their drinks.

"I'm tempted, but I'd better not," Fenella told her. "Jack and I are going to the wildlife park tomorrow, so I should probably have an early night."

"And I can't have more than one, not when I'm driving," Daniel said. "Thank you both, though. I enjoyed your company. We should do this more often."

Shelly laughed. "Fenella and I do this all the time," she told him. "You're always welcome to join us."

He nodded. "I may just start taking you up on that."

Fenella wondered if he really would start spending more time with her and Shelly. If he did, would that lead to him spending more time with just her, as well? They'd been working toward something like a relationship before he'd gone to Milton Keynes and met another woman. Maybe they could get back to where they were before, once Jack was gone.

They took the elevator back down to the ground floor and then Daniel insisted on walking them home.

"You have an uncanny knack for bumping into the men and women involved in the murder cases you get wrapped up in," Daniel said at Fenella's door. "Ring me if you happen to come across anyone from this case, please."

"I will, for sure," Fenella promised before Daniel walked away.

Shelly gave her a quick hug. "I want to meet Jack," she said. "Do you want me to cook dinner for you both tomorrow night?"

"Jack's a very fussy eater."

"I'll make a roast chicken. He'll eat that, won't he?"

"Probably, but don't be offended if he doesn't."

"You'll eat it, right?"

"Yes, of course."

"Then that's what we'll have. If Jack doesn't want to eat it, you can take him home before dinner."

Fenella was very tempted to ask Shelly to make something strange and exotic instead of the roast chicken, to increase the likelihood of Jack wanting to go home early. "What about Tim?"

"What about Tim?" Shelly echoed.

"Is he going to be at the dinner? I just want to let Jack know what to expect," Fenella explained.

"Oh, yes, he will be. The band is playing later, though. I thought maybe we could go and listen to them."

"Are they playing at the pub?"

"No, they're at one of the restaurants further down the promenade. It's some sort of Christmas party thing, but Tim assures me that it's open to the public."

"Let's see how dinner goes," Fenella suggested. "I suspect I'm going to need a drink after that, anyway."

"I'll have wine with dinner," Shelly promised.

"Except I'll have to take Jack back to Poppy Drive after dinner."

"We can put him in a taxi," Shelly said. "He'll be fine."

Fenella laughed and then let herself into her apartment. Katie had gone to bed again, so she undressed quietly and then slid under the covers.

"Merrow," Katie said softly as Fenella put her head on the pillow. It didn't seem a moment later when the kitten began to tap on Fenella's nose.

"It can't be seven," Fenella groaned, opening one eye to check the clock. It was exactly seven. "How do you do that?" she asked Katie as she climbed out of bed.

Katie winked at her and then dashed away to complain loudly in front of her empty bowls. Fenella filled them both and then started coffee before she headed for the shower.

"I'm taking Jack to the wildlife park today," she told Katie as she poured herself a cup of coffee. "I'll tell all of the animals you said hello."

Katie shrugged and then left the room, clearly not interested in the animals at the wildlife park. Fenella made herself a plate of pancakes and then smothered them in maple syrup.

"You're only eating those because you're feeling stressed," Mona said as she appeared in the kitchen. "All that sugar is just going to add to the problem."

"I'm eating these because they sounded good," Fenella argued. "I do feel as if I deserve a small treat, though, I will admit."

"What about Jack? What does he have for breakfast?" Mona asked.

"Cereal, bread for toast, yogurt," Fenella rattled off a list. "He didn't want the ingredients for pancakes because he doesn't like to cook."

"Which made them all the more tempting for your own breakfast," Mona suggested.

"Probably," Fenella shrugged. "Regardless, they taste wonderful. I needed something hot and filling. We're going to the wildlife park today and it's going to be cold."

"Maybe you should make other plans," Mona told her.

"I'm open to suggestions."

"You could spend the day tracking down the four women you met at Dr. Grady's," Mona said eagerly.

"I'm not getting involved in the investigation," Fenella replied. "Anyway, Jack is looking forward to seeing the animals."

"Why are we going to the wildlife park, exactly?" Jack demanded a short time later as Fenella drove Mona's car away from the house on Poppy Drive.

"Because it's fun and it gets you out of the house," Fenella replied after counting to ten in her head. "If you'd prefer, you can stay home all day."

"It's cold," he grumbled. "Maybe we should do something indoors."

"We could go to the House of Manannan. It's that other museum I mentioned."

"You know I don't like museums."

"You're a historian. How can you not like museums?"

"Museums are stale and boring. Take me out to a battlefield and I'll spend a day studying vantage points and retracing the steps of the armies involved. That's the sort of historian I am."

"Unfortunately, the island is lacking in terms of battlefields," Fenella told him.

"So let's go to the wildlife park," Jack sighed. "It's better than sitting at home and waiting for a killer to find me."

"You really don't think the killer is after you, do you?"

"I don't know. He or she could be. The more I think about it, the more I worry. What if Peter wasn't dead when I arrived?"

"Then you slept through his murder," Fenella said baldly, "but the killer doesn't know that. He or she probably doesn't even know you exist."

"I was thinking last night that if the killer had known I was there, he or she probably would have killed me, too," Jack said quietly.

Fenella glanced over at him and then leaned over and squeezed his hand. "You need to stop worrying about such things and try to enjoy your visit to the island," she said. "It's a unique and fascinating place and I want you to like it."

"Why? Are you thinking about asking me to move here?" Jack asked. "I'm not sure, in light of everything that's happened, that I want to do that."

"I just want you to enjoy your vacation," Fenella told him. "You've spent a lot of money on flights, and you don't take vacations very often. I want you to go back to Buffalo feeling like you've enjoyed everything the island has to offer."

"Do you miss Buffalo?" Jack asked a short while later.

"Not really. I don't miss the snow and ice, that's for sure."

"But do you miss your old life, even just a little bit?"

Fenella thought carefully before she replied. "I do miss teaching," she said, slightly surprised to realize it. "I miss sharing history with undergraduates and watching just a very few of them become passionate about what they're learning. I don't miss the others who were only in whatever class it was because they needed the credits."

"What about your house? I always loved your little house."

Fenella grinned. She'd always loved her house, too. It had been small and cozy, and when she'd bought it she'd thought she'd live there forever. "I like my apartment here a lot more than that house," she told Jack. "I never would have believed it, but there are a lot of advantages to living in a large apartment building."

"Like what?"

"I don't have to cut the grass, for one thing," Fenella told him. "That was always one of my least favorite chores." Her house had had a fairly small yard, but keeping the grass cut and the yard tidy still took time every summer weekend. "I don't have to worry about the roof, and if we did get snow, I wouldn't have to shovel it."

Jack nodded. "I've been thinking about getting a condo."

"Really? I thought you loved your house." Jack had a large house in one of the nicest suburbs of the city. It was far too large for one person, but Jack had always insisted that he needed the space.

"I like my house, but as I get older it seems like too much house for just me. I always thought that I'd get married and have children to fill the rooms, but now that seems unlikely."

Fenella frowned. After a miscarriage, she'd been told that she'd never be able to have children of her own, something that she'd told Jack as soon as they'd started dating. With whom had he been planning to have children, then?

"We were together for over ten years," Jack said. "It doesn't seem like that many, though, does it?"

"Not really," Fenella agreed. "Time passes so very quickly, especially as we get older."

"I haven't been to your apartment here yet. I'd like to see it."

"I thought we might go there after the wildlife park," Fenella told him. "My neighbor, Shelly, has invited us over for dinner tonight."

Jack made a face. "What is she making?"

"Roast chicken."

"I suppose I could eat that," Jack conceded.

"Shelly is a very good cook. I'm sure it will be delicious."

"Tell me about Shelly, then."

Fenella told Jack all about her closest friend as they made their way across the island. "Shelly has a boyfriend, Tim. He might be there tonight as well."

"You'd better tell me about Tim, then."

"He's an architect who plays in a band in his spare time. He's in the same band as Todd Hughes. I'm sure I told you about them."

Todd was a semi-retired world-famous musician, who happened to live on the island when he wasn't traveling to perform at venues across the globe. He and Fenella had dated for a short while, but Fenella hadn't wanted to travel with him and he hadn't been willing to stay in one place for very long. They'd parted friends, and Fenella knew he was spending Christmas somewhere exotic with a famous acting legend.

"Really? Fascinating," Jack said.

Fenella glanced at him, wondering if he was being sarcastic, but he looked genuinely interested.

"As I said, he may not be there," she warned. "It might just be Shelly."

"I'm looking forward to meeting her, anyway. I'm curious about your friends on the island."

Fenella wanted to question what he meant, but then she missed the entrance to the wildlife park. By the time she'd found a safe place to turn the car around and gotten parked, it was too late.

"Here we are," she said brightly, gesturing toward the park's entrance.

"It doesn't look like much," Jack said.

"No, it isn't a huge zoo like you'd find at home," Fenella agreed. "It's a lovely small park, though."

Jack nodded and then climbed out of the car. Fenella did the same and then they walked down a small incline to the entrance gate. The sign said open, but there wasn't anyone in the ticket booth.

"What now?" Jack asked.

"There's a box into which you insert your admission fee," she told him, leading him through the entrance. She pushed the required fee into the box and then led Jack into the park.

"Pelicans?" he asked as they walked into the first enclosure. "Shouldn't they be behind bars?"

"Unlike American zoos, a lot of the enclosures here let the animals roam freely," Fenella told him. "That's why there are two sets of gates. You never open the second gate until the first one is shut behind you. That keeps the animals where they belong."

"What other animals are wandering around?" Jack asked nervously.

"Capybaras, wallabies, some deer, a few rheas, things like that."

"Nothing dangerous?"

"Of course not. I'm told you don't want to take a stroller though the lemur enclosure unless you want a lemur to climb inside, but none of the animals are dangerous."

"I don't like the looks of that pelican," Jack said. "We may have to rethink this visit."

"He's not going to bother you," Fenella replied confidently. "Just walk past him and ignore him. Once we get past the pelicans, the other animals are all charming."

Jack didn't look like he believed her, but he followed her along the winding path through the first enclosure. As they passed a group of pelicans, one of them stretched out his neck and gave Fenella a hard stare. Jack picked up his pace, nearly tripping over Fenella in his rush to get away.

"That wasn't so bad," she said as they shut the first gate behind them.

"It was different," Jack replied. "Quite unlike anything I've experienced at a zoo before."

"When was the last time you went to a zoo?" Fenella asked.

"It's been some years, and that one was nothing like this."

They wandered through several more enclosures. Fenella enjoyed seeing the various animals, especially the wallabies.

"The island has a wild wallaby population," she told Jack. "A breeding pair escaped many years ago, and I've been told there are probably seventy-five to a hundred animals living wild on the island."

A short while later they found themselves at the café.

"Want to stop for a coffee or something?" Fenella asked.

"It's too early for lunch, isn't it?" Jack replied. "I didn't have any breakfast, so I'm rather hungry."

"I thought you bought cereal and yoghurt yesterday."

"I did, but the cereal didn't taste the same as it does at home. Maybe it was the milk. I don't know, but it didn't taste right. Do they do plain sandwiches here?"

"I'm not sure what they do, but we can find out," Fenella suggested.

The café was as empty as the rest of the park had been.

"Ah, good morning," a young, dark-haired man called as they walked inside. "I'll be with you in a minute." He was sitting on the floor behind a large freezer that had pictures of frozen treats all over it. As Fenella crossed the room she could see what looked like hundreds of pieces of the freezer's components spread across the floor next to him. He was holding a screwdriver and frowning at the back of the machine.

Jack went and stood at the counter, frowning over the menu. After a minute, Fenella joined him. The other man wasn't far behind. Fenella would have guessed him to be around thirty. He was smiling as he wiped his hands on a towel.

"I'll get it working before the summer," he laughed. "What can I do for you today?"

Jack opened his mouth to reply, but was interrupted as the café's door swung open.

"Robert, what have you been telling the police now?" a voice shouted from the doorway.

Fenella turned around and nearly gasped as Bev Martin stormed into the room.

7

"Bev, darling, what are you doing here?" Robert asked with a huge grin on his face.

The woman looked at him for a minute and then frowned at Fenella. "What are you two doing here?" she demanded.

"Visiting the animals," Fenella replied.

"Really? What an odd coincidence," she said suspiciously.

"Maggie, who is this woman?" Jack asked.

Fenella looked at Jack and had to hide a smile at the confused look on his face. He was terrible at remembering people, but he was usually more subtle when he didn't recognize someone.

"Don't play dumb with me," Bev snapped. "I'm not stupid."

Jack nodded. "Of course not. I'm terribly sorry, but I don't have any idea who you are, though. I have a terrible memory for faces. Should I assume you were one of the young women I met on Monday at Dr. Peter Grady's home?"

Bev frowned as the man behind the counter cleared his throat. "I thought you said you weren't at that man's house on Monday," he said to Bev.

She glared at Jack for a moment and then turned a huge, fake smile on the younger man. "I'm not sure what I said. It was all so upsetting and you know how fragile I am right now," she told him.

Robert nodded. "But what did happen on Monday?" he asked.

Bev shook her head. "Let's not worry about that right now. I didn't mean to interrupt anything. It never occurred to me that you'd have customers, not at this time of year."

"We were just going to get a snack," Fenella said.

"I'm quite hungry," Jack complained. "I'd like something more than a snack."

"We're serving our full menu," Robert told him. "What would you like?"

Jack seemed to take ages to read through the board. Fenella knew him well enough to know what he was thinking. "I'm sure they can adjust things if you need them to," she said after a while.

"As you're my only customers, I can do whatever you want," Robert agreed cheerfully.

Jack finally ordered one of the sandwiches, asking to leave off nearly everything by the time he was done. Robert carefully wrote down exactly what Jack wanted and then grinned at Fenella. "What can I get for you?"

"I'll have the tomato soup," she said.

"Give me a few minutes," he said. "What about drinks?"

"Coffee," Jack replied.

"Make that two," Fenella said.

"Make it three," Bev interjected. "I'll chat with your customers while you're busy in the kitchen."

"Great," the man said. He disappeared into the kitchen.

"Let's sit by the window," Bev suggested, leading Fenella and Jack to a table as far from the kitchen as it was possible to get.

"What are you doing here?" she asked as the trio took seats.

"I told you, we came to see the animals," Fenella replied. "We certainly weren't expecting to bump into you out here."

"You didn't know that Robert was the manager of the café?" she demanded.

"Is that Robert, then, your husband?" Fenella asked, even though she was sure she knew the answer.

"Yes, that's my husband, and I'd appreciate it if you'd stop talking about Dr. Grady in front of him," Bev replied.

"He doesn't know that you found the body?" Fenella wondered.

"No, and I'd rather he didn't." She looked around the room and then slid her chair closer to Fenella's. "We're trying to make our marriage work, and it will be easier to do that if Robert thinks I'd already ended things with Peter before his death."

"I think you'd be better off telling him everything," Fenella said. "You'll have trouble explaining when you have to appear at the inquest or the trial, won't you?"

"Inquest? Trial? Why would I have to appear at either of those?"

"You found the body. The police may well want you to testify."

Bev sighed. "Can't you just tell everyone that you found the body? I mean, you were right behind me. You saw the same thing I saw."

"The police already know you were there," Fenella pointed out.

Bev sighed. "I don't want Robert to know the whole story. He'll be upset."

"He seems like a really nice guy," Fenella told her.

"Yes, he's very nice. That's part of the problem. He was heart-broken when I told him I was leaving and he was thrilled when I came back to him. I don't want to hurt him again."

"Lying to him isn't a good idea, especially not during a murder investigation," Fenella replied.

"He's already said something to the police that's causing trouble," Bev sighed. "I'm just not sure what he said."

"What do you mean?" Jack asked.

"The police have been asking more questions about my relation-ship with Robert. He must have said something to them that's different to what I told them."

"Here we are," Robert said brightly as he carried in a small tray. He unloaded Fenella's soup, Jack's sandwich, and four cups of coffee. "I thought I might take a break and join you for a few minutes," he explained.

"You're more than welcome," Fenella said quickly.

"But I interrupted your conversation. What were you talking about?" he asked.

"The police have been asking me more questions," Bev told him. "What did you tell them?"

Robert glanced at Fenella and Jack and then looked at Bev. "I told them that I'd thought we were happy together until you left me, and that I was delighted when you rang me on Monday and wanted to talk about maybe getting back together."

Bev shrugged. "That's okay, then."

"What happened on Monday?" Robert asked. "Why are the police asking all these questions? Something happened to the man you left me for, didn't it? I heard something on the news a little while ago about a body found in a house in Douglas. He lived in Douglas, didn't he?"

"You don't need to worry about it," Bev told him. "He's dead and he can't come between us now."

"He's dead? How did he die?" Robert demanded.

"I believe the police think he was murdered," Fenella said after a long, awkward silence.

"Murdered? But that doesn't happen on the island. Murder is for television shows. Real people have heart attacks or get cancer. They don't get murdered," Robert said firmly.

"I went to see him, to tell him that we were through," Bev said. "I found the body. He was definitely murdered."

Robert stared at her for a minute and then shook his head. "You told me you hadn't seen him in weeks," he said.

"I hadn't, and I didn't see him on Monday, not alive, anyway," she replied.

"What time did you find the body?" he asked.

Bev glanced at Fenella and then looked back to Robert. "I'm not sure, maybe around five or six, maybe a little earlier."

"And then you rang me around seven asking me to take you back," he said in a low voice. "You weren't going to see him to end things, were you?"

"Of course I was," Bev replied. "I'd realized that I'd been an idiot and that I had everything I needed with you. I knew Peter was meant to be back on the island on Monday, so I went over to tell him that I didn't want to see him anymore. Then I was going to come home to you."

Robert stared at her for a full minute, not speaking.

"This is good," Jack said in the silence. "The sandwich, I mean. It's exactly what I wanted."

Robert looked at him and then nodded. "I'm glad," he said.

"You have to believe me," Bev said in a pleading voice. "I was a fool, getting involved with another man. I love you."

Robert got up and began to pile empty dishes onto his tray. "I'll think about it," he said before he left the room.

Bev sat back and sighed. "You see?" she asked Fenella. "He was happier not knowing."

"Does he know that you were at Dr. Grady's house earlier in the day? Does he know that you met some of his other girlfriends? Maybe that would help him understand why you suddenly decided that you still loved him," Fenella said cynically.

"It wasn't like that," Bev snapped. "Peter was charming, and I met him when Robert and I were having difficulties. He made me feel clever and funny and interesting. Robert is sweet and kind, but he's not a university professor. Peter was smart, and we talked about things like the meaning of life and whether there could be alternate realities or not. Robert isn't interested in things like that."

"Robert deserves a woman who loves him exactly as he is," Fenella suggested.

"I do love him," Bev replied. "I'll be a good wife to him, too, now. Everything that happened with Peter was the wake-up call that I needed to truly appreciate Robert and what we have together. I really was going to end things with Peter if I'd been able to find him the other night."

"I hope, for Robert's sake, that you're telling the truth," Fenella said.

"I wish he'd been alive when I found him," Bev said. "I don't think he's ever been dumped by a woman before. It would have been incredibly satisfying telling him that I was going back to my husband."

"He didn't know you had a husband, did he?"

"Well, no, but I would have told him that, too, as I ended things. I had it all planned and it would have been epic. I can't believe that someone killed him before I got the chance."

"Who killed him?" Jack asked.

Bev blinked at him and then shrugged. "How should I know?"

"What about Robert? Was he jealous enough to kill him?" Jack pushed.

"That's a crazy idea," Bev replied, laughing. The laughter sounded forced to Fenella, as if the woman wasn't quite sure the idea was all that crazy.

"He was upset about losing you," Jack said. "How upset?"

"Not upset enough to kill anyone," Bev retorted. "Besides, he didn't even know where Peter lived."

"He knew Peter lived in Douglas," Jack pointed out. "Maybe Robert followed you the first time you went to the house and then, after you and the other women went for a drink, he went back and killed Peter."

Bev stared at Jack for a minute and then forced out another flat chuckle. "Maybe you're just trying to find other suspects because the police suspect you," she said.

"Why would the police suspect me?" Jack replied. "I didn't even know Peter."

"Maybe you met him and heard about his house that was sitting empty, and decided to break in and stay there while you thought Peter would be away. Maybe he came home and found you in the spare bedroom and you killed him so you could stay," Bev suggested.

"I had the key and the code for the security system," Jack pointed out. "I also have witnesses to the conversation that took place in Buffalo."

"Who else might have wanted to kill Dr. Grady?" Fenella asked, more to stop the pair from arguing than anything else.

"Any one of the other women," Bev suggested. "Oh, they all pretended that they didn't care that Peter had other women in his life, but I didn't believe them."

"Had you ever met any of them before Monday?" Fenella asked.

"Not really, although I'd sort of met Hannah Lawson once. Her boyfriend knows Robert."

"Hannah has a boyfriend?" Fenella was surprised, even though she told herself she shouldn't have been.

"Yeah, or at least she did. They may have split up for all I know, but they were together a few months ago, anyway."

"How does he know Robert?" was Fenella's next question.

"His name is George Norris and he works for one of the companies that supplies the café. I've met George a few times, and he brought Hannah to the summer picnic that the park had for all of the suppliers and their families. We never actually got introduced because there were like a zillion people here, but I saw them together."

Fenella sat back in her seat and tried to think. Was it possible that all of the women had other men in their lives? Maybe none of the men minded about Peter Grady. Or maybe one of the other men murdered the man.

"You don't think George killed Peter, do you?" Bev asked.

"That's for the police to work out," she replied.

"I'd suspect Hannah before I'd suspect George," Bev told her. "He's nice, and I know Robert likes him."

"What about pudding?" Robert asked as he rejoined them.

"Pudding? I don't think so," Jack said.

"Pudding means dessert," Fenella told him. "I'd love a slice of chocolate gateau."

"I know what pudding means," Jack replied. "I don't want anything."

"One slice of chocolate gateau," Robert said.

"Make it two," Bev said, winking at him.

Robert nodded. "And I'll bring the coffee pot, too. You all need refills."

No one spoke while he was gone. Fenella was lost in thought, wondering about Hannah and her boyfriend and the other two women. She couldn't imagine what Jack or Bev was thinking about.

"Here we are," Robert said a minute later. He handed Fenella a generous slice of cake and then gave Bev hers. After refilling all of the coffee cups, he sat back down next to Bev and smiled at her.

"I'm sorry," she said softly.

He nodded. "You need to tell me everything about Monday," he said. "I want to try again, but I have to be able to trust you, and I can't do that if you aren't telling me everything."

"Peter was supposed to be back on Monday. That's what he'd told me when he left. I went to see him, but he wasn't there. Instead, I met Fenella, and two other women who'd also been expecting Peter to be back," Bev said in a rush. "We all went for a drink, and the other two women told me all about how Peter always had lots of girlfriends at the same time and couldn't be trusted. That's when I realized how much better off I was with you, so I went back to Peter's house to tell him that I didn't want to see him again. Instead, I found his body."

Robert took her hand and squeezed it tightly. "That must have been horrible."

"It was. Now every time I close my eyes, all I can see is Peter's body on the bed with blood everywhere," Bev said as a tear slid down her cheek.

"I'm not sure that I believe you," Robert told her.

"I don't blame you," Bev replied. "I've been terrible to you. I don't deserve you, really I don't."

"But I still love you," Robert added. "I need some time to think. Maybe we can try again, but first I need to think."

"Of course," Bev said. "I'll stay at my parents' for now, until you're ready for me to move back in with you."

"If I decide to try again," Robert replied.

"Yes, of course," Bev said, but Fenella was sure she could see confidence in the woman's eyes. Bev seemed certain that Robert would take her back eventually.

"Aren't you meant to be at work?" Robert asked as he looked at the clock on the wall.

"I took the day off," Bev explained. "I'm a bit shaken up after Monday. I was going to spend the day in bed, but then the police came and kept asking more and more questions. When they were done, I wanted to see you."

"You should go home and get some more rest," Robert suggested.

"Yes, I think I should," Bev agreed. She got to her feet and then looked down at Robert. "Can I have a hug?" she asked softly.

For a minute Fenella thought Robert was going to refuse, but then he got to his feet and pulled his wife close. When she leaned back and tried to kiss him, though, he released her.

"We have a long way to go before we get back to that," he told her firmly.

Bev looked surprised and disappointed, but she didn't argue. Instead, she picked up her handbag and then looked at Fenella and Jack. "I won't say it was nice to see you again, because it wasn't, but I do think our conversation was productive in a way. I hope I never see you again, though."

Robert frowned as Bev left the café. "That wasn't very nice," he said as the door swung shut behind her.

"I quite agree with the sentiment," Jack said. "I'd be quite happy to never see her again."

"That might be best for me, too," Robert sighed. "I'm afraid I'm too much in love with her to live without her, though."

Fenella bit her tongue before she could urge him to try. It really wasn't her place to offer him relationship advice.

"The cake is delicious," she said instead.

"I'm glad you like it. We have a specialist supplier who does our cakes and pies. I don't think we've ever had a single complaint about any of them."

"Is that George Norris?" Fenella asked.

"George? No, do you know George? He supplies paper goods, mostly, paper towels and napkins, paper plates, that sort of thing. He's a good guy. Do you know him?" he repeated the question.

"No, Bev mentioned him, that's all. She said something about his girlfriend, Hannah," Fenella explained.

"Hannah's a sweetheart," Robert told her. "She's beautiful and smart, and I keep telling her that she could do a lot better than George, but she just laughs. I don't mean it, of course. Like I said, George is a good guy."

Fenella wanted to ask more questions, but Jack clearly had other ideas. "We should go," he said as he got to his feet. "How much do we owe you?" he asked, reaching for his wallet.

"I'll get the bill," Robert told him.

Jack opened his wallet and frowned at the contents. "I don't have any Manx money," he told Fenella. "Do you think he'll take a credit card?"

"Probably, but you'll have to pay all sorts of fees to use your card over here."

"I should have thought about that before I bought groceries yesterday," Jack sighed. "Can I pay for lunch with dollars?"

"No, but I'll get lunch," Fenella replied. "We can find a bank later and get some of your dollars converted into pounds."

"They can do that at a bank?"

"I hope so," Fenella replied, trying not to think of how much Jack's visit would cost her if they couldn't. She could afford it, but she really didn't want to have to pay for everything.

Robert returned and handed Jack the bill, which he immediately gave to Fenella. She smiled at the low total. "Are you sure this is right? It doesn't seem like enough."

"I only charged you for the ingredients I actually used in the sandwich," Robert told her. "That made it a lot less expensive. I didn't charge you for the coffee, either, since I joined you while you were drinking it."

Fenella pulled out a twenty-pound note, which was more than double what the bill for the meal totaled.

"I'll get your change," Robert said.

"Keep it," Fenella told him. "Thank you."

Robert was still protesting as Fenella led Jack out of the building.

"Thank you for lunch," Jack said as they continued on their way around the park.

"It was an odd experience," Fenella said.

"Yes, I really don't remember that young woman from Monday. Are you quite sure she was at the house?"

"Yes, quite," Fenella replied. "She found Dr. Grady's body."

Jack shrugged. "I was very tired on Monday. The entire day, from when I arrived on the island until the time I went to bed, is very fuzzy."

"I'm sure the police love that," Fenella muttered.

"Jet lag is a medical condition," Jack said. "It wasn't my fault."

"Of course not," Fenella replied. "It was strange seeing her again, and meeting her husband."

"You knew she had a husband?"

"She told us she was married. That might have been when we were out having our drink, though. You might have missed that part."

"I don't understand why she'd cheat on Robert. He seemed like a very nice young man."

"That's between her and him, and not our concern," Fenella said.

"Do you think that Bev killed Peter?" Jack asked as they walked through the last enclosure.

Fenella stopped to admire the penguins as she thought about her reply. "If she had, I don't think she would have deliberately found the body," she said eventually. "I don't think Robert killed him, either, if you were wondering."

"Not really. I discounted him myself. He's not the type."

Fenella thought about arguing. If the last nine months had taught her anything, it was that anyone could be a killer under the right circumstances, but she held her tongue because she agreed with Jack on this one. Robert definitely didn't seem the type to have killed his rival, no matter how much he loved his wife.

"So now what?" Jack asked as they walked back to Fenella's car.

"How about a long drive down to the south of the island," Fenella suggested. "You could see some of the gorgeous scenery along the way and then we'll head back to my apartment for a while before dinner."

"Sure, that sounds good," Jack replied easily.

Fenella wondered why he was being so agreeable, but she didn't question it. It only took her a minute to point the car south.

"This isn't the sort of car I'd expected you to be driving," Jack said after a few minutes.

"You said that about my other car, too," Fenella reminded him.

"Yes, well, that one seems too boring and ordinary. I thought you came over to reinvent yourself, and that car would have fit in perfectly with your old life."

Fenella couldn't argue with that. "And this one?" she asked.

"This one is too, I don't know, wild and crazy for you. You aren't wild and crazy, even if you aren't the same woman I used to know."

"This car was Mona's," Fenella explained. "She was wild and crazy."

"I thought she was really old when she died."

"She was, but she was still wild, or at least adventurous."

"Really? How interesting."

"I love driving this car, though. It handles beautifully."

"It should," Jack told her. He rattled off a bunch of facts about the car's engine and other components that left Fenella shaking her head.

"I didn't know you knew that much about cars," she said when he was done.

"I looked this one up on the Internet after I saw it on Monday," he told her. "Do you know what it's worth?"

Fenella hesitated and then nodded. "My lawyer gave me an approximate value for it."

"I'm surprised you're happy to drive it, then."

Fenella made herself laugh, even though Jack had a good point. "It's insured," she reminded them both. "It's too fun to leave just sitting it the garage, and I can't imagine ever selling it."

Jack dutifully admired the views as Fenella drove him around the island. Although she felt as if she'd never get tired of driving Mona's car, Fenella headed for home when she could tell that Jack was completely bored.

"I didn't realize you lived right on the water," Jack said as Fenella turned into the parking garage under her apartment building.

"There is a road and the promenade between me and the sea," she replied. "The views are amazing, though."

Hoping that Mona would be out, Fenella led Jack down the corridor to her door. "This is it," she said, not sure why she was so nervous. Being alone with Jack was nothing new. Her nerves were probably all down to worry about what Mona would think of him, she decided.

"The views are amazing." Jack echoed her earlier words as he walked into the living room. "I'm sure everything in here is antique. Your furniture must be worth a fortune," he added as he looked around the room.

"Don't tell him that I bought everything new," Mona said as she appeared in the corner. "I'd hate for him to think that I was old."

Fenella swallowed a laugh. "I'm glad you like it," she told Jack.

"I don't think that I'd want to live here," he said thoughtfully. "It does suit you, though."

"Thank you," Fenella replied. "Would you like some coffee or something else to drink?"

"Coffee would be good. I usually drink a lot of it and I've only had a few cups today."

Fenella nodded. Jack's coffee habit was almost legendary at the university where they'd worked together. She'd been surprised to see that he hadn't bothered to make himself a pot that morning. She headed to the kitchen and gave Katie a late lunch before she started the coffee brewing. Jack came and sat on one of the counter stools.

"It does suit you, this apartment," he said after a minute. "You look, I don't know, content here, in a way I don't remember you looking back in Buffalo."

"I love it here. The island is beautiful, my apartment is gorgeous, and I don't have to work. Why would I ever want to leave?"

Jack nodded. "And why would you want to share all of this with me?"

Fenella opened her mouth to reply, but Mona interrupted. "Don't let him make you feel guilty," she said quickly.

"I don't want to share all of this with anyone," Fenella said. It's bad enough sharing with a ghost, she added to herself. Mona made a face at her, suggesting that she could hear Fenella's thoughts, a worrying idea.

"No, I don't blame you. We always had our own homes, for all the years that we were together. Maybe I should have asked you to move in with me when we first started dating. Maybe things would have gone differently if I had."

"I would have said no," Fenella told him. "After everything that had happened to that point, I needed my own space. I didn't want to live with anyone again, not after having my heart broken."

Jack nodded. "You were fiercely independent. That was one of the things that I found attractive. My mother hated you, though."

"Because I started taking over all of the little jobs that she was used to doing for you. I did your laundry and your grocery shopping and paid all of your bills for you."

"And having had Mother to do it before you came along, it never occurred to me that I should have been doing all of those things myself," Jack sighed. "I'm nearly sixty, you know. My life hasn't exactly gone the way I'd planned."

"I hope that in some ways it's gone better," Fenella told him.

He studied her for a minute and then nodded slowly. "I hadn't thought about that," he admitted. "I've been thinking a lot lately about growing old alone. I always thought I'd have a wife and children, and I feel as if I've suddenly reached sixty and missed out on everything. I have had a good and interesting life, though. Perhaps I should focus on the things I have done, rather than what I haven't."

"It's not too late," Mona said. "He could still find someone and have children, you know."

Fenella felt a familiar pang of sadness as she considered the idea. She'd always wanted children, and not being able to have them was a sorrow that she'd carry to her grave. "You could still meet someone," she told Jack as she poured them each a cup of coffee. "Sixty is the new forty, or so I'm told."

He chuckled and then took a sip of his drink. "You say that because you're not quite fifty. If your creative math is correct, that would mean you're going to be the new thirty in another year. It's a great idea, but it isn't really true."

"Whatever age you are, you could still meet someone," Fenella insisted. "I hope that you do."

"I'd like to, I think," Jack replied. "I am rather set in my ways, though. Women are something of a mystery to me, as well. I'm never quite sure if a woman likes me or not. You made it easy."

Fenella laughed as she remembered the early days of their relationship. She'd done most of the work, setting up their dates and making all of their plans. In the beginning, she'd only been interested in becoming friends with Jack, who'd already been working for the university for years before she'd been hired. It was only after weeks of spending time together that she'd finally kissed him one evening. "I wasn't even sure I wanted a relationship," she recalled.

"And I was crazy about you, but thought you were too young and too beautiful for me," Jack replied.

"How sweet," Mona said flatly. "If he can get you to remember your first date and your first kiss you'll be well on the way to falling in love with him again."

Fenella glared at her. "That was a very long time ago," she told Jack. "I think we're both ready to move on with our lives."

The pair spent some time reminiscing about the earliest days of the relationship while Mona made the odd disparaging remark behind Jack's back. Fenella was grateful when it was finally time to go over to Shelly's for dinner.

"You'll like Shelly," she told Jack. "She's incredibly sweet." Not like Aunt Mona, she added to herself, frowning at the woman as they headed for the door.

Mona winked at her and then laughed.

❧ 8 ❧

"It's lovely to meet you," Shelly told Jack as she let the pair into her apartment. She introduced him to Tim before excusing herself. "I just have a few last-minute things to do for dinner," she explained.

"What can I get you to drink?" Tim asked, moving over to a low table that had been set up as a small bar.

Jack shrugged. "I'm not much of a drinker, but I suppose a glass of wine wouldn't hurt."

"Fenella?" Tim asked.

"One glass of white wine, but that's all, as I'll be driving Jack home later."

The trio sat together, admiring the view and nibbling on cheese and crackers until Shelly returned.

"So what did you two do today?" she asked brightly.

"We went to the wildlife park," Fenella told her. "We saw the animals, and we managed to bump into one of the women who was involved with Dr. Grady."

"Which one?" Shelly wanted to know.

"Bev Martin," Fenella replied. "Her husband actually manages the park's café."

"Robert Martin?" Tim asked. "He's a good guy. Someone told me he was married now."

"You know him?" Fenella asked.

"Not well, but we play a few gigs at the wildlife park in the summer months for special events. Robert has always been great to us, making sure we get cold drinks and snacks, and he usually forgets to charge us for them," Tim replied.

"He seemed really nice," Fenella told him.

"I didn't realize he was caught up in your murder investigation," Tim frowned. "Shelly was telling me about the case before you arrived."

"His wife found the body," Fenella said.

"Oh, dear. How upsetting for both of them. Did you say she was having an affair with the dead man?" Tim asked, looking confused.

"As I understand it, she'd left Robert for him," Fenella replied. "It's all a bit complicated, but I believe they're trying to work things out."

Tim shook his head. "When my wife cheated on me, I ended things immediately. She wanted to get back with me afterwards, but I wasn't going to let her hurt me again. I should give Robert a ring and have a little chat with him."

"What did Daniel say when you told him you'd run into Bev?" Shelly asked.

Fenella gasped. "I never called him," she exclaimed. "I should have done that right away."

"The phone is on the table," Shelly gestured.

Fenella stood up and took a step toward it and then shook her head. "I'll just go back over to my apartment and do it," she said. "That way the rest of you don't have to sit silently while I'm on the phone."

She didn't wait for anyone to disagree before she headed to her own apartment. After a moment's hesitation, she rang the police non-emergency number.

"Could I possibly speak with Inspector Robinson?" she asked the receptionist.

"Please hold," the woman replied.

"Hello?" Daniel's voice came down the line a moment later.

Rats, Fenella thought. She'd been hoping to simply leave a message for him. "It's Fenella," she said. "Jack and I went to the wildlife park today. While we were there, we met Robert Martin, and talked to Bev as well."

Daniel sighed. "I knew Robert Martin worked there. I did wonder if you'd manage to meet him and work out who he is, but I wasn't expecting you to see Bev, too."

"She came in while we were ordering food in the café, otherwise we wouldn't have known who Robert was," Fenella explained.

"Run me through the whole thing," Daniel told her. "Start with what time you woke up this morning."

Fenella glanced at the clock and then launched into a very brief account of the start of her day. When she got to the part where Bev walked into the café, though, she slowed down and tried to remember every detail. Daniel didn't interrupt.

"I wish I knew how you do it," he said when she was done. "Neither of them have been very forthcoming with me or Mark. You learned more over coffee than we've been able to find out through direct questioning."

"Maybe you should have given her coffee," Fenella suggested.

Daniel laughed. "If only it were that easy. Seriously, though, she never mentioned knowing Hannah and her boyfriend to me, and that's useful information. Is that it for today or did you see Diane Jenkins on the promenade this afternoon?"

"I told you what we did this afternoon. Mostly we hung out at my apartment, waiting until time to go to Shelly's. I should tell you that Shelly's boyfriend, Tim, knows Robert, too, though."

"Of course he does," Daniel sighed. "I can't interview everyone on the island who knows any of the sus, er, witnesses, but if Tim says anything interesting about any of them, please let me know."

"All he's said so far is that Robert is a really nice guy."

"Everyone seems to say that, but nice guys can be pushed too far."

"I don't think he seemed like a killer," Fenella said.

"I'll keep that in mind," Daniel told her. "Ring me back later tonight at home if you learn anything else."

"I will."

"Or stop over when you drive Jack home," Daniel suggested. "If there are lights on in my house, I'll still be up."

"We'll see what time I take him home. Shelly said something about going to see the band later tonight. I'm not sure if I'll take Jack home before or after that."

"I'd hate to interrupt your fun, but please remember that this is a murder investigation. If Tim says anything that might be useful, I'd like to hear about it sooner rather than later."

"I'll call," Fenella promised, "before we go to hear the band."

"Thank you."

She put the phone down and then frowned at the receiver. If Daniel was that interested in what Tim knew about Robert, he should talk to him himself.

"Stop making that face. You'll get horrible wrinkles," Mona said.

"Why doesn't Daniel just talk to Tim himself?" she demanded.

"Because he doesn't really think that Tim knows anything, but he's looking for excuses to talk to you," Mona told her.

Hoping that Mona was right about Daniel wanting to talk to her, Fenella hurried back to Shelly's. "I hope I didn't keep you all waiting too long," she said as Shelly let her in. "Daniel wanted a minute-by-minute account of my day, as always."

"Not at all," Shelly assured. "We were enjoying getting to know Jack."

Fenella raised an eyebrow but didn't question her friend's words.

"Dinner is ready," Shelly announced just a minute later. They all crowded into the small dining room where Shelly had laid out all of the food on a long table along one wall.

"Ladies first," Jack insisted, motioning for Fenella to fix her plate first. A short while later they were all sitting around the table with very full plates. Even Jack had taken large helpings of just about everything.

As she ate, Fenella sat back and watched as Jack turned on the charm. It had been years since she'd seen him around people he didn't know. She'd forgotten how interesting he could be when he made an effort.

"Everything is delicious," she told Shelly during a short gap in the conversation.

"Thank you," Shelly replied. "It's such an easy meal, but it always comes out nicely."

"I wish I could cook like this," Jack sighed. "I'm rather hopeless in the kitchen, really. Fenella did all of the cooking when we were together."

"You could do this," Shelly told him. She rattled off the instructions for roasting a chicken. When she was done, Jack grinned at her.

"I might just be able to manage that," he said. "It certainly tastes like a lot more work went into it than what you've told me."

"It truly is simple," Shelly replied. "Once you've mastered the basics, you can try different spices and herbs and things, if you'd like, but you really don't need to change a thing."

"I just have time for pudding before I have to go and warm up," Tim said as he helped Shelly clear the dirty plates.

"It's a good thing I made a pudding, then," Shelly laughed. She brought in plates with generous slices of Victoria sponge on them a moment later.

"Daniel wanted me to ask you if you knew anything else about Robert Martin," Fenella said as everyone dug into his or her slice of cake.

"Not really. As I said earlier, he always treats us well when we perform at the park. I've probably not said more than ten words to him in the last five years, though," Tim told her.

"Maybe you know some of the other women," Jack suggested. "Women love men in bands, don't they?"

Tim laughed and then squeezed Shelly's hand. "I wanted to join a band because I believed that was the case, but it hasn't exactly worked out that way. Lead singers from big bands do well with women, or so I'm led to believe. I've never had much luck myself."

"What were the women's names, then?" Shelly asked. "Tim may not have had much luck with women, but he does seem to know just about everyone on the island."

"Thanks to my job at ShopFast, not the band," Tim clarified.

"Please don't repeat any of this," Fenella said. "I don't know how much the police are releasing to the general public."

Tim raised an eyebrow. "I won't repeat anything."

"The women we met at Dr. Grady's were Bev Martin, Hannah Lawson, Diane Jenkins, and Carol Houston," Fenella told him.

"I was trying to remember the names earlier," Shelly said, "when Tim and I were talking about the case, but I got them all muddled up."

"I've already told you that I don't know Bev Martin," Tim said. "Although I might, but under her maiden name. Do you know what it was?"

Fenella shook her head. "I've no idea."

"Hannah Lawson sounds vaguely familiar. What does she look like?"

"She's probably in her late twenties and she has long and beautiful red hair," Fenella said.

"From the description, I'm going to say that I don't know her. She sounds pretty unforgettable."

"What about Diane Jenkins?"

"I don't think so, but I do know Carol Houston," Tim said.

"You do?"

"Thirty-something blonde?" he asked. "She drives a really cool blue sports car and only goes out with men who have money, if I'm thinking of the right woman."

"That sounds like her," Fenella agreed.

"How do you know her?" Shelly asked.

Tim laughed. "She spent some time hanging around with the band. I think she had her sights set on Todd, but he isn't really into much younger women. I think she may have gone out with Paul once or twice, but he does his best to avoid relationships."

Paul was a very talented musician in his thirties who sometimes fronted Tim's band. He spent a lot of his time in the UK, chasing after his big break, and Fenella really hoped that he'd find success one day soon.

"What did you think of her?" she asked Tim.

"I thought she was okay. She seemed like fun, and she was willing to help out sometimes with moving equipment and things like that. It was pretty obvious fairly quickly that she was just there looking to find a man, though. Once she discovered that Todd wasn't interested and that Paul wouldn't commit, she stopped coming around."

"How long ago was that?" Fenella wondered.

"Oh, goodness, it's probably been six months or more since I saw her last. Let me think. Todd was here in the spring for a few months, which is when I first met her. Paul did some shows with us in March. I believe he played with us through Easter, if I'm remembering rightly. I can't say for sure if Carol was around during all of that time or not."

"Interesting," Fenella remarked. "I'll have to call Daniel and tell him what you've told me."

"Now that I think about it, I think she found herself a boyfriend in the end," Tim said thoughtfully. "The last time I saw her, she was with Matthew Arkwright, or at least they seemed to be together."

"Who is Matthew Arkwright?" Fenella asked.

"He owns a few of the hotels and restaurants on the island," Shelly told her. "He's probably one of the island's most eligible bachelors, given that he's wealthy, single, and under fifty. He doesn't spend much time on the island these days, though, or at least that's what I've heard."

"You're right," Tim confirmed. "We play at a lot of his places and I haven't seen him in a while. In fact, I think the last time I saw him was back in April when he was with Carol."

"She didn't mention a boyfriend when we spoke at Dr. Grady's house," Fenella said thoughtfully.

"They may well have split up by now," Tim said. "April was a long time ago. Matthew isn't known for having long relationships."

Tim insisted on helping Shelly clear the dessert plates before he rushed away to get ready for his show. "You are coming later, right?" he asked Shelly in the doorway.

Fenella hid a smile and turned away as he pulled her friend into a kiss. After all of the uncertainty that Shelly had felt with Gordon, she had to know exactly where she stood with Tim.

"I'd better go and call Daniel," Fenella said as Shelly shut the door behind Tim. "He'll want to hear everything that Tim said."

"And then you're coming with me to enjoy the band, right?" Shelly asked.

"Yes, of course. Jack, do you want to go home or do you want to go and see the band?" Fenella asked.

"If you don't mind driving me home late, I think I'd quite like to see the band," he replied.

"Let me make my phone call, then," Fenella said.

"You can stay and chat with me," Shelly told Jack. "I want to hear more about your research."

Fenella mouthed the words "don't encourage him" at her friend, but Shelly just laughed and then let Fenella out.

"It's me, again," she told Daniel when he answered his home phone. "Tim knows everyone in the world, or at least everyone on the island."

"I hope you're exaggerating," Daniel sighed.

"I am, a bit. He doesn't know Hannah or Diane, but he does know Carol Houston," Fenella told him. She recounted as much of the conversation they'd had over dessert as she could remember.

"I may have to talk to Tim myself," Daniel said when she was done. "It may even be smart to talk to everyone in the band. Where are they playing tonight?"

Fenella told him. "It's a Christmas party. Tickets are available at the door, or so I'm told. Tim gave Shelly a handful of them, though. She can probably leave one for you at the door."

"That would be great. I won't do any formal questioning tonight, but I may stop in for a short chat with the guys in the band. They may tell me more informally than they would in an interview."

"They'll be drinking," Fenella warned him.

"As I'm only looking for background information at this point, I'll just see how it goes. I could do with a night out anyway."

"I'll see you there, then," Fenella told him.

Shelly and Jack were both ready to go when Fenella got back to Shelly's apartment.

"Jack's charming," Shelly whispered as they started down the corridor. Jack had dashed ahead to summon the elevator for them.

"Yeah, he's great," Fenella replied.

Shelly laughed. "Well, he's been charming to me."

"He's available, if you want him."

Shelly just laughed again, and then they caught up to Jack, who was holding the elevator door open with his leg.

"I was afraid I might get stuck in there," he said as he stepped backward into the elevator car.

If anyone could, it would be you, Fenella thought but didn't say.

The restaurant they were heading for was only a short walk away. It was crisp and cold outside, and Fenella pulled her coat more tightly around her as they went. "It feels like it might snow," she said.

"Except that it's far too warm," Shelly told her. "It's like six or seven out here."

"That's well below freezing," Fenella complained.

"Six or seven Celsius," Shelly replied.

"Oh, what's that in Fahrenheit?" Fenella asked.

"Around forty-four," Jack said.

"So, too warm for snow," Fenella sighed. "I don't suppose we'll get a white Christmas, either."

"If you want a white Christmas, you just have to go back to Buffalo," Jack told her.

"I don't want a white Christmas that badly," Fenella laughed.

The restaurant looked warm and inviting as they made their way toward it. "I've never been here before," Fenella whispered to Shelly as they crossed to the door.

"Me either. I've been told the food is good, but there a lot of other places to eat. I've never even consider coming here, really" she replied.

"Good evening, ladies, gentleman," the man who'd opened the door for them said. "Are you here for tonight's special Christmas performance by The Islanders?"

"Yes, we have tickets," Shelly said, pulling the tickets from her bag.

"Excellent. The band will be performing in the ballroom," he told her. "You can follow the red carpet all the way there."

Shelly left a ticket with Daniel's name on it with him, and then the trio did as they were told and followed the red carpet to the ballroom.

Tim must have been watching for them because he met them before they'd gone more than a few steps into the room. "There are tables over here for guests of the band," he told them, leading them to a corner near the stage. While they would be close to the performers, the view wasn't the best.

"It's a good thing we came to hear the band rather than see them," Shelly laughed.

"Todd's away, obviously," Tim said, glancing at Fenella. "Paul's going to be performing, though. He's going to be on the island until after Christmas."

"That's good news," Shelly said. "He's so talented."

"I would have told you sooner, but I only found out when I got here," Tim replied. "He was talking about going back across after all the, um, well, trouble in October, but he hasn't."

The ballroom was about half-full when the band began their first set. By the time they took a break, there were only a handful of empty seats left in the room.

"They're very good," Jack said as soon as the music stopped. "I'm impressed."

"They're even better when Todd plays with them," Shelly told him. "He's celebrating Christmas somewhere exotic, though."

"There you are," Daniel said as he joined them. "I arrived just after the first song and didn't dare try to find you in the crowd."

"No one is sitting here," Jack said, pointing to the seat next to him.

The only other empty seat at the table was on the other side of Fenella. Daniel grinned and then slid into that seat.

"I hope no one is sitting here, either," he said in a questioning tone.

"It looks like you are," Jack said grumpily.

"Not for long," Daniel replied. "I need to go and talk to the guys in the band."

"The break won't last long," Shelly warned him. "The owners want them to do three sets, so they'll have to keep things moving."

Daniel picked up his glass and headed for the cluster of band members near the stage.

"I wasn't expecting to see you here," a familiar voice said from behind Fenella.

She turned around and smiled at Carol Houston, not feeling the slightest bit surprised to see the woman. "Hello," she said brightly.

Carol was clinging to the arm of a very handsome dark-haired man. He looked Fenella over and then gave her a small smile. "Friends of yours?" he asked Carol.

"I wouldn't quite put it that way," Carol replied. "Why don't you go and get me another drink while I chat with them?"

The man raised an eyebrow and then shrugged. "If you need another drink."

"Oh, I definitely do," she told him. She leaned over and whispered something in his ear. He nodded and then turned and walked away without so much as another glance toward Fenella.

Carol dropped into the chair next to her. "I should have just stayed away from you, but I need a favor. Please don't tell Matthew anything about how we met," she said plaintively.

"As I don't even know who Matthew is, I'm unlikely to tell him anything," Fenella replied.

Carol shut her eyes, and Fenella could almost hear her counting to ten before she spoke again. "You told the police I was at Peter's house the day he died," she said.

"Yes, I did," Fenella agreed.

"They've questioned me twice," Carol complained.

"They've questioned me a good many more times than that," Fenella told her. "They're just doing their job."

"Yes, I understand that, but I'd rather people didn't know that I knew Peter," Carol said in a low voice. "It would complicate things."

"You were seeing him behind Matthew's back," Fenella suggested.

Carol winced. "That makes it sound a good deal nastier than it was. Matthew and I have an understanding."

"Then what's the problem?"

"The understanding doesn't include either of us getting caught up in a murder investigation. Matthew has a certain image to uphold and being questioned by the police doesn't fit in with that image."

"I think finding out who killed Peter Grady is more important than anything else," Fenella told her. "He was murdered."

"Perhaps he shouldn't have been involved with so many women at the same time."

"Are you suggesting that one of the women he was seeing killed him?"

"One of them, or one of their husbands or boyfriends."

"Then you can clearly see why the police have had so many questions for you. All things considered, they're probably going to want to talk to Matthew, too."

Carol shook her head. "I'd really rather they didn't. He didn't approve of Peter."

"But you were still seeing Dr. Grady behind his back."

"I was going to end things with Peter once he was back on the island. I was tired of him playing games with me. It was obvious that that was all he was ever going to do, too, play games. Peter wasn't looking for anything serious. I'm hoping Matthew might be, but he won't be if he gets dragged into the mess."

"It's amazing how many women were planning to dump Dr. Grady," Fenella said thoughtfully. "It seems as if he would have been spending Christmas all alone."

"I truly was going to end things with him," Carol insisted. "You have to believe me."

"Okay, I'll believe you," Fenella said. She didn't really care whether the woman was planning to dump Dr. Grady or not. All she wanted was for the police to find out who had killed him.

"Good, then you can tell the police you were wrong," Carol said happily.

"Tell the police I was wrong about what?" Fenella asked.

"About my being there that day. Tell them that you met me here tonight and realized that you had the wrong woman. Tell them that whoever you did meet was using my name but wasn't me."

"You've told them that you weren't there?" Fenella asked, shocked.

"Yes, and I need you to back me up," Carol said. "It's the only way to keep Matthew out of everything."

"What if Matthew killed Dr. Grady?"

Carol shook her head. "He wouldn't have done that. If he found out that Peter and I were still seeing one another, he simply would have ended things with me and broken my heart."

"I'm sorry, but I won't lie to the police for you."

"But you have to," Carol insisted.

"Ms. Houston?" Daniel's voice interrupted the conversation. "I think we need to talk."

Carol looked up at the police inspector and the color drained from her face. "How long have you been standing there?" she asked softly.

"Long enough," Daniel replied. "I think we should probably have our conversation down at the station."

"The station? I don't think that's necessary. I can get us a room here at the hotel," Carol suggested. "That would be a good deal more comfortable, wouldn't it?"

Daniel glanced at Fenella, who raised her eyebrows. She wasn't entirely sure what Carol was suggesting, but she knew Daniel was going to refuse.

"I think the station is a better idea," Daniel told her. "I'd rather not make a scene, so maybe we could just walk out together?"

Carol looked very much like she wanted to argue, but after a minute she shrugged. "I don't have much choice, do I?" she muttered as she stood up. "Don't tell Matthew where I've gone," she told Fenella. "Just tell him I wasn't feeling well."

Fenella opened her mouth to reply, but Carol was already walking away. Daniel followed, and Fenella was pretty sure Carol was doing everything she could to pretend she didn't know the inspector was behind her. The band started the second set a moment later and Fenella sat back to enjoy the music.

"They're very good," Jack said between songs. "I'm really enjoying this."

Fenella spent the next song trying to work out why Jack had never wanted to go anywhere when they'd been together. She'd asked him to go with her to plays, musicals, band concerts, lectures, and a dozen other places, and he'd never agreed. The look on his face tonight suggested that he was having fun, which made her think that he'd missed out on a lot he would have enjoyed over the years.

"I should have let you drag me to more things back in Buffalo," he said as another song finished. "This is amazing."

"Do you think he's just pretending to have fun in an effort to win you back?" Shelly whispered in her ear.

"I think he's genuinely enjoying himself," Fenella told her. "I also think that we wasted ten years together not doing things like this."

When the band stopped for their second break, Jack headed to the bar to get another round of drinks. Fenella insisted on soda as she had to drive later, but Shelly could walk home, so she was happy to have another glass of wine with Jack.

"She's left me, then," a voice said in Fenella's ear.

She turned and discovered that Matthew had taken the seat next to her. "I'm sorry?" she replied.

"Carol's gone home, has she?" he asked.

"Oh, yes, I believe she wasn't feeling well."

He chuckled. "I'm sure as soon as she saw the police inspector she began to feel quite unwell."

Fenella shrugged, unsure of how best to reply to his words.

"I'm Matthew Arkwright," he said after a moment. "Carol and I are, well, I'm not sure what we are, but she came with me this evening."

"It's nice to meet you. I'm Fenella Woods."

"Yes, of course, Mona's niece. I've been wanting to meet you. I have some investment ideas I'd love to share with you."

"Doncan Quayle handles all of my investments. You'd have to talk to him," she replied firmly.

He chuckled. "Maybe not, then. Doncan has very exacting standards for investment. Never mind. Let's talk about why Carol was escorted out of here by the police instead."

"Was she?" Fenella played dumb.

"Come now, you saw her talking to Inspector Robinson, and I'm sure you saw them leave together. No doubt you know why he wanted to speak with her, as well."

"It really isn't my place to discuss it, though."

Matthew frowned and then nodded slowly. "Shall I tell you what I think happened? Carol was involved with a man called Peter Grady. I think you know something about him or about his relationship with Carol. No doubt she was asking you to keep that quiet when Inspector Robinson joined in the conversation. As Dr. Grady was murdered just a few days ago, I'm sure the inspector is investigating all of the women who were involved with Peter. That should take him up to retirement, I reckon."

"You didn't mind that she was seeing Dr. Grady?" Fenella asked.

"We have an understanding," Matthew replied. "Neither of us is looking for anything serious. We're just having a bit of fun. We both see other people and no one minds as long as everyone is reasonably discreet."

"I see," Fenella said after discarding a dozen other replies.

Matthew laughed. "It works for us, or at least it was working for us. Carol getting herself involved in a murder investigation complicates things."

"It's hardly her fault."

"Oh, I know, but it also isn't very discreet. My advocate has advised me that I may even be questioned about the murder. I'd rather not be involved."

"But you already are involved," Fenella pointed out. "The police will probably want to ask you about your whereabouts the day Dr. Grady died, just to cross you off their list."

"Do you really think I'm on their list?" Matthew looked amused. "Perhaps I should be enjoying this rather unique experience. How often does someone get questioned about a murder, after all?"

In my case, far too often, Fenella thought. "I think Carol is worried that you'll be angry with her if you get questioned," she said.

"As you said earlier, it's not her fault. I just hope I have a suitable alibi. If I don't, I might even be a suspect. What a thought. When did Dr. Grady die?"

"I've no idea," Fenella said.

"I shall have to ring my advocate and have him ring the police," Matthew said as he got to his feet. "Maybe they can talk to me at home. I'm sure that would be nicer than going to a police station, anyway." As he walked away, he pulled out his phone, and Fenella suspected that the man's advocate was about to get an unexpected call.

The third set was every bit as good as the first two had been, but Fenella was feeling incredibly tired when it finished.

"I can't wait to get to bed," she said after the band played their final encore.

"There's a party at Mark's," Tim said when he joined them a minute later. "It's sort of the band's unofficial Christmas party. Everyone is welcome."

"Sorry. I'm going home to bed," Fenella told him. "After I drop Jack off where he's staying."

"I'd love to come," Jack said, "but it appears I'd lose my ride home."

"Someone can make sure you get home eventually," Tim replied. "Come and have a few drinks with the band. It's Christmas, after all. Shelly is coming, aren't you?"

Shelly nodded. "Just for one drink, though. I'm pretty tired, too. I've been drinking all night, so I can't drive Jack home. Are you sure there will be someone there who will be fit to drive?"

"He can get a taxi," Tim said, clearly unconcerned. "He could always just crash on a couch, too. Lots of options."

Fenella hid a smile at the thought of Jack sleeping on a couch in Mark's apartment. She'd only been there once. It was nice enough, but clearly belonged to a single man who wasn't too overly concerned about housework.

"What's the plan for tomorrow?" Jack asked Fenella.

"House of Manannan, maybe," she replied.

"Sure, why not. What time do you want to pick me up?"

They ended up agreeing on eleven to give Jack a slow start after his late night. Fenella knew that Katie would have her up at seven, regardless. Shelly, Tim, and Jack walked Fenella back to her building before they continued on to the party.

"I saw a side of Jack tonight that I hadn't known existed," she told Katie as she got ready for bed. "He was actually having fun and being charming. Where was that man for the ten years we were together?"

Katie, fast asleep in bed, didn't reply.

Fenella crawled in to join her and fell asleep as soon as her head touched the pillow.

✺ 9 ✺

When Katie woke her the next morning at seven, Fenella was happy to discover that she wasn't as tired as she'd expected she would be. She gave the kitten her breakfast and then took her shower and got dressed.

"How was your evening?" Mona asked as Fenella put on her makeup.

Fenella winced as she jumped and drew a line of eyeliner across her forehead. "Oh, good morning," she said. "I didn't see you there."

"Clearly," Mona chuckled.

Fenella wiped away the mess before she replied. "The evening was, well, interesting. Tim knows some of the women involved in the case, so that was interesting. Then we went to hear the band perform and I ran into Carol Houston again. In the end, Daniel took her back to the station to answer more questions. I think the strangest part of the evening was that Jack had fun, though."

Mona looked surprised and then shook her head. "Maybe he was just pretending to have fun in an effort to convince you to give him another chance. If you were to try again with him, he'd probably go right back to never wanting to do anything."

"I think he truly was having fun," Fenella told her. "He even went to the party at Mark's after the gig, even though I came home and went to bed."

"How very odd."

"Yes, it was."

"But tell me about Carol and what Tim knows about the suspects. Maybe we can work out who killed Peter Grady before Daniel does."

"Let's leave the case to Daniel. He's the one who questioned Carol last night."

"Why? Tell me everything."

Fenella thought about refusing, but she knew that Mona loved playing detective. She gave her aunt a complete rundown of everything that Tim had said and then repeated the conversation she'd had with Carol in the ballroom.

"She actually wanted you to lie to the police," Mona said. "I can't believe she thought you'd agree."

"She seemed desperate. I think she's a good deal more interested in Matthew than he is in her."

"And yet she was also involved with Dr. Grady. I really wish I could have met the man. He must have been incredibly attractive and charming," Mona said.

"You should see if he's still wandering around the spirit world," Fenella suggested. "You'd be about the right age for him, I suppose."

Mona's ghost appeared to be somewhere in her mid-thirties, even though the woman had been over ninety when she'd died.

"It's a tempting idea, but it might upset Max. You know I try not to upset Max."

"Of course not," Fenella agreed, wondering if Mona was telling the truth or not. "Although from what I've heard, you used to upset him quite regularly when you were both alive."

Mona laughed. "We had a very volatile relationship, yes, but underneath it all was a firm foundation built on love and trust. Anyway, we've both mellowed a lot over the years. Max was ill for quite a long time, and we never had a single quarrel during his illness."

As she didn't need to pick up Jack until later, Fenella took advantage of the unexpected free time and did some more Christmas shopping. She found small treats for Winston and Fiona and bought a large box of chocolates for Harvey. After a moment's hesitation, she added a few extra boxes of chocolates to her shopping basket. It would be good to have them on hand if she needed any last-minute gifts, and if she didn't end up giving them away, she would happily eat the chocolates herself.

She was only a few minutes late to the house on Poppy Drive. Wondering what time Jack got home, she knocked loudly and then waited.

"Maggie, darling, good morning," Jack said brightly as he opened the door. "I'm nearly ready to go. I just need to finish my breakfast."

"It's nearly time for lunch," Fenella pointed out as she followed Jack through the house to the kitchen.

"Yes, of course. I'm only having a little bit of cereal." Jack spooned up the last few mouthfuls from the bowl on the counter and then sighed. "I'm still hungry, but you'll want to get lunch somewhere, won't you?"

"I'd like to, yes," Fenella told him.

He nodded and then stuck his bowl and spoon in the dishwasher. "Let's go, then."

They were headed across the island before Jack spoke again. "Thank you so much for taking me to see the band last night. It was wonderful."

"I'm glad you enjoyed it."

Jack sighed. "I'm incredibly jealous of you, you know."

"Because I can hear The Islanders anytime?"

"Well, yes, that, but more than that. I'm jealous that you were able to leave your old life behind and start fresh where no one knew you. You were able to reinvent yourself. What a wonderful opportunity to be given."

"You're right, of course, and I'm hugely grateful to my Aunt Mona for everything."

"I was thinking last night, after a few too many drinks, how wonderful it would be to start over again. I'm sure I'd be a completely different person."

"You aren't happy the way you are?"

"I don't know. I'm not unhappy, but I'm, well, stuck, I guess. When

I first earned my doctorate and started teaching, I was young and I worried that the students wouldn't take me seriously. I started behaving like I thought I should behave, like a senior professor, and I stopped thinking about having fun. Now, all these years later, I am a senior professor, and I feel as if I missed out on things when I was younger."

Fenella wasn't sure how best to reply to Jack's words. She'd done the same thing when she'd first started teaching, eliminating swear words from her vocabulary and trying to act older than she had been. Getting involved with Jack was probably part of her attempt to be taken seriously, and it had led to her becoming more staid and even boring. While she knew she'd been having a lot more fun since she'd been on the island, she'd credited the fact that she no longer needed to work for a lot of that. The opportunity to reinvent herself as someone who'd date more than one man at a time and who spent most evenings at the pub was also a factor, though.

"Maybe you should think about taking early retirement," she said cautiously. Jack seemed to have been coming to terms with the idea that they weren't getting back together. She didn't want to say anything that might make him think she was changing her mind.

"I don't know what I'd do with myself if I retired."

"What do you want to do?"

"I've never really thought about it," Jack sighed. "I don't like to travel, not really. I'm enjoying my stay here, but it's also very stressful for me. I enjoyed the band last night and I even had fun at the party afterward, but the whole experience was draining. I'm not good at socializing and I'm too old to want to learn to be better at it."

"You're here for a few more weeks. Spend some of that time thinking seriously about what you'd like to change in your life," Fenella suggested. "Even if you just start with really small changes, it will be worth it if it makes you happier."

"I miss you. Shelly and I were talking about you last night and she told me about all the other men you've been seeing. I hope they all appreciate how wonderful you are. Are you in love with any of them?"

"I think we should talk about something else. How was the party?"

"It was fun, although the apartment was something of a mess. I'm not very good at housework, but even I don't have piles of dirty laundry in my bathroom."

Fenella grinned. "That's good to hear."

Jack chuckled. "I really do need to try harder," he admitted. "It was so much easier when my mother did everything for me. Then you took over and you did everything and that was wonderful too. Sometimes I get really angry with myself when I don't know how to do something I should have learned to do when I was twenty-one."

"You seem to have been doing okay since I've been gone."

"I've been sulking and miserable," he countered. "I truly thought you'd come back, you know. I still can't quite believe that you won't, even though I wouldn't if I were you. Your life here is much better than anything I could offer you back in Buffalo."

"I am a lot happier here," Fenella admitted. "That doesn't mean that I don't miss you, or Buffalo, but somehow I feel more like I belong here."

"I can understand that. There's something wonderful about this island. It's given me a new perspective on life."

"That's good to hear. Even though we aren't together anymore, I do want you to be happy."

"And I'm happy for you," Jack said. "If you ever change your mind, though, I'd do everything I could to make you happy."

Fenella didn't reply. Instead she pointed out Tynwald Hill, which was conveniently on their right. Telling Jack about the hill and the island's annual Tynwald Day festivities filled the rest of the drive to the House of Manannan.

"The ship sailing right through the window is well done," Jack said as they approached the building. "This isn't a typical museum, is it?"

"Not at all. It's very different."

Two hours later they'd made their way through the entire building. Fenella had done it before, but she still found herself learning more about the island's rich history. The tour concluded by showcasing Peel Castle, which was only a short distance away.

"Unfortunately, the castle is shut at the moment," the guide told them. "You can walk around some of the perimeter, but it's quite steep and rocky in places."

"I'd like to at least drive as close as we can to the castle," Jack said as they headed back toward the museum's entrance. "I'm rather more interested in the island's history than I thought I'd be."

Fenella wondered what sort of magic the island had used on Jack. He wasn't the same person she'd left behind in Buffalo, that was for sure.

"Maybe we should have lunch first," she suggested.

"There's a café here now," a passing museum staff member interjected. "They do really good jacket potatoes and great cakes."

"Jacket potatoes?" Jack asked as the woman disappeared through a door marked "Staff Only."

"Baked potatoes with toppings like cheese or beans," Fenella explained. "You can just get them plain with butter, too."

"Does that sound good to you?"

"It sounds better than trying to find somewhere else to eat," she laughed.

"And they have cakes," Jack added.

"Yes, that may be part of the temptation," Fenella admitted.

The café had been tucked into a small corner of the building, but the size didn't matter as Fenella and Jack were their only customers. They ordered and then sat near the counter to save anyone having to walk too far.

"Ah, George, I hope you've brought lots of napkins. We seem to run out nearly every day," the girl behind the counter said as a man pushing a cart walked into the café.

"Aye, I brought three cases this time," he replied. "That should keep you going until after Christmas, anyway."

"Oh, it should, especially as we're shut after tomorrow until the new year," the girl laughed.

George chuckled and then began to unload boxes off the cart and into an empty corner.

"I'm all alone here today," the girl said. "I don't suppose I could persuade you to unload in the kitchen?"

He frowned. "I'm not supposed to bring things any further than the door," he said. "I'm already several feet inside of the door."

"Can I borrow your cart, then?" the girl asked. "Otherwise the boxes are probably going to have to sit out here until January."

After a deep sigh, he shrugged. "If I sit down with a cuppa I might not notice if you move the cart a little bit," he suggested.

The girl quickly made him a cup of tea and then began reloading the boxes back onto the cart. Jack jumped up.

"Let me help you," he said.

The other man shrugged and then walked over and sat down next to Fenella. "Your husband?" he asked.

"No, just a friend," she replied.

"He probably thinks I should be helping, but I do this all day every day and if I start doing more than I'm being paid to do, I'll end up being taken advantage of everywhere."

Fenella nodded. "I'm sure it's a tough job, hauling heavy boxes all over the place."

"It isn't easy, but it pays okay."

"I'm Fenella, by the way," she added.

"George, George Norris. It's nice to meet you. I don't normally talk to strangers, but I didn't want your husband to think badly of me."

"It's Christmas," Fenella said. "That's the best time of year to talk to strangers."

George grinned. "It's going to be a good Christmas, too," he said. "I'm going to ask my girlfriend to marry me."

"Oh, good luck."

"She'll say yes," he replied confidently. "I'm perfect for her."

Fenella swallowed her reply. George's phone rang suddenly, saving her from having to find a suitable response.

"Hello? Hey, baby, how are you?" he said into his phone. Fenella listened closely to his half of the conversation, fairly certain that he was talking to Hannah.

"The police? Again? Just answer their questions. We both know you barely knew the man, right?"

"Let's talk about it over dinner, okay?"

"But I wanted to see you tonight."

"If you're upset, we should be together."

He didn't say anything else, and after a minute he put his phone back into his pocket while muttering a curse under his breath.

"I hope everything is okay," Fenella said.

"It will be once the police stop bothering my girlfriend."

"The police?"

He shrugged. "She went out with this guy a few times, months ago, and he managed to get himself murdered. They keep asking her questions, that's all."

"How upsetting for her."

"Yeah, she's very sensitive. Things will be better once we're married. I'll be able to protect her better then."

Fenella nodded, wondering if Hannah was aware of how strong George's feelings for her were. "She may need some time to recover from everything that happened," she suggested.

"Yeah, maybe. Maybe I'll wait until New Year's Eve to propose. That might be better."

Or maybe you should wait for about a year, Fenella thought. She was trying to frame the idea more diplomatically when Jack and the girl from the café returned from the kitchen.

"I can't thank you enough," the girl was saying to Jack. "That would have taken me ages, if I could have even managed some of those boxes."

"It wasn't a problem," Jack replied. "I was happy to help."

The girl smiled. "But I haven't even given you your food yet," she exclaimed. "Let me get that."

"I could do with a little something," George called after her. "Just a slice of cake, maybe."

Fenella heard the woman mutter something, but she couldn't make out the words. That was probably for the best, she thought.

"Jack, this is George," Fenella said.

"Yes, hello," Jack said.

"I was just telling your wife that I can't do more than what I'm getting paid to do," George said. "Otherwise people will start to expect it."

Jack nodded and sat back down next to Fenella. The girl from the café delivered their potatoes a moment later.

"What about me?" George asked.

"I only have two hands," the girl replied. She went back into the kitchen and then returned with a slice of jam roly-poly for George.

"Thank you so much," he exclaimed.

He cleared his plate within seconds as Fenella and Jack ate at a more leisurely pace. "Must get back to it," he said as soon as he was done. "Thanks," he called to the girl behind the counter. He grabbed his cart and pushed it out of the room, leaving the girl frowning behind him.

"He could have offered to pay for his cake," she muttered as she cleared away his plate and coffee cup.

"You won't have to pay for it, will you?" Fenella asked.

"No, I can leave a note in the till that George was here. The manager knows what that means," the girl sighed.

"I'm surprised Manx National Heritage does business with him, all things considered," Fenella remarked.

"He's not that bad," the girl told her. "He's reliable, anyway. I used to work at the café at the Manx Museum, which is a lot busier than we are here. I lost track of the times I had to run out to ShopFast to buy napkins or coffee stirrers because we'd run out and our supplier hadn't turned up on time. Since we've started using George's company, we've not had that problem, anyway."

"He could have helped you with the boxes, though," Fenella suggested.

"He used to, when he first started delivering at the museum. He used to hint that maybe I'd like to go out with him sometime, too, but once he found a girlfriend he stopped being so helpful."

"Do you know his girlfriend?" Fenella asked.

"Hannah? I've met her once or twice at MNH events when suppliers are invited, too. She's, well, she wasn't what I was expecting when I heard that George had a girlfriend."

"Really? Why?" Fenella was intrigued.

"She's very pretty, for one thing. I mean, George isn't ugly or anything, but I would have thought she was out of his league, really. I did wonder if she was after his money. That would make sense."

"George's money?" Jack said. "He has money?"

"He owns the supply company that he delivers for," the girl explained. "I'm sure he could afford to hire a bunch of helpers, but he likes to do it all himself. That way he gets to keep all of the money, I suppose. I've seen how much MNH is paying him just for this site, and he supplies about a dozen sites all over the island. I'm sure he's doing really well for himself."

Fenella thought about the pretty redhead that she'd met on Monday. Would Hannah really date George just for money, she wondered.

After she and Jack finished their potatoes, the girl insisted on giving them each a slice of cake to thank Jack for his help. Fenella made sure she added a very generous tip to the bill when she finally received it.

"Keep the change," she told the girl as she handed her the money. "Thank you."

"Are you sure?" the girl gasped. "Thank you so much."

"Do you still want to get a closer look at Peel Castle, then?" Fenella asked as she and Jack headed back to her car.

"Yes, please," Jack replied. "You seemed very interested in George," he added as he fastened his seatbelt.

"Robert mentioned him when we were at the wildlife park," Fenella reminded him. "His girlfriend is Hannah Lawson."

"Do I know Hannah Lawson?"

"She was one of the women who came to the house looking for Peter Grady."

"Really? That whole day is something of a blur now. I believe I was more jet-lagged than I realized at the time."

"Hannah is a very pretty redhead."

"Oh, I remember her, although only vaguely. Did all of the women have boyfriends, then?"

"It seems like it, except for Bev, who is married."

"I suppose it makes sense in a way. If Peter wasn't looking for anything serious, it was probably smart for him to get involved with women who were already in other relationships."

"What was he like?" Fenella asked. "I'm finding it hard to believe that he was so charming and handsome that so many women were prepared to cheat to spend time with him."

"He was very likeable, really," Jack said. "You know I don't generally talk to strangers, but then I don't often go out in the evening, either. We'd met earlier in the day and he talked me into going out that night. We drank together and talked for hours about women and how much trouble they were." Jack stopped and took a deep breath.

"What?" Fenella demanded.

"I may have told him something about being madly in love with you, but not being able to be with you since you were here," Jack confessed. "That's when he offered me the use of his house on the island."

"And you accepted and that's how we ended up in the middle of a murder investigation," Fenella sighed.

"All while he was talking to me, he was talking to everyone else, too," Jack added. "Sue and Hazel were both very taken with him, and I believe he left with one of the older graduate students."

"Really?"

"He really seemed to listen to me and to sympathize with my problems. He also genuinely seemed to want to help. I suppose I can see women falling for him. By the end of the evening, I wanted to be his friend, and you know I don't make friends easily."

Fenella nodded. "Do you remember anything specific that he said about his problems with women?"

"Not really, why?"

"I just wondered if he mentioned any of the women that we've met, that's all."

"Inspector Robinson asked that too, but I told him the same thing I'm telling you. I wasn't paying close enough attention and I don't really remember what he said."

"That's a shame," Fenella sighed. She started the car and drove down the causeway to Peel Castle. After parking as close as she could to the site, she turned to Jack. "Do you want to get out and explore?"

"Yes, please. I may never get another chance to see Peel Castle."

Fenella nodded and then led Jack up the steps to the castle's door, which was shut tightly and locked.

"We can try walking around some of it," she suggested. "We might get a good view from the beach below here, too."

They spent an hour walking around the area, trying to see as much as they could of the castle from the distance. A cold wind was blowing and Fenella was happy to get back to the car.

"Did you say there was another castle on the island?" Jack asked as Fenella switched on the car's heaters on full blast.

"Yes, Castle Rushen. That one is in much better condition. That's where Christmas at the Castle is being held tomorrow night."

"Ah, yes, the charity thing. Who knows, maybe I'll even find that I enjoy that," Jack replied.

"The Islanders are doing a set or two. You'll enjoy that part."

"Are they? That is good news."

"But what do you want to do now?" Fenella asked.

"What would you be doing if I wasn't here?"

"Maybe having a walk on the promenade, but probably I'd be curled up in my apartment reading a good book and drinking hot chocolate," Fenella answered honestly.

"I still need to get to a bank," Jack reminded her. "I need to try to change some money so that you don't have to keep paying for everything."

"Let's go back to Douglas. There are several banks in between the shops."

"Speaking of shops, I need to do some Christmas shopping, too," Jack said. "I'd like to get something little for Shelly, as she was very kind to me last night. Maybe a little something for Tim, too."

"I'm always happy to go shopping," Fenella laughed.

"I usually hate it, but I'm trying to be more open to different experiences now."

"The shops in Douglas are unique, anyway. It's nothing like going to a shopping mall in Buffalo, that's for sure."

Fenella started the car and headed back toward Douglas. "Dr. Grady didn't give you any names for the women who were causing his troubles?" she asked as they went.

"He seemed to trying to avoid using names," Jack told her. "He said something about never getting involved with anyone ginger, whatever that means."

"It means someone with red hair," Fenella told him. "He might have been talking about Hannah."

"Do you think so? He said something about her having a terrible temper, but being irresistible when she wanted to be."

"What else did he say?"

"He said something about women who were too young being too much work," Jack remembered.

"I wonder if he meant Bev," Fenella speculated. "She was the youngest of the women we met, anyway."

Jack shrugged. "Like I said, he never mentioned any names."

"But he was unhappy with all of the women in his life?" Fenella asked.

"He seemed to be. He said something about letting things get too complicated and having to hide in America until it all calmed down."

"Interesting."

"But then he laughed and said something about variety keeping life interesting and that it wasn't his problem if other men were jealous."

"We need to talk to Daniel," Fenella said. "I should have called him and told him about my conversation with Matthew Arkwright last night. I definitely need to tell him about meeting George today, and you need to tell him everything you can remember from your conversation with Dr. Grady."

"I don't really like talking to the police," Jack complained, "and especially not Inspector Rockwell, now that I know that you and he dated."

"We didn't exactly date, and we aren't dating at the moment. I can call Inspector Hammersmith if you'd prefer."

Jack shook his head. "He looked like a used car salesman. I hate used car salesmen."

Fenella laughed. "I've always thought the same thing about him. I'll call Daniel."

"After we do our shopping?" Jack asked.

"Only if we're quick."

The bank where Fenella had her accounts was happy to change Jack's dollars into pounds.

"We'll give him our preferred exchange rate, since you're one of our best customers," the girl behind the counter told Fenella.

"Thanks," Fenella said.

She helped Jack pick out a nice brightly colored scarf for Shelly. "It will suit her, and everyone can always use a scarf," she reasoned.

It was harder to find something for Tim, but they finally settled on a bottle of whiskey. "We were talking about whiskey last night," Jack told her. "He knows a lot more about it than I do, but I know enough to know that he'll appreciate this bottle."

With the purchases out of the way, they headed back to Fenella's apartment. She called the police station, but Daniel was out.

"Just tell him that Fenella Woods called. I have a few things I need to discuss with him," she told the woman on the other end of the phone.

"I'll make sure he gets the message when he returns," she promised.

Jack sat down on the couch. "The view is incredible," he sighed.

Fenella smiled as she watched Katie wander in from the bedroom. The kitten approached Jack slowly, seemingly studying him as she went.

"Hello," Jack said when he noticed her. "I wondered where you were yesterday when I was here."

"Meorow," Katie said before she jumped up into Jack's lap.

"I don't really like animals," he said conversationally. "I might just be prepared to make an exception for you, though."

Katie began to purr loudly as Jack rubbed her head. "She's lovely," he said.

"I'm glad you like her."

"I'm surprised that Katie has come out of hiding," Mona said. "She seemed determined to avoid Jack."

Fenella very nearly replied to her, only stopping herself at the last second. A moment later someone knocked on the door.

🦂 10 🦂

"I was told you rang me," Daniel said when Fenella opened the door.

"As usual, I keep bumping into suspects," she replied. "I thought you'd like to know."

Daniel sighed. "I should have Mark come and talk to you. It is his case, after all."

"Let me tell you everything, and then if you think that any of it is important, you can have him join us," Fenella suggested. "Jack has a few things to tell you, too."

"Is he here?"

"Yes, but come in," Fenella laughed and then stepped back to let him into the apartment. They walked together into the living room. Daniel greeted Jack and then sat down on the chair next to him. Katie opened her eyes and then shouted a greeting. She jumped down from Jack's lap and quickly climbed into Daniel's.

Mona laughed. "She's making her feelings clear," she said.

"Drinks?" Fenella said quickly. "I need to get Katie's dinner, anyway."

"She doesn't seem hungry," Daniel said with a chuckle as the kitten curled up under his hand.

"She will be any minute now," Fenella said, feeling slightly embarrassed by the animal's behavior.

"Are you making coffee?" Jack asked.

"I can. Do you want some?"

"Yes, please," both men said at the same time.

Fenella filled the coffee maker and switched it on before she refilled Katie's bowls and then got down her bag of treats.

"Katie, treat," she called.

The animal didn't move.

"You're just making it worse by drawing attention to it," Mona told her.

Fenella frowned and dropped the treats on top of Katie's food bowl.

"So tell me whom you've seen since we last spoke," Daniel suggested once they all had cups of coffee in hand.

"You know I saw Carol," Fenella replied. "After the band's next set, I had an interesting chat with Matthew Arkwright."

She repeated everything she could remember from the conversation and then moved on to tell him about their bumping into George Norris at the café in Ramsey.

"It's uncanny," Daniel said. "I know it's a small island, but I think you've met more of the witnesses than I have."

"I'm not going looking for them," Fenella told him.

"I never suggested that you were," he replied. "Is that everything or is there more?"

"Jack remembered some things that Dr. Grady said about the women in his life," Fenella said.

"Really? What have you remembered?" he asked Jack.

Jack repeated the same things he'd already told Fenella. "He also said something about blondes not being nearly as much fun as everyone suggested," he added when he was done.

"A criticism of Carol, perhaps," Mona wondered.

"I wonder if that was aimed at Carol," Fenella said.

"That's one possibility," Daniel said.

"Have you found many other women who were involved with Peter?" Jack asked.

"I can't talk about an active investigation," Daniel replied. "Let's just say we're still looking into Dr. Grady's rather busy social life."

"He lived in Liverpool, didn't he?" Fenella asked. "Did he have a string of girlfriends there, too?"

"As I said, we're still looking into things."

"I don't think he had women in Liverpool," Jack said. "He said something about keeping the house on the island for romantic encounters and keeping his life in Liverpool simpler."

"Interesting," Daniel said, making a note. "You're remembering a lot more now than you did when we first spoke."

"I'm less tired," Jack said defensively. "Anyway, I'm only remembering because Maggie and I have been chatting about it, that's all."

"That happens sometimes," Daniel replied.

"I'm surprised he wasn't married," Mona said.

"How often did he come to the island?" Fenella asked.

"He told me that he tried to get over here most weekends and every time the university had a break," Jack said.

"That's consistent with what his colleague in Liverpool said," Daniel remarked.

"From what he told me, he was a very different person in Liverpool. He was able to behave differently on the island to what was expected of him at home."

"The island let him reinvent himself," Fenella said thoughtfully.

Jack nodded. "Something like that, anyway."

"Thank you both for your time," Daniel said. "I need to go and share all of this with Mark. He may have more questions for you, so please make sure you're available."

Fenella looked at the clock. "We're going to go and get something to eat soon," she said. "I want an early night tonight."

Jack chuckled. "I was thinking the same thing. I enjoyed last night, but I'm exhausted now. Is it too early for me to go to bed now?"

"I'll take you home right after dinner," Fenella promised.

"Can we get fast food for dinner?" Jack asked.

"I'm going to leave you two arguing about that and get back to work," Daniel said. "Katie, I'm afraid I have to go."

The kitten opened her eyes and then scowled at Daniel. She

jumped off his lap and dashed to the kitchen, no doubt to enjoy the treats that Fenella had left for her. Daniel got to his feet and headed for the door.

"If Mark has more questions, I'll encourage him to ring you early," he told them. "Jack will be at the house on Poppy Drive. Where will you be?" he asked Fenella.

"Here," she said quickly, "after I drop Jack off, of course."

Daniel nodded. "What about your plans for tomorrow?"

"We haven't discussed it," Fenella said, looking at Jack.

Jack frowned. "We have that fundraiser in the evening right?"

"Yes."

"I think I'd quite like some time at home on my own," Jack said. "Is there going to be food at the castle?"

"There's a finger-food buffet, whatever that means," Fenella replied.

"So we'll need dinner before we go, but I think I'd rather just stay home and fix myself something for breakfast and lunch. What time does the thing at the castle start?"

"Seven."

"Maybe you could pick me up around five and we could get some dinner before we head there?" Jack suggested. "After everything that's happened since I've been here, I think I could do with some time on my own."

"That works for me, if you're sure," Fenella told him, thinking that she'd quite like some time away from Jack.

"So you'll be at the house on Poppy Drive all day tomorrow," Daniel said to Jack. "Mark or I might have more questions for you."

Jack nodded. "I actually brought some work with me. I have a new class I have to start developing, so I'll be doing the planning for that if you come by."

Daniel nodded. "And you'll be here?" he asked Fenella.

"I might run some errands or take a walk on the promenade, but otherwise I should be here," she confirmed.

"Thank you both for your time tonight," Daniel said. "Every little bit of information helps us build up the bigger picture."

"Does that mean you don't have any idea who killed Dr. Grady?" Jack asked. He flushed. "That came out rather badly."

Daniel shrugged. "I can't comment on an active investigation. We won't comment until we make an arrest."

"I hope that's soon," Fenella said. She walked him to the door and then pulled it open. "Thanks for coming over," she said softly.

Daniel looked as if he wanted to say something, but after a moment he simply nodded and left.

"You should have kissed him," Mona told her. "It's what he wanted."

Fenella sighed. It was what she'd wanted, too, but there was no way she could kiss Daniel in front of Jack. Anyway, he was investigating a murder and she was tangled up in the case. He wasn't thinking about kissing her at the moment.

"He was, though," Mona said softly.

Fenella frowned at the idea that Mona could read her mind, and then turned and smiled at Jack. "How about some dinner, then?"

"I wasn't kidding about fast food," he said as he slowly got to his feet. "My late night has caught up to me, and the coffee isn't helping."

"The island doesn't have much to offer in terms of fast food," Fenella told him. "There is a great little Chinese restaurant next door that does takeout and is super quick."

Jack frowned. "I don't know that I like Chinese food."

"You don't like bands or traveling, either," she retorted. "Try it."

He shrugged. "At this point I'll eat anything."

Fenella found the menu and went through it with Jack, pointing out the items she thought he'd most likely enjoy. In the end, she ordered a dozen different things and then she and Jack went down to pick it up. The car smelled wonderful as they drove back to Poppy Drive.

"I forgot you don't have any plates," Fenella sighed as Jack began opening food boxes in the house's kitchen.

"Let's just eat out of the boxes," Jack said tiredly.

Fenella grinned at him. "Who are you and what have you done with the real Jack Dawson?"

He laughed. "I'm still the same man, but I'm hungry and I'm tired. I just want to eat something and go to bed."

It didn't take Jack long to decide that he only liked two of the things that Fenella had ordered. She happily let him eat all of them while she nibbled her way through many of the others. Eventually she was too full to want to move and Jack was yawning as he broke open a fortune cookie.

"You will be lucky in love in the future," he read out.

"Really? I hope it's right," Fenella told him. She opened her own cookie and then grinned. "There is a tall, dark, handsome man in your future," she read out.

Jack frowned. "I suppose I can't be jealous of a fortune cookie," he muttered.

"I'm not jealous of how lucky you're going to be in the future," Fenella told him.

Jack opened his mouth, but yawned instead of replying. Fenella laughed. "I think I should go. You need sleep."

"I do, and I was serious when I told the police inspector that I brought work with me, too. I'm hoping to start a new course next year and I need to get a draft syllabus ready along with a reading list."

"What sort of new course?" Fenella asked.

"An in-depth look at battlefield strategy, based around the US Civil War," Jack said, looking excited in spite of his tiredness.

Fenella fought back a yawn of her own. "Okay, well, good luck with that," she said. "I'm going to go."

Jack walked her to the door. She waited until he'd locked the door behind her before she headed back to her car. For the first time in a while, Katie was still up when Fenella got back.

"I'm glad you like Daniel better than Jack," Fenella told her, "but maybe you could be a little less obvious about it next time?"

Katie just shrugged and then settled into Fenella's lap. Mona joined them and they watched an old James Bond film together until bedtime.

"I need to find something fabulous to wear to Christmas at the Castle," Fenella told Mona as she got ready for bed.

"There's a wonderful red dress on the right side of the wardrobe," Mona told her. "It's very festive."

Fenella nodded. She'd never seen anything she'd considered festive in the wardrobe, but she had no doubt she'd find the red dress when she looked tomorrow. There was something odd, almost magical, about the wardrobe full of gorgeous designer clothes that Mona had left behind. Thus far everything Fenella had tried on had fit her perfectly, which was strange in itself, as Mona had had a very different shape from Fenella's. It seemed smarter not to question Mona about anything, though, just in case asking interfered with the magic.

Katie wasn't in bed when Fenella climbed in. She took advantage of the opportunity to stretch across as much of the bed as she could, bouncing back and forth as she tried to get comfortable. Within a minute, she found herself curled up in her normal spot, leaving plenty of room for Katie to join her, which she did a short time later.

"I'm joining the band," Jack said firmly. "There's nothing you can do to stop me."

"You can't play any instruments," Fenella pointed out. "You can't sing, either."

Jack shrugged. "I'm going to learn to do both. Tim is going to help me."

"But you can't stay on the island, not without some sort of visa or something."

"I'll figure it all out. You don't have to worry about it. It's all going to be fine."

"What about your life in Buffalo? You have a job and a house," Fenella said.

"I'm not going back. The island has worked its magic on me. I'm never leaving."

Fenella stared at him. "That's impossible," she said.

"That's the way the island works," Daniel told her as he walked into the room. "It's done the same to me. I can't imagine living anywhere else now."

"I'm staying, too," Hazel said as she appeared behind Daniel. "You can't keep this wonderful place all to yourself forever, you know."

"But there are rules about who can live and work here," Fenella protested. "You can't just decide to come and then stay."

"But we are," Fenella's brother James announced from the other side of the room. "Anyway, I was born here. I'm allowed to stay."

"We're all staying," Jack said, "and we're all staying with you, as well. You've plenty of room in your apartment."

"I don't," Fenella said. "You all have to leave."

"All of us?" Daniel asked.

"No, not you," Fenella replied. "This can't be happening."

"Meroow," Katie said.

Fenella sat up in bed and looked around the room. Aside from Katie, she was alone. "What a horrible dream," she told her pet. "Everyone wanted to come and live on the island. I don't blame them, really, but it was horrible."

Katie shrugged and then snuggled back into a ball. A glance at the clock had Fenella doing much the same thing. It was only just after midnight, and she needed a lot more sleep before her planned late night out the next night. Her sleep was restless and she had to drag herself out of bed when Katie woke her at seven.

"I should have asked you to wait until eight," she told Katie as she filled her bowls. "You usually do, when I ask nicely, and I could have used the extra sleep."

Katie didn't bother to reply, preferring instead to eat her breakfast. Fenella thought hard about going back to bed, but decided that a shower and a lot of hot coffee would have to do for today. She got dressed but didn't bother doing anything with her hair or makeup. There would be time later to put more effort in before she left for Castletown.

"What are you doing with your morning at home, then?" Mona asked a short while later.

Fenella had finished combing her hair, and had been sitting and staring at her reflection in the mirror, feeling too tired to move, when Mona appeared. The woman's words made her jump and reminded her that she had coffee brewing in the kitchen.

"I don't know. I don't have any plans," she said. "I should probably work on my research, but I told Marjorie that I was going to take a break until after Christmas."

Having mostly given up on the idea of writing about Anne Boleyn, Fenella had started doing some research at the Manx Museum, just delving into various documents and enjoying spending time studying history again. Marjorie Stevens, the museum's librarian and archivist, had a long list of topics she was hoping people might research, but thus far Fenella had resisted getting tied into any one particular thing. She'd promised Marjorie that she'd have a serious chat with her after the holidays, though, and in some ways she was looking forward to taking on some serious research and writing.

"We should talk about the suspects, then," Mona said. "I've barely heard anything about the case this time. You've been too busy with Jack to talk about murder."

"Or maybe I just don't like talking about murder."

"Whichever, we've helped Daniel solve cases before and I'm sure we can do it again. I've been thinking, and I believe the killer must be one of the women who visited the house the day the body was found."

Fenella shrugged. "They seem most likely, because whatever they said about seeing cars in the driveway, I suspect they all knew that Dr. Grady was due back on the island that day."

"Exactly. If it wasn't one of them, it had to be one of the men in one of those women's lives."

"There may well have been other women who knew he was coming back to the island that day," Fenella pointed out. "Dozens more could have shown up when I wasn't there. Jack was fast asleep. He wouldn't have heard them knocking."

"If they knocked," Mona said. "Dr. Grady may have given at least some of them keys."

"He gave Jack keys, and he'd only just met him," Fenella said thoughtfully. "Jack could have slept through several people coming and going. He didn't wake up when Dr. Grady came home, after all."

"Are you sure about that?"

"No, of course not. I'm just guessing that he came home at some point after Jack arrived because there was so much blood and it looked, well, fresh," Fenella replied. "I don't see how Jack could have slept through Dr. Grady's arrival, the murderer's arrival, and the murder, but he seems to have done just that."

"Unless Dr. Grady woke him and the pair got into a fight," Mona suggested. "Maybe Dr. Grady told Jack he couldn't stay at the house and that made Jack so mad that he killed the man."

Fenella laughed. "That's the craziest idea you've come up with yet. If Dr. Grady had told Jack to leave, he would have gone quietly. Well, quietly after he'd shouted into the phone for me to come and get him, anyway. There's no way Jack had anything to do with Dr. Grady's death."

"You said something about Jack having all of his bags in the bedroom he was using. Was there nothing left anywhere that might have told Dr. Grady or any other visitors that Jack was there?"

Fenella shut her eyes and tried to remember what Jack had done on his arrival at the house. "He took off his shoes," Fenella exclaimed. "He's funny about shoes, actually. He never wears them in the house, and he doesn't like it when other people do, either. He took off his shoes right inside the door and left them on the mat that was there."

"Dr. Grady must have realized that Jack was there, then. He'd have known that the shoes weren't his. His guests, on the other hand, may not have realized."

"I wonder why Dr. Grady didn't wake Jack up and, I don't know, welcomed him or something."

"Perhaps he was in too much of a hurry to get to bed," Mona suggested.

"Maybe he brought someone back to the house with him and they headed straight to the bedroom," Fenella speculated.

"Or he'd rung or texted someone to invite her over and then went up to the bedroom to wait for her."

"And that brings up back to the four women."

"Indeed it does. Let's talk about each of them in turn."

"I met Carol first, and I quite liked her. I'm less fond of her now, after the other night."

Mona nodded. "Asking you to lie on her behalf was not a very smart thing to do. You said she knew about Dr. Grady's other women, though, didn't you?"

"Yes, and I told her that Jack was in the house, as well. That should have been a deterrent, right?"

"All four of the women knew Jack was there," Mona said. "That might suggest that the killer was someone other than those four women."

"Maybe it was Matthew Arkwright, although I doubt it. He didn't seem to care all that much about Carol. I can't see him caring about his rivals."

"From what you've told me, I'm inclined to agree. What about Hannah Lawson and her boyfriend? He sounded like a more likely candidate, really."

"I think you're right. I can't see Hannah killing anyone, although I did only speak to her briefly, but I didn't like George at all."

"Put him on the top of the suspect list," Mona told her.

Fenella knew exactly what Mona meant. She sighed and then went and found a notebook. "George Norris," she said as she wrote the man's name on the top of the first blank page. "Where does Hannah go?"

"Under George, but not too far down. It sounds as if she's only after George for his money, and if that's true, then she could be more ruthless than she first appeared."

"I'll put her down a few lines, in case we have others to put above her," Fenella said.

"Put Matthew Arkwright above her," Mona instructed, "only because he may not have known that Jack was there. I'm inclined the think that the killer would have killed Jack, too, if he or she had known Jack was in the house."

Fenella shivered. "I can't imagine. He makes me crazy, but I'd have been devastated if anything had happened to him."

"He seems to be improving nicely. By the time he's ready to go home, he'll be a new man."

A dozen questions sprang into Fenella's head, but she didn't ask any of them. If Mona was doing something to help change Jack, she really didn't want to know about it. "Where does Carol go?" she asked instead.

"Above Hannah, for asking you to lie to the police."

"Let's talk about Bev and Robert," Fenella suggested after she'd added Carol's name to their list.

"She belongs right under George, as she didn't know that Dr. Grady had other women in his life."

"But she did know that Jack was in the house."

"Maybe she would have killed him, too, if he'd woken up, but since he didn't, she just quietly went away after killing Dr. Grady."

"I suppose that's possible."

"She'd ended her marriage for Dr. Grady. That's pretty serious. Finding out that he was just playing with her must have made her very angry."

Fenella nodded. "She seemed to be taking it pretty well by the time we'd finished our drinks, but that might have been an act. I find it odd that she's trying to get back with her husband so quickly now that Dr. Grady is dead. I feel sorry for Robert, really."

"I'd put him at the bottom of the list of suspects. Everything you've said about him suggests that he's a nice person who had the misfortune to fall in love with the wrong woman."

Fenella added both names to the list in the places Mona had suggested. "What about Diane Jenkins?"

"You've barely mentioned her," Mona complained. "Does she have another man in her life?"

"Not that I know of, although that doesn't prove anything. I've told you everything I know about her. She was the one who suggested that we get a drink together, and I probably liked her the best of the three women at the pub. I haven't seen her since the murder, though."

"You should ring her."

"I don't have her number, and even if I did, what would I say to her?"

"Tell her you're sorry for her loss," Mona suggested. "You could offer to buy her a drink at the Tale and Tail."

"I could, but I'm not going to," Fenella replied. "I'm not interfering in a police investigation. It's bad enough I've seen two of the women since the murder without even trying. Daniel understands that it's all coincidental, but I'm not sure Mark Hammersmith agrees."

"All things considered, you should probably put Diane at the very bottom of the list, then. We don't know enough about her to properly assess the likelihood that she killed Dr. Grady, so we're going to have to go with your initial impression of the woman from the day you met her."

Fenella wrote Diane's name on the bottom of the sheet of paper and then pushed the tablet away. "The killer is probably someone else entirely," she told her aunt. "Dr. Grady could have been sleeping with a dozen other women and they might all have jealous boyfriends."

"You need to ask Daniel how many other women they've discovered."

"Except I'm not getting involved in the case."

Mona sighed. "You're already involved. Won't you feel better once the killer is behind bars? Until then, Jack is in danger."

"I can't imagine why. If the killer didn't know Jack was there, he or she still doesn't know about him. If the killer did know Jack was there, he or she chose not to kill him, which should mean he's fine."

Mona argued for a while longer, trying to persuade Fenella to call Daniel and try to get more information about the case.

"That's quite enough," Fenella said eventually. "I've made your list of suspects for you. Now I have to start thinking about tonight. I need to find something to wear."

"I already told you what to wear," Mona reminded her. "The red dress is perfect. Don't even bother trying on anything else."

Fenella found the dress in question and held it against herself. "It's very, well, red," she said doubtfully.

"Which makes it perfect for a Christmas party."

"I suppose." Fenella slipped into the gown and then stood in front of the mirror frowning at herself. Mona was right, of course. There was something about the dress that suggested Christmas in some way.

"Put your hair up and pin the red ribbon in the bottom drawer through it. It matches the dress perfectly," Mona told her.

With her outfit decided and the matching shoes and handbag found, Fenella could relax for a short while. She watched some television with a snack and then soaked in a hot tub before she got ready.

"Add a bit more eye shadow," Mona suggested. "It's a formal evening. You need formal makeup."

"I'm wearing a gown. That should be enough."

Mona sighed. "Sometimes I wonder if we truly are related."

"If we weren't, I wouldn't be able to see you."

"Are you sure about that?"

"No, of course I'm not sure about that. Every time I ask you questions about the afterlife, you make up your answers. Maybe you get to decide who sees you and who doesn't and it's nothing to do with me. Or maybe you aren't even here and I'm just talking to myself and making myself crazy."

Mona chuckled. "Any one of those things could be true. I'd tell you more if I properly understood it all myself. I'm still fairly new to being dead, you know. There's still a lot more I have to learn about how it all works."

"Can you choose who gets to see you?"

"I don't believe so. I was rather surprised to find that you could see and hear me, actually. No one who'd been in the flat before you arrived reacted at all when I talked to them."

"James said you talked to him in his dreams."

"Yes, and I have some control over how that works, but he couldn't see me when he was awake, even though he and I are related in the same way you and I are."

Fenella shrugged. "Perhaps it's best if I don't understand."

"That's what I've been saying all along."

"Where can Jack and I get dinner?" Fenella asked as she powdered her nose. "It needs to be fairly quick, and I'd prefer somewhere between here and Castletown rather than having to go out of my way."

"You can't possibly be considering takeaway food when you're dressed like that." Mona sounded appalled at the idea.

"That's why I'm asking you for advice."

"There's actually a lovely little place tucked away near the Fairy Bridge. It probably won't be busy tonight, so it should be fairly quick. The owner, Michael, was a dear friend. Give him my best."

"Sure, and then wait for the authorities to lock me up." She got directions from Mona and then checked that she had everything she needed in her handbag.

"Christmas at the Castle was always one of my favorite holiday traditions," Mona sighed. "I always used to go twice, once to see the decorations and then again on the last night for the auction. That auction is the main reason why I have so many boxes of Christmas decorations in my storage room. I'm going to have to pop down and have a look at the decorations later."

Fenella looked around her apartment. "These decorations came from Christmas at the Castle?"

"Some of them did, anyway. Max nearly always bought me at least one room full of decorations every year. He used to buy several for the public spaces in the various buildings he owned, and then he'd add one for me, too. He was incredibly generous."

"I didn't get tickets for the auction. I think I have enough Christmas decorations, anyway."

"You can bid on the rooms even if you don't go to the auction. They'll have sealed bid forms for everyone tonight. You can bid on other things, too. There's usually some stunning jewelry and a few trips to exotic places."

"I was already looking forward to it. Now I'm even more excited," Fenella told her aunt. "I hope Jack is ready and suitably attired." She headed for the door.

"I'll see you later," Mona told her with a wink.

🦂 I I 🦂

Jack was both ready and wearing his nicest suit. It was one that Fenella had selected for him a few years earlier. She smiled when he opened the door. The suit was still gorgeous and seemed to fit Jack perfectly.

"You look stunning," Jack said, sounding slightly surprised.

"Thanks," Fenella replied.

"I don't think I've ever seen you that dressed up before," he added. "You never wore dresses like that in Buffalo."

"We never went anywhere where a dress like this would have been appropriate."

"Yes, I suppose that's true," Jack frowned. "Perhaps we should have done more."

Fenella didn't bother to reply to Jack's comment. "Ready to go?" she asked instead.

"Yes, I think so. I'm rather hungry, though. You did say we'd get some food first, didn't you?"

"There's a little restaurant along the way that I'm told is very good. I thought we could stop there."

Jack nodded and then put on his shiny black shoes. Shining his shoes was one job that Jack had always insisted on doing for himself.

Fenella could remember more than one occasion when they'd been late to something because Jack had needed extra time to give his shoes an extra polish.

The drive south didn't take long in Mona's little red car. Fenella found the restaurant easily and parked right in front of it.

"It's very small, and it doesn't look as if anyone else is here," Jack said doubtfully as he studied the front of what looked like a tiny cottage rather than a restaurant.

"Maybe they aren't open," Fenella replied, even though there seemed to be lights on inside the building.

"There must be other places we could go," Jack suggested.

"I'm sure, but as I said, this one came very highly recommended."

Jack shrugged. "Are we going inside, then?"

Fenella hesitated for a moment and then nodded. Mona had never let her down before. She climbed out of the car and headed for the small door that was set in the center of the building's façade, with Jack on her heels. The door opened into a tiny foyer. The door into the restaurant itself was shut, giving Fenella no indication of its size or how busy it might be.

"Ah, you must be Fenella Woods," the man standing behind the podium in the corner of the foyer said. "No one else would be driving Mona's car, would they?"

"I hope not," Fenella replied with a nervous smile. She was starting to get used to total strangers knowing who she was, but that didn't make it any less uncomfortable for her.

"Two for dinner?" he asked.

"Yes, please."

He made a note in the book on the podium and then bowed and stepped over to open the door into the rest of the building. Fenella and Jack followed him into a tiny but beautifully decorated dining room. It felt cozy and intimate, and Fenella was almost sorry she was there with Jack. It would have been the perfect venue for a romantic date, which this most assuredly was not.

There were three other couples scattered around the room, which could only accommodate around thirty people at best. At another table, a single woman was sitting staring at her phone. Fenella and Jack were shown to a table near a large window that looked out at acres of farmland behind the building. Fenella also spotted a large parking lot. Clearly all of the other customers knew to park around the back of the building, something she'd try to remember if she ever came again.

A tuxedoed waiter was at their table before they'd even opened their menus. He read off a list of specials, each one sounding more delicious than the previous choice. When he was done, he took their drink order.

"I always suggest the specials, if any of them sounded good," he added. "Chef is at his most creative with them, and sometimes even the most popular ones are never repeated."

Jack insisted on ordering off the menu, something plain and boring that Fenella hadn't even noticed. After much internal debate, Fenella chose one of the specials.

"The fire makes it feel very cozy in here," Fenella said.

"Yes, I suppose so," Jack replied.

Fenella looked around the room and then gasped as she recognized the woman who was sitting on her own. Their eyes met, and even from a distance Fenella thought she could see Diane Jenkins blushing. Turning her attention back to Jack, Fenella did her best to ignore the other woman, but she found her eyes returning to her repeatedly for the next few minutes. When their eyes met for a second time, Diane seemed to sigh before she rose to her feet.

"Good evening," she greeted Fenella, nodding at Jack. "I thought I was just far enough off the beaten path here that I wouldn't see anyone I know."

"Sorry," Fenella said, even though she'd done nothing wrong.

Diane shrugged. "It isn't your fault. I should have known the island is too small for there to be anywhere truly safe."

"Safe?" Fenella echoed.

Blushing, Diane nodded. "I'm on a blind date, or rather, I'm meant to be on a blind date, but he hasn't arrived yet. I'm starting to think that I've been dumped before we've even met."

"Blind dates are the worst," Jack said. "Every time I go on one I promise myself I'll never do it again."

"You go on blind dates?" Fenella asked.

Jack frowned. "I've gone on a few since you left. I wasn't going to mention that, though. I don't want you to feel bad about it or anything. It was mostly work colleagues who insisted on setting me up with friends of theirs, that sort of thing. None of them worked out at all, though."

"Yes, well, this one isn't working out, either," Diane said. "I think I'm going to leave."

"I would have at least expected the man to text you and cancel, rather than just leave you sitting here on your own," Fenella said, feeling angry on the other woman's behalf.

"Yes, that would have been nice," Diane agreed. The words were barely out of her mouth when the phone in her hand buzzed. She glanced at the screen. "He's two minutes away and very sorry," she told Fenella.

"Good luck," Fenella told her.

Diane nodded and then rushed back to her table. Fenella smiled when, a few minutes later, a very handsome man in a nice suit was escorted to Diane's table. The look of relief on Diane's face almost made Fenella laugh out loud.

The food was delicious, at least as good as Mona had suggested it would be, and after chocolate mousse for dessert, Fenella felt happy and satisfied. Jack paid the bill as Fenella gathered up her handbag and got to her feet. She glanced over at Diane and then nodded when their eyes met. Diane winked and then turned back to her date.

"It wasn't bad," Jack conceded as they headed back to the car.

They arrived in Castletown just a few minutes after Christmas at the Castle had opened for the evening. Fenella found a parking spot across the street from the huge medieval fortress. People seemed to be arriving from all directions and Fenella was happy to see that the women were nearly all in evening gowns like her own. The uneven steps, worn down by centuries of use, were tricky to navigate in her heels, but she managed. After showing their tickets, Fenella and Jack headed into the castle building to take a tour of the decorated rooms.

"Welcome," a woman dressed in a seventeenth-century gown said. "Here are your voting cards. Score each room from one to ten and then write the number of your favorite room on the back of the card. It's all anonymous, but I do need to mark your tickets so that we know that you've had voting cards. We can't have people going through multiple times just to vote for their friends."

Fenella dug out the tickets again and handed them to the woman. She wrote something across them both and then thanked Fenella. "Oh, and don't forget pencils," she added, handing them each a small pencil.

"This is gorgeous," Fenella said as she walked into the first room. Everything was white, from the trees that lined both sides of the room to the lights that twinkled on them and just about everywhere else. Each tree was decorated in white baubles, aside from a single ball near the middle of each tree. That one had a name painted in red across it.

"Thank you," the girl standing in the doorway said. "The names on the trees represent lives lost to cancer. We're part of the island's largest cancer charity."

Fenella gave the room a nine on her card and then walked into the next room. After the white, the riot of colors there was something a shock. Each tree was decorated in a different color, and they moved in a rainbow pattern from the entrance door to the exit. There were toys under every tree and the walls were decorated with oversized puzzle pieces and board game tokens.

The woman from the children's charity who'd decorated the room was helping a handful of children write letters to Father Christmas at a table in the corner. Fenella gave that room a nine as well, before she and Jack moved on to the next space.

An hour later, the pair had toured all twelve rooms and Fenella had given every single one of them the same score. "They were all so beautiful," she said as she and Jack sat together on some folding chairs in the castle's throne room.

"I suppose, if you like Christmas decorations," Jack replied.

"I love Christmas decorations," Fenella told him. "Which was your favorite?"

Jack shrugged. "I gave them all fives. They were all fine, but none of them were spectacular."

Fenella didn't bother to argue. Instead, she mentally walked back through each room, trying to chose a favorite.

"Room five was the best," a familiar voice said in her ear.

Fenella jumped and then looked at Mona. "How..." she began, stopping when she remembered that no one else could see Mona.

"You can't give them all the same mark," Mona told her. "That won't help any of them. Make a few of the nines into eights, although I wouldn't have given room seven anything higher than a four, myself."

Fenella frowned. It wasn't any of Mona's business how she rated the rooms.

"I can't vote this year, as I came in without a ticket," Mona told her. "The least you can do is give me a say in how you vote."

With Mona egging her on, Fenella finished filling out her voting card and then got to her feet. "I'll just go and turn this in," she told Jack.

"Here, take mine, too," he said, handing her his card. "Is that all there is to this? Do we go home now?"

"There's food and drinks downstairs," Mona told Fenella. "The Islanders will be playing down there in a few minutes, too."

"The Islanders are playing downstairs," Fenella told Jack. "I believe there's food, as well."

Jack got his feet. "I'll go down and watch the band for a bit. I did enjoy them the other night, but I hope they aren't going to be playing nothing but Christmas music. I'm not a huge fan of Christmas music."

"Or Christmas," Fenella muttered. "You go and get some food and watch the band. I'll be right behind you, although I do want to check out the items on auction first."

"As I can't exactly bid on anything, I'll leave that to you. You'll find me sitting as close to the band as I can get."

Fenella nodded and then watched as Jack left the room. She checked his voting card against hers. Even though he'd said he'd given everyone fives, she found a few slightly higher numbers. He'd given room seven a zero.

"He has better taste than I'd realized," Mona said as she looked over Fenella's shoulder. "Room seven was terrible."

"Perhaps I should bid on the decorations from room seven," Fenella said in a thoughtful voice.

"Did you like it?" an elderly woman who was standing nearby asked.

"I thought it was ghastly. All those feathers and beads didn't say Christmas to me, either."

Fenella nodded. "It didn't feel very much like Christmas," she agreed.

"It felt like a teenaged boy's fantasy fetish den," the woman replied.

Mona and Fenella both laughed at the description, which Fenella was forced to admit was apt. "Okay, I'll lower my score for them," she said. "It was never going to get my vote for favorite, anyway."

The other woman nodded and then walked away. Fenella amended her card and then walked across the room to drop them in the large box in the corner. When she turned back around, she smiled as she realized she was alone in the spacious throne room. It was gorgeously decorated for Christmas, done by Manx National Heritage and therefore not a contender in the voting. She walked slowly around the space, wondering what life might have been like for those who had lived in the castle.

When she reached the door, she glanced back and was surprised to see a woman in an elaborate costume crying quietly in the corner. Where had she come from and what had upset her, Fenella wondered. She took a few steps closer to her and then stopped when someone else joined the crying woman. As it was Mona who was now patting the woman's back, Fenella could only assume that the beautifully dressed woman was also a ghost. Making a mental note to ask Mona about it, she turned and left the room.

Her next stop was the large room where the auction items were being displayed. Fenella walked past the cards that described the contents of each of the decorated rooms. She really did not need any additional Christmas decorations. That left rows upon rows of jewelry, electronics, gift cards, and vacations, with each item carefully described on a card at each display.

"We have forms for the auction items," a young man with a scraggly beard told her. "The current highest bid is displayed on each item so you can best judge how much to bid yourself," he told her, handing her a form on a clipboard.

Knowing she could afford to be generous, Fenella walked around a second time, determined to bid on a few items. The gift cards and certificates all already had bids in excess of their face value, something that confused Fenella. The various vacations were somewhat tempting, but they were all for two people or families of four. The ones for couples all seemed to be geared toward romance, and Fenella didn't want to take Shelly away with her if the prize included romantic dinners and "spa dates for him and her."

She studied a mobile phone that was being touted as having all of the latest features, but as she barely used any of the features on her current model, it seemed silly to buy anything else.

"Just bid on the necklace that you know you want and be done with it," Mona told her as Fenella began a third circuit of the room.

Fenella's eyes were drawn again to the necklace in question. It was a long gold chain made of interlocking links that suggested the triskelion of the Manx flag. She loved it, but it had already been bid up to a very high price.

"You can afford it," Mona reminded her. "Bid a thousand pounds over the current bid and you should get it."

Unable to stop herself, Fenella quickly worked out what that would equate to in US dollars. The amount made her eyes water. "Maybe not," she said softly.

"You'll love it and wear it all the time," Mona told her, "and if you don't buy it, someone else will grab it and put it in a drawer somewhere."

The idea made Fenella frown. The beautiful piece deserved to worn as much as possible. She took another good look at the chain and then wrote down her bid, two thousand pounds higher than the current bid. Mona chuckled when she saw it.

"I knew you loved it," she said.

After turning in her bid paperwork, Fenella went to find Jack and the band. The band was hard to miss, as they were on a large stage in the center of a spacious room. There were tables full of food along the back wall and a large bar on one side of the space. Dozens of tables with chairs around them filled the rest of the space. A single Christmas tree with flashing colored lights provided the only hint of Christmas in the room.

Fenella waved to a few familiar faces as she walked around the room, looking for Jack. They were mostly people she'd met while out with Donald. Donald Donaldson was a very wealthy businessman in his late fifties. Fenella had met him not long after her arrival on the island, and she'd been surprised when he'd asked her out for dinner. The pair had gone out several times after that, most usually to fancy charity events where Donald's attendance was practically required. On a small island, successful businessmen were expected to support local charitable endeavors.

Because Donald often traveled for work, and because Fenella was determined not to get seriously involved with anyone so soon after ending her relationship with Jack, the pair had done little more than share a few kisses before Donald had ended things. His excuse was that he was looking for more commitment than Fenella was offering, an idea that seemed foreign to Donald's reputation on the island.

They'd just begun seeing one another again when Donald's daughter, Phoebe, had been injured in a car accident in New York City. Donald had rushed to her side, and he was still in the US trying to work out how best to facilitate her recovery. He rang Fenella sporadically, sometimes sending flowers or small gifts in an effort to apologize for his absence. Now, as Fenella waved to yet another man she vaguely recalled Donald introducing her to, she wondered if their relationship was over. She hadn't heard from him in more than a week and she felt no inclination to reach out to him herself.

"There you are," Jack's voice interrupted her thoughts.

"Sorry, I got caught up bidding on a few things," Fenella replied as she dropped onto the chair next to his.

"I had a terrible time trying to keep a chair free for you," Jack complained.

Fenella flushed as she glanced around. She'd just taken the only empty seat at the table, and when she looked around the rest of the room, she couldn't see any other seats available.

The dark-haired woman next to her frowned. "My husband was going to sit there," she snapped.

"I told you that seat was taken when you sat down," Jack shot back.

The woman made a face at him and then turned and began an animated conversation with her other neighbor.

"I am sorry," Fenella said to Jack as words like "selfish" and "rude" floated past her from her other side.

"I was here first," Jack replied. "The table was empty when I sat down, so it should be up to me who gets the seats."

Fenella shrugged. "I'm surprised they don't have more chairs out, really. They must have known how many tickets they sold."

"I believe the band is a big draw," Jack said. "Perhaps if the band wasn't here the guests would be more spread out throughout the castle."

A moment later two men in dark suits began setting up additional chairs. Within minutes, everyone who was standing around was seated, and a moment later the band began its first set. Fenella was delighted when the woman next to her got up and joined a man on the other side of the room. That left an empty seat, which Mona quickly filled.

"I hope no one sits on you," Fenella said to her in a low voice as the band played.

"They wouldn't dare," Mona replied.

A few minutes later, as the band played a Christmas song, Fenella noticed Carol Houston sitting a few tables away from her. She was whispering in a man's ear and when he sat back in his seat, Fenella recognized Matthew Arkwright.

"When you said his name, I didn't realize that I knew him," Mona said, sounding amused. "Of course, the last time I saw Matthew Arkwright, he was only about seven years old. He's grown into a rather handsome man, really."

A dozen questions popped into Fenella's head, but she didn't dare ask any of them. Instead, she tried to give her aunt an inquisitive look.

Mona laughed. "My goodness, that's quite scary. I wish I could tell you lots of interesting things about him, but as I said, I haven't seen him in years. It was his father with whom I was friendly, but that was even before Matthew was born. Once Michael Arkwright married Angela, he was a model husband."

"How unusual," Fenella muttered.

"He still did business with Max, which meant we sometimes had dinner with them, but they didn't socialize all that much. Angela was devoted to her son. He was an only child, although I'm sure Angela would have welcomed more. We usually took the couple out for a meal, but once in a while Angela had a dinner party at their home. Matthew was usually tucked up in bed when we went, but I recall one occasion when he was still up. I believe we were going to the theater after dinner, so we were eating earlier than normal."

Fenella resisted the urge to roll her eyes at the woman. While she enjoyed hearing about Mona's past, none of this was relevant to Peter Grady's murder, and that was what she was most interested in at the moment.

"Yes, well, I don't remember thinking that Matthew seemed like a future murderer when I spoke with him that night," Mona said, seemingly replying to Fenella's thoughts. "He was only a child, though, so perhaps his murderous tendencies hadn't yet developed."

When the band took a break, Fenella jumped to her feet. "I'm going to check out the food," she told Jack.

"I don't want anything," he replied. "I would go and say hello to Tim, but I suppose I should stay here to guard our seats."

"There are plenty of chairs out now. You can do whatever you like," Fenella told him, not really caring if she got to sit again or not. What she really wanted to do was talk to Carol and Matthew.

Jack looked around and then shrugged. "We'll see."

Fenella headed toward the tables of food along the wall, making sure to walk a path that would take her past Carol and Matthew. She waited until she was just a step away from them before she did her fake double take.

"Carol? How nice to see you again," she exclaimed.

The other woman looked up from her seat, and after a moment, forced a phony smile onto her face. "Fenella, you do seem to turn up everywhere, don't you?"

Matthew stood up and held out his hand. "It's nice to see you again," he told her. "If you've had any second thoughts about investing with me, I'd love to share some ideas with you."

"Oh, stop it," Carol snapped. "This is meant to be a romantic evening, remember? You know I hate that you're always working."

Matthew shrugged. "You seem to run into Fenella everywhere, but

I haven't been that fortunate. This is only the second time I've had a chance to pitch my services to her."

"The answer is still the same," Fenella said. "You need to talk to Doncan Quayle, not me."

"I'd never let someone else handle my investments," Carol said. "I don't trust anyone else."

"So you don't have your money invested with Matthew?" Fenella asked.

Matthew looked amused as Carol flushed. "I don't have enough money to invest to interest Matthew," she told Fenella. "He's far more interested in women like you with millions in the bank than he is in my insignificant funds."

"You know that isn't true," Matthew interjected. "I've offered a number of times to invest for you, at any level you'd find comfortable."

Carol shrugged. "What I said earlier still holds. I don't trust anyone else with my money."

"Thus far Doncan has done a wonderful job with mine," Fenella told her. "I will be keeping a closer eye on things now that I'm more settled, but I can't imagine dealing with it all myself."

"Perhaps if Carol owned as many properties and other assets as you do she'd find someone she felt she could trust to help her, as well," Matthew said.

"In that case, of course I'd invest with you," Carol told Matthew.

He grinned at her and then winked at Fenella. "As long as she had money she could afford to lose," he suggested.

"Have the police arrested anyone yet?" Carol asked as she blushed again. "For Peter's murder, I mean."

"Not that I know of, but I'm not privy to what the police are doing," Fenella replied.

"I thought I'd heard that you and Inspector Robinson were a couple," Carol replied. "I'm sure someone told me that you've been seeing one another."

"We're friends, but nothing more," Fenella told her. At least so far, she added to herself.

"Surely your friends talk about their work with you," Carol suggested.

"Some do, when I see them. I haven't seen Daniel in a few days, though."

"Of course you still have Jack visiting, don't you? How incredibly awkward," Carol said.

"It isn't awkward at all," Fenella told her. She bit her tongue before she could say anything nasty back. There was no way she was going to stoop to Carol's level, but she found satisfaction in moving Carol a line higher on her mental list of suspects.

"Perhaps we could have lunch one day," Matthew said, holding out his business card to Fenella. "You choose a place and I'll buy."

Fenella took the card and dropped it into her handbag. "I'm really not interested in investing with you."

"Then maybe we could become friends," he suggested with a bright smile. "I have very fond memories of your aunt. She came to dinner one night when I was about seven or eight, and I thought she was a princess or something. She was gorgeous. I still compare every woman I meet to her."

Fenella glanced at Carol, who frowned at Matthew. "I suppose I can't ever live up to your childhood memories," she said angrily.

Matthew shrugged. "I don't think anyone can. That doesn't mean I don't care for you, though."

Carol opened her mouth to reply and then shut it again. She shook her head and then picked up her handbag, stood up, and spun on her heel. Matthew and Fenella watched as she stormed out of the room.

"I didn't mean to upset her," Matthew said mildly. "Perhaps it's for the best. She was getting rather too serious, anyway."

"And you aren't interested in getting serious?"

"No, at least not with Carol. She's lots of fun, but not someone I'd considering marrying. She wants children, too, which aren't in my plans."

"His mother would probably love grandchildren," Mona said thoughtfully.

"I'm sure Mona would be flattered to know that you still remember her from so long ago," Fenella said, earning a frown from Mona.

"It wasn't that long ago," Mona hissed, "and I expect to be memorable."

Matthew laughed. "She was someone truly special. I'm sure there aren't many women in the world like her. If I met one, I'd marry her in a heartbeat."

Fenella remembered what Carol had said about wanting to be just like Mona. How much of that desire was driven by Matthew's attitude toward Mona?

"I am sorry that I upset Carol, really," Matthew told her. "She hasn't been herself since Peter Grady died. I do wonder if she had stronger feelings for him than she's willing to admit."

"Maybe she's just upset because of the rather horrible way in which he died," Fenella suggested.

"I suppose that could be the case," Matthew shrugged. "Let's just hope whoever killed Peter isn't targeting Carol's lovers, shall we?" He laughed, but it sounded forced.

"Does Carol have other men in her life?" Fenella asked.

Matthew shrugged. "I've no idea. I didn't know about Peter until they'd been seeing each other for several weeks, or even months. Carol can be very good at keeping secrets when it suits her. I only found out about Peter when she wanted to make me jealous."

"That doesn't seem to have worked," Mona said.

"Did you end up having to talk to the police?" Fenella asked.

"I did, actually," Matthew said with a grin. "It was fascinating, like being in a television episode of some detective show that I'd never actually watch. I enjoyed it in a very odd way."

Fenella wasn't sure how to reply to that, so she simply nodded. A ringing mobile phone interrupted the conversation. Matthew sighed and then pulled his phone out of his pocket.

"Yes?"

"Give me five minutes." He ended the call and then dropped the phone back into his pocket. "Carol has just realized that I drove and she doesn't have any money to pay for a taxi home. I'm not sure if I'm going to actually drive her home or just hand her taxi fare, but I need to go and do something."

"It was nice seeing you again," Fenella said.

He nodded. "I meant what I said about lunch. I would like to get to know you better. Bring Doncan if you'd prefer. I might just be able to persuade him to invest a few of your millions in one of my schemes if I work hard enough."

Fenella was trying to work out the best way to reply to that as Matthew turned and walked out of the room.

"Don't invest a penny with him," Mona told her. "I don't trust him, not one bit, even if he is still in love with his memory of me."

Fenella filled a plate with several delicious-looking items from the food tables. Dinner felt as if it had been a very long time ago for some reason. After grabbing a glass of wine from a passing waiter, she made her way back toward the table she'd been sitting at with Jack. He wasn't there and a quick look around revealed that he was talking animatedly with Tim. The table was now filled with strangers, so Fenella looked around for somewhere else to sit with her snack.

"Fenella? Come and join us," a familiar voice called.

She looked around and spotted Hannah Lawson waving at her. George was sitting next to her, scowling at the plate in front of him.

"Hello," Fenella said brightly as she slid into a chair next to the woman. "I wasn't expecting to see you here."

"George does a lot of work with Manx National Heritage. He's expected to buy tickets to a lot of their events because they put so much business his way," Hannah explained.

"And I have to bid on overpriced bits of rubbish in order to look as if I'm supporting their hard work," George grumbled.

"He's bid a fortune on a necklace for me," Hannah confided in Fenella. "He's really hoping he gets outbid, though."

"Which necklace?" Fenella asked, trying to sound only slightly interested.

"The ruby and diamond one," Hannah replied.

Fenella nodded. She'd admired it, but the current bid had had far too many zeros for her to even briefly consider adding a bid of her own to it. "It's stunning," she told Hannah.

Hannah giggled. "I love it, but it's awfully expensive."

"I could buy you something nicer at the jewelers for that much money," George said.

"Yes, of course, but isn't it nice to support the hard work that the various charities do?" Hannah asked. She put a hand on George's arm and waited until he was looking at her to smile brightly at him. "You don't really mind, do you?"

George hesitated and then shook his head. "Of course not, darling, not for you."

Hannah patted his arm and then sat back looking satisfied.

"How are you?" Fenella asked her.

"Me, I'm fine," she replied. "Why wouldn't I be?"

"Just making conversation," Fenella replied. She turned to George. "We met at the café in the House of Manannan the other day, didn't we?"

He stared at her for a minute and then nodded. "I knew you looked familiar, but I couldn't place you. I didn't realize you knew Hannah, though."

"I didn't know I knew her either," Fenella laughed. "That is, I knew I'd met her, but I didn't know she was your girlfriend."

"How did you two meet, then?" George asked.

"We have some mutual friends," Hannah said quickly. "We only met in passing, once, but that seemed enough to warrant letting Fenella sit with us, as there aren't many empty seats."

"When we met, George told me that you'd been spending a lot of time with the police," Fenella said. "I hope everything is okay."

Hannah frowned. "It's fine. Some time back, I was briefly involved with a man who ended up getting himself murdered. The police just wanted to talk to me about the man. He was involved with several women at the same time, so there's no shortage of suspects."

Fenella nodded. "Former girlfriends and their significant others, I would imagine," she said.

"They haven't questioned you, have they?" Hannah asked George in a joking tone.

"They have, actually," he said tightly. "I didn't tell you because I didn't want to talk about it, but yes, they have spoken to me."

Hannah frowned. "You should have told me."

"Why?"

"I worry about you, that's why," she said, rubbing his arm. "Talking to the police isn't very pleasant."

"It was fine," George told her.

Fenella sat and watched as the pair simply stared at one another for a moment. She took a bite of food and chewed slowly, waiting to see who would speak next.

"There's a lot going on without any words," Mona said thoughtfully as she settled into the empty chair next to Fenella.

Fenella nodded and then took another bite, determine to keep quiet until one of the others spoke. Another ringing mobile broke the uncomfortable silence.

"That's mine," Hannah said quickly. She grabbed her handbag and dug around in it for a minute. The ringing seemed to get louder as she frowned into the bag's interior. "Where is that phone?" she muttered, starting to pull things out of the bag and piling them on the table.

"I have it," George told her. "You left it on the table in my house before we came out, and I picked it up for you." He reached into his pocket and handed her the phone. The ringing stopped as she grabbed it.

She frowned and then clicked through a few screens. "I need to go and ring my mother back," she said, quickly getting to her feet. She disappeared a moment later.

"That wasn't her mother," George said morosely.

"Are you okay?" Fenella asked.

George just looked at her for a minute and then shrugged. "Sure, fine."

"He thinks Hannah is cheating on him and he's devastated," was Mona's verdict. Fenella was inclined to agree with the assessment. She was trying to think of something to say when Jack walked over and dropped into the seat that Hannah had vacated.

"Hello," he said. "I hope I'm not interrupting anything."

George shook his head. "Fenella was just keeping me company because Hannah had to step outside to take a phone call. She'll be back in a minute."

"The band will be starting again any second now," Jack told him. The words were hardly out of his mouth when Paul jumped back up on the stage and launched into a disco/rap version of "Jingle Bells" that had nearly everyone in the audience trying to sing along.

George just sipped his drink and stared at the door through which Hannah had exited. After a few songs, he pulled out his phone and stared at it. "Hannah's ready to go," he shouted to Fenella. "Bye."

She didn't get a chance to reply before George was gone. Jack frowned at her. "That was almost rude."

"He said Hannah was ready to go. I'm sure he didn't want to keep her waiting."

"Hannah is the redhead, isn't she? He doesn't seem like the type of man that a woman like her would go for," Jack said thoughtfully. "She's far too attractive for him. He must have money."

The band started up again before Fenella could reply. She sat back, feeling surprised that Jack had made such an observation.

"I told you he's a new man," Mona said in her ear. "He's improving in leaps and bounds."

When the band took their second break, Jack went with Fenella for more food.

"I enjoyed dinner," he said. "I shouldn't be hungry." As Fenella watched in surprise, he filled a plate with foods that she had never seen him eat before. She quickly piled a generous helping of everything she'd enjoyed from her first trip to the tables onto a plate of her own and then followed Jack back to the table they'd just left. While they'd been away, two of the seats had been taken. Fenella felt it was almost inevitable that the new arrivals were Bev and Robert Martin.

"You again?" Bev asked. "I know it's a small island, but really."

"It's nice to see you again, too," Fenella said, smiling a sweetly fake smile.

"Hello," Robert said. "You were at the café at the park the other day, right?"

"Yes, that's right," Fenella agreed.

He chuckled. "We don't get many visitors this time of year, but I'd remember you, anyway, because you know Bev. Are you enjoying Christmas at the Castle?"

"It's wonderful," Fenella told him. "I've never been before and I can't believe how beautiful everything is."

"Except for room seven," Bev interjected.

"That's what I said," Jack said.

Fenella laughed. "I didn't hate room seven. I didn't like it, exactly, but I didn't hate it."

"Too much color without any clear design," Bev pronounced. "It was done by a designer from across. I believe he was hoping to get a few commissions around the island once his work was seen. I don't think he's done himself any favors, though."

"My goodness, I wouldn't pay him to decorate a room for me," Jack said.

"I wouldn't, either," Fenella admitted. "Anyway, the other rooms are all beautiful, and the food is delicious."

"They did a good job on the food," Robert said. "I had a hand in developing the menu. We needed lots of simple things that could be kept warm or eaten at room temperature. Christmas at the Castle has been around for a long time, and we try to introduce at least a few new food items every year. A few things have always been on the menu, like the mince pies. You can't have a Christmas party of any kind without mince pies."

Fenella nodded, even though the tiny pastry shells filled with mincemeat weren't at all to her taste. Jack had taken one, but he hadn't tried it yet. She was looking forward to his reaction when he finally bit into it.

"Have you heard anything about Peter yet?" Bev asked in a low voice.

"Not a thing," Fenella told her.

"We were hoping the police would find the killer fairly quickly," Robert said. "Neither of us is sleeping well knowing that there's a murderer loose on the island."

"Unless he or she went across or elsewhere," Bev suggested. "Maybe someone from Liverpool came over and killed him and then simply went home."

"You keep saying that," Robert sighed. "I hope you're right, although I feel guilty for feeling that way. I don't wish anything bad on the good people of Liverpool, obviously, but I'd rather the killer was there than here."

"I'm sure we all feel that way," Fenella assured him.

"Are the police looking into Peter's life in Liverpool?" Bev asked.

"They must be," Fenella replied.

"I wondered if, because he died here, they were assuming his death was tied to something or someone on the island," she explained.

"I've been involved in police investigations before. They'll be looking at every possible motive from every imaginable angle," Fenella told her. "I'm sure they have officers in Liverpool looking into his life there in the same way they'll be investigating his life here. They'll be able to check flights and ferry records, too."

"Will they?" Bev asked, suddenly looking nervous.

"I believe so," Fenella replied.

"Great," Bev said weakly.

"You've gone pale," Robert told his wife. "Are you okay?"

She nodded and then shrugged. "If the police are checking ferry records, they'll find out soon enough. I went to Liverpool a fortnight ago to see Peter," she told him.

Robert frowned. "You said that you'd told me everything," he said with a sigh. "You promised no more lies, too."

"I have told you everything," Bev protested. "I went across to meet him, but he never showed up."

"Tell me the whole story," Robert said sternly.

Mona slid into an empty chair as Bev cleared her throat. "Peter texted that he was coming back to the island for Christmas, but that he wasn't going to get here until later in December. He said he didn't want to wait that long to see me and invited me to come over to spend some time with him in Liverpool."

"And you went running to him," Robert muttered.

"I was infatuated," Bev said. "I've admitted that several times. Peter was smart and funny and gorgeous and he managed to convince me that he thought we were perfect together. I felt swept off my feet and, well, I did stupid things. I can only apologize so many times, but I will keep doing it, because I am incredibly sorry."

"Tell us the rest of the story," Mona demanded.

Fenella frowned at the woman and then remembered that no one else could hear her. It was just as well.

"What happened in Liverpool, then?" Robert asked tiredly.

"I took the ferry over and checked into the hotel that Peter had booked," Bev told him, staring at the table, her cheeks bright red. "It was a huge room with a balcony and everything. I've never been anywhere that nice before."

Robert frowned. "I've been saving to take you on a belated honeymoon, you know that, but with all of my mother's problems, well, it's difficult."

Bev nodded. "I know, and I love you for taking care of your mother. We'll get our honeymoon one day."

"What happened when Peter arrived, then, or don't I want to know?" Robert asked.

"That's just it, he never arrived. He texted not long after I got there and said he was busy with something and that I should order room service and then get some sleep. He told me he'd be there when I woke up in the morning, but then he wasn't. Instead, I got another text message, telling me that he'd unexpectedly been asked to teach a seminar or something, but that he'd see me at six. I spent the day wandering around Liverpool, wondering what I was doing and feeling guilty. By the time I got back to the hotel, I'd decided to come home. I packed my things and sent Peter a text to let him know. I took the late ferry back to the island and never even saw Peter."

Robert looked at her for a minute and then shrugged. "I don't know whether to believe you or not."

"I'm sorry," she said. "I'm telling the truth, though."

"You need to tell the police all of that," Fenella said. "It will help them work out where Dr. Grady was and when, at least."

"I already told them," Bev replied. "The only thing I didn't tell them was that I saw someone I know on the ferry."

"Who?" Fenella asked.

"That's not strictly true," Bev corrected herself. "I didn't know her at the time, but I met her later, at Peter's house."

"Who?" Mona shouted.

"Which woman?" Fenella asked.

"Diane," Bev replied. "I didn't know her at the time, but I noticed her because she was arguing with her traveling companion. The argument seemed to get quite heated until she noticed that everyone in the room was staring at her. Then she stopped talking and simply sat and stared out the window for the rest of the journey."

"Tell me about her traveling companion," Fenella said.

"He was probably forty, with dark hair and glasses. I don't really remember much about him except he was really angry with Diane, although I didn't know that was her name at the time."

"Could you hear any of the argument?" Fenella asked.

Bev flushed. "Everyone in the room heard part of it," she said. "The man said something about wanting to spend time with her and her disappearing for almost the entire weekend. Then she said something about needing to have time to herself."

"Diane was with Peter," Mona said excitedly.

Fenella really wanted to discuss the possibility, but she couldn't, not at the moment. "Was that all?" she asked Bev.

"Then he said something about having trust issues, and Diane laughed and made some comment about not having enough time to go off, meet someone, start an affair, and then get back to him in time for breakfast." Bev started at Fenella for a minute and then drew a deep breath. "You don't think she was with Peter for some of the weekend, do you?" she asked.

"I have no idea, but I'm sure the police would like to hear all of this," Fenella told her. "You should call them right away."

"When we get home," Robert said.

Fenella wanted to argue, but Bev patted her hand. "I'll ring them the minute we get home," she promised. "I should be grateful to Diane if she was with Peter that weekend, since she saved me from, well, getting even more involved with him, but mostly I want to help the police solve Peter's murder so that Robert and I can move on with our lives."

"Do you remember anything else about the fight or the man with Diane on the ferry?" Fenella asked.

Bev sat back and looked thoughtful. "He tried to talk to her a few more times during the journey, but she wouldn't speak to him. Eventually, he began to apologize for doubting her and said something about taking her away somewhere nicer than Liverpool. Diane didn't even look at him, though."

"I wonder who he was," Fenella said softly.

"He wasn't anyone I've ever seen before," Bev said. "I don't even know if he was Manx or was from across."

"Hopefully, the police will be able to track him down," Jack said.

"It sounds as if he might have had a motive for murdering Peter Grady," Robert said. "They seem to think that I had one, after all."

"You wouldn't hurt a fly," Bev said softly. "I told them that, too."

Robert nodded. "When you left me, I thought about killing myself, but I never thought about killing anyone else."

Bev flushed and then sat up straighter in her seat. "I'm such an idiot," she sighed. "I can't believe what I put you through. You shouldn't be giving me another chance. You should run away and find yourself a better woman."

Robert took her hand and squeezed it tightly. "I'm not sure we're going to be able to work this out," he told her, "but I'm willing to try if you are."

"I am," she whispered with tears in her eyes.

Robert nodded. "Let's go home and ring the police. Maybe this will be the clue they need to wrap up the case."

The pair walked out of the room as the band began their third set. Fenella sat back in her seat and tried to think as the band played a few of their own songs, some traditional Manx tunes, and a string of Christmas favorites. When they were done, Fenella joined everyone else in giving them a huge round of applause.

"That was fun," Jack said as he and Fenella joined the mass exodus toward the door when the band finished. "I need to do this sort of thing more often."

"I should have dragged you out more when we were together," Fenella said with a sigh.

"I should have dragged you out more when we were together," he countered. "We were both too lackadaisical. If I ever have the good fortune to fall in love again, I won't make the same mistake."

Fenella nodded. She felt the same way about her own future relationships, if they ever happened. "We had fun," she reminded Jack.

"Yes, we did," he agreed. He reached over and took her hand, giving it an affectionate squeeze. She squeezed back and then let him hold her hand all the way to the car. The drive back to Douglas didn't seem to take any time at all.

"Do you want to come in for a short while?" Jack asked as Fenella pulled into the driveway on Poppy Drive.

She hesitated, glancing toward Daniel's house. "I should call Daniel and tell him about everything that happened at Christmas at the Castle," she said.

"Call him from here. Maybe he can just come over and hear everything from both of us at the same time," Jack suggested.

Fenella nodded. "That makes sense."

She followed Jack to the door. As he was digging for his keys, she heard another door open behind them. Daniel waved as he locked his door and then crossed the road.

"I hope I'm not interrupting anything," he said as he approached.

"We were just about to call you," Fenella told him. "I think we saw just about every suspect in the case tonight, well, every suspect that I know of, anyway."

Daniel grinned at her. "If you were anyone else, I'd be surprised, but as it's you, I'm just eager to hear what you learned."

"Come in," Jack invited him. "I'll put coffee on."

Jack led them into the kitchen where, true to his word, he started a pot of coffee without asking Fenella for any help. Daniel sat down at the table and pulled out a notebook while Fenella found a packet of cookies and opened them.

"I need the sugar rush," she explained as she grabbed a few cookies. "Help yourself."

Daniel took one and nibbled his way through it while they all waited for the coffee to brew. Once Jack had filled cups for all of them, he sat down next to Fenella. "We should start with dinner, shouldn't we?" he asked Fenella. "That's where we saw Diane."

An hour later, the pair had just about finished recounting the conversation that they'd had with Bev and Robert. Daniel was taking notes as quickly as he could, shaking his head slightly with each new revelation.

"Quite an evening," he said when Fenella finished. "I need to ring Mark and pass all of this along to him. I think the first priority is talking to Bev again."

"She said she was going to get in touch with the police. I expected her to call someone right away," Fenella said.

"She may have rung someone who hasn't yet worked out the significance of what she's sharing. I'll talk to Mark and then one of us will go and interview both Bev and Robert," Daniel replied.

Fenella walked Daniel to the door while Jack started clearing up the coffee cups and the half-eaten packet of cookies.

"I wish I knew your secret," Daniel said in the doorway. "I only ever see suspects, or rather witnesses, when I hunt them down. You find them everywhere you go."

"It's a small island, and with Jack here, I'm out and about all the time. You're busy working, rather than sightseeing."

Daniel nodded, but he didn't look convinced. He glanced back toward the kitchen and then leaned in close to Fenella. "Is everything going okay with you and Jack? He seems like a nice guy, really."

"Things are going well. He's, well, he's mellowed some since he's been here. Maybe he just needed a vacation for the last ten years. Anyway, he seems to have accepted that we aren't getting back together and now we're just enjoying seeing the sights together."

"When does he leave?"

"Not until the middle of January, but you're coming for Christmas dinner, aren't you? I can't quite believe it's Christmas in two days."

"Yes, tomorrow is Christmas Eve and I still haven't done any shopping," Daniel sighed. "I'll have to send my sister a check to buy things for the boys."

"I would have thought that shopping for your nephews would be fun. I love toys."

"It is fun, when I have the time, although the older they get the harder it is to be sure I'm getting the right things. Apparently little boys who are nearly eight don't want cuddly toys anymore."

Fenella shrugged. "I wouldn't have the first clue what to buy little boys, but I think it would be fun to look, anyway."

"Nathan's birthday is in January. You can come shopping with me and learn for yourself just how difficult it is," Daniel told her.

"It will be fun."

"I hope so."

Daniel glanced back at the kitchen door again and then leaned down and kissed Fenella on the forehead. "Take care of yourself," he said in a low voice. "Hopefully, I'll see you on Christmas Day."

Fenella nodded and then watched as he walked back across the street to his own house. She shut the door as he was closing his and then made her way back into the kitchen.

"I should go," she told Jack, who was washing dishes.

"Tomorrow is Christmas Eve. What are we going to do?"

"I don't think we can do anything to stop it from being Christmas Eve," Fenella laughed.

Jack frowned. "That isn't what I meant and you know it. What are you planning for the day? What about our traditional Christmas Eve meal?"

Fenella stared at him. "What traditional Christmas Eve meal?"

"We always have beef stew on Christmas Eve."

"We do? I don't remember that at all."

Jack sighed. "When my mother lived in town we used to visit her on Christmas Eve. You do remember that, I hope."

"Yes, of course." And not fondly, Fenella added to herself.

"You always used to throw beef stew into the slow cooker before we left in the morning, and then we'd eat it when we got home."

Fenella tried to think back. "I remember doing that a few times," she admitted eventually, "but not every year."

"You did it last year. Hazel had that Christmas party at her new house, remember? You started the stew and then we drove over to the party for a few hours."

"Yes, but we only stayed for about half an hour because you weren't enjoying yourself," Fenella reminded him.

Jack flushed. "That isn't the point. The point is that we've had beef stew nearly every year for Christmas Eve. I thought it would be nice to follow our tradition again, especially as you're making a turkey for Christmas. We always had ham, remember?"

"I suppose I could make beef stew, or we could go out somewhere. I'm sure we could find it on a restaurant menu somewhere on the island."

"But I do love it the way you make it. It will bring back lots of fond memories."

Fenella didn't bother to argue. Jack had been trying hard to be easier to get along with in the last few days. Making a pot of beef stew wasn't that much work. They had to eat anyway, and now that she thought about it, finding a restaurant that could accommodate them on Christmas Eve might not be easy.

"I'll make beef stew," she said, "but first I'll need a trip to the grocery store. I still need to get everything for Christmas dinner as well. You'll have to entertain yourself tomorrow morning. I'll be shopping."

"Would you like me to come along and help?"

"Not unless you really want to see what the shops here are like when they're insanely busy. I suspect three quarters of the island's population will be shopping tomorrow. You'd be smart to stay home and rest."

"Can I help with the preparations, then?" Jack asked. "There must be lots you have to do tomorrow to get ready for Christmas."

"I'll have a few things to do, but not too much. I'll plan on picking you up here around one o'clock. Eat some lunch here and we'll have the stew for dinner. If I still have things to do for Christmas, we'll go back to my apartment. Otherwise, we'll find something else to do for the afternoon."

"That sounds good. I'm really looking forward to spending Christmas with you. I bought you something very special this year."

Fenella struggled not to make a face. Over the years, Jack's idea of something special for Christmas had run the gamut from anti-aging cream to socks with individual sections for each toe. He never kept receipts and always insisted that Fenella make use of whatever he'd purchased. The cream had made her face break out, which had at least reminded her of her teen years. The socks had just been too uncomfortable to stand. She'd blocked out any memory of what she'd been given the other eight Christmases they'd spent together.

"I'll see you tomorrow," she said. "Enjoy your quiet morning."

Jack nodded and then walked her to the door. "I really hope you like your present this year. I spent ages picking it out."

"I'm sure I'll love it," Fenella replied automatically. She was halfway to the car before she started to worry. What if Jack had bought her an engagement ring?

❧ 13 ❧

"What did Daniel say?" Mona asked when Fenella walked into her apartment a short time later.

"Lots of things, mostly along the lines of 'that's interesting' and 'how do you keep bumping into these people?' That sort of thing, really."

"We have to talk about the suspects again in light of all of the new evidence."

"You do what you like. I'm going to bed," Fenella said with a yawn. "I have to go grocery shopping in the morning and I'm expecting the stores to be crazy busy."

"Yes, they probably will be busy. You shouldn't have left your Christmas food shopping for the last minute."

"I have to pick up the turkey tomorrow, anyway, so even if I'd done all of my shopping last week, I'd still have to go to the store tomorrow."

"It would be much easier if all you had to do was get the turkey, though. They have them in a separate area. You could skip the rest of the store."

Fenella sighed. "You didn't tell me that part when you told me I had to order a turkey in advance," she complained. The idea of pre-ordering her Christmas turkey still felt strange, but Mona had insisted that pre-ordering was essential if she wanted to be sure to get a bird.

"They may have some available for customers who failed to pre-order, but they may not," Mona had said. "You know you want one, so you may as well get it ordered and be sure you'll have it."

Reasoning that it could always be frozen if she'd changed her mind about cooking her own Christmas dinner, Fenella had gone ahead and ordered her turkey in early December. Now she just had to remember where she'd put the order form with the receipt for the deposit. It was somewhere in the apartment. She'd find it in the morning.

"Meerow," Katie grumbled as Fenella switched on the light in her bedroom.

"So sorry to bother you," Fenella laughed. She turned on her bedside lamp and then turned off the overhead lighting, earning a tiny smile from the kitten.

"I think Peter invited all of his women to Liverpool that weekend and was moving between them," Mona said as Fenella washed her face. "What a horrible man."

"Maybe he only invited Bev, but Diane found out he was back and surprised him," Fenella suggested.

"What about her traveling companion? We need to hear the whole story. You should ring Diane and ask her to meet you for a drink."

"That's not going to happen. I'm not getting in Daniel's way. I'm sure he's going to talk to Diane once he's spoken to Bev."

"You need to add Diane's mystery companion to the list of suspects," Mona told her.

"I need sleep. The man that Bev described didn't sound anything like the man Diane was with tonight, anyway."

"Where did you see Diane?" Mona demanded.

"I forgot you missed that part." Fenella quickly told Mona about her conversation with Diane at the restaurant and about the woman's blind date.

"Interesting. I don't think we need to add the man from tonight to the list, but we should add the man from the ferry," Mona said when Fenella was done.

"We'll talk about it tomorrow," Fenella replied, yawning again. She crawled into bed next to Katie and fell asleep almost instantly.

"Seven? Already?" she asked as Katie patted on the her nose. A one-eyed squint at the clock revealed that it was indeed seven. Fenella shuffled into the kitchen and fixed Katie's breakfast. Arguing with herself all the way back to the bedroom, Fenella only just managed to convince herself to head for the shower rather than back to bed.

"The stores are only going to get busier," she reminded her reflection as she did her makeup. "Going now is the smart thing to do." Her mirror image stuck out its tongue, but Fenella knew she was right.

It only took her a few minutes of digging through drawers to find the missing order form. She read through it, happy to see that she'd ticked the box next to "early morning (7 a.m. to 9 a.m.) collection" for Christmas Eve. It was a good thing she hadn't gone back to bed. They might have given her turkey to someone else.

As she pushed her desk drawer shut, she noticed the sheet of paper on the top. It was the list of suspects in the Peter Grady murder. About halfway down the page in an old-fashioned script, someone had written "Diane's mystery ferry companion" on the list.

"How did she do that?" Fenella asked Katie.

The animal shrugged and then headed back into the bedroom. "Sure, take a nap," Fenella called after her. "You have to get lots of rest so you can drag me out of bed at seven again tomorrow. Tomorrow is Christmas, though. Maybe you could let me sleep until eight, or even nine. If you're really good, you'll get a present from Santa."

"Do stop shouting," Mona said. "Shelly will be able to hear you, although she's far too polite to complain."

"I was talking to Katie, but she's in the bedroom."

"Her bad manners are no excuse for bad manners yourself," Mona scolded. "I thought you needed to get to the shops?"

"I do. I'm going right now," Fenella replied. She slid on her shoes and grabbed her handbag. After tucking the order form into her coat pocket, she let herself out of her apartment, only just resisting the temptation to slam the door behind herself.

In her haste, she'd grabbed the keys to Mona's sports car rather than her own more sensible car. Too annoyed with Mona to go back, she climbed into the little red car and drove out of the garage. It would be difficult to fit all of the shopping she needed for both today and Christmas dinner into the tiny trunk, but she wasn't going back for the other keys.

Even though it wasn't quite eight o'clock yet, the grocery store was packed. Fenella was grateful to find that the shelves were fully stocked, at least. She worked her way through the produce department, trying to think of everything she might want for her beef stew and for Christmas dinner. She hesitated over a small bag of Brussels sprouts. Shelly had said that a British or Manx Christmas dinner wasn't complete without them, but Fenella had never cooked them before. She'd have to get Shelly to tell her what to do with the little green balls, she decided as she added them to her shopping cart.

Mona was right; the pre-ordered turkeys were being distributed in a different part of the store. Fenella paid for everything else and then took it out to the car. She loaded a dozen bags into the car's tiny trunk, which somehow seemed just big enough for everything. There was just enough room left for the turkey, Fenella thought as she shut the trunk and headed back into the chaos.

"I'll just get this for you," the young and incredibly cheerful girl behind the desk in the order department said when Fenella handed her the order form for her turkey. The girl was back a moment later with a large bag. Fenella paid the balance due on the bird and then carried it out to the car. It fit perfectly between the bags that were already inside the trunk.

"Everything about Mona is a little bit magic," Fenella muttered to herself as she turned the car toward home.

She had to make three trips from the car to the apartment to get everything inside. Unpacking seemed to take ages, and when she was done the refrigerator and cupboards were all nicely full. Now she just had to start the beef stew before she could have some lunch and then go and get Jack.

"Ring Daniel," Mona suggested as Fenella was slicing vegetables for the stew. "Pretend you're ringing to check his plans for Christmas and see if he'll tell you what he learned from Bev and Diane."

"I can't do that. Daniel and I talked about Christmas dinner last night. Everything is as arranged as it can be, what with his work and all."

"So find another excuse to ring him. We can't solve the case if don't know what Diane was doing in Liverpool while Bev was there."

"Her trip to Liverpool might not have anything to do with the murder."

"But it might be the key to solving it. I think the man she was with on the ferry has to be a serious suspect."

Fenella nodded. "I think he certainly needs to be considered, and I'm sure Daniel is taking a good look at him."

"I think you should move Diane up the list of suspects. She never mentioned her trip to Liverpool when you talked to her."

"Neither did Bev before last night, and Bev was going specifically to see Dr. Grady. Diane may have been going across for a dozen different reasons that have nothing to do with Dr. Grady"

"It's an odd coincidence, then, that Dr. Grady was back and that he'd invited Bev across for that weekend."

"I think it would be more odd if he'd actually invited both women," Fenella argued. "Why would he do that? He ended up paying for a hotel room for Bev that he never actually even visited. It doesn't make any sense."

"Maybe there was some miscommunication somewhere and he didn't mean to invite them both for the same weekend, but he did."

"From what I've heard about Dr. Grady, he was always juggling multiple women. Surely he wouldn't have made such an elementary and costly mistake?"

"Having invited Bev and paid for her trip, I can't see him canceling his plans with her for anything other than another woman," Mona replied. "The excuses he gave Bev about being busy with at work don't ring true to me at all."

Fenella nodded. "They don't to me, either. I worked for a university. It would be very unusual for a professor to be asked to do anything extra on such short notice."

"So there was another woman involved. We just can't be certain that woman was Diane. Her argument on the ferry, however, suggests that it was."

"Maybe she really did just want some time away from him. From everything Bev said about him, he wasn't very nice."

"And last night she was out on a blind date," Mona said thoughtfully. "That suggests that the man from the ferry didn't stay in her life for long. Only a fortnight ago they were on holiday in Liverpool together and last night she was out with another man."

"How long is a fortnight?"

Mona chuckled. "Two weeks. It's a lovely old-fashioned word, really, one that I'm pleased is still in common usage. No one uses sennight any longer, which is a shame."

"Sennight?"

"A week."

"Maybe because week is a better word," Fenella suggested. "There isn't a single word for two weeks other than fortnight, so I can appreciate the usefulness of that one."

"Sennight just sounds better than week," Mona sighed. "Never mind. It seems odd to me that Diane was on holiday with a man only two weeks ago and now she's out looking for someone new."

"Maybe they never made up after their fight on the ferry. Bev said Diane wasn't even talking to the man for most of the journey."

"Maybe you should ask Daniel about all of this."

"Maybe I should get some lunch and then go and pick up Jack."

"Oh, yes, do. It's so much fun watching him change."

"What are you doing to him?"

Mona chuckled. "Nothing, my dear. Nothing at all."

She faded away before Fenella could ask her any additional questions. The fact that Jack seemed happier than she'd ever seen him before would have kept Fenella from demanding more answers from her aunt anyway. She finished putting the stew together and switched on the slow cooker. In six hours they would have a lovely meal. A quick sandwich and an apple were enough to keep her going until then, she decided. Once she'd fed Katie, Fenella headed back out to get Jack.

Daniel's house looked empty as Fenella pulled into the driveway of the house on Poppy Drive. He was probably at the station or out interviewing suspects. Crime didn't stop just because it was Christmas Eve.

Jack had the door open before Fenella was out of the car.

"Hello," she said, trying not to sound worried as she walked toward him. "Were you watching for me?"

"I've just been thinking all morning," he replied. "What about Christmas cookies?"

Fenella shrugged. "What about them? They aren't a tradition over here. They do Christmas cake and mince pies for their dessert on Christmas."

"I'll admit the mince pie I had last night was surprisingly good," Jack said, "but it isn't Christmas without Christmas cookies. I can't believe you haven't baked any."

"I didn't really think about it," Fenella said, feeling surprised now that the subject had come up. "I suppose with you visiting and with the murder and all, the idea just slipped my mind."

"We'll have to buy some," Jack said firmly. "At least a few dozen of my favorites."

"Except, as I said, they don't really do them here. I don't think you'll find cookies in the shops, not like the ones we get at home."

Jack frowned. "At the risk of sounding like a spoiled child, I want proper Christmas cookies for tomorrow."

Fenella nodded. "Now that you've mentioned them, so do I. We'll just have to bake all afternoon."

"Really?" Jack asked, his face lighting up. "I don't want you to go to any trouble on my behalf."

"I'll be doing them for both of us, and for Shelly and Tim and Daniel, since they'll be joining us for dinner. Anyway, cookies aren't that difficult, they're just time consuming. We didn't have any firm plans for this afternoon anyway."

"I'll help as much as I can," Jack promised.

"I may need to go to the store again," Fenella sighed. "I don't know that I have the right ingredients for everything I'll want to make."

Jack locked up the house and then he and Fenella made their way back to Promenade View Apartments. Katie looked surprised when the door opened. She jumped off of Mona's lap and raced into the bedroom.

"I thought you were going to be out this afternoon," Mona said before fading away.

Fenella grinned to herself as she walked into the kitchen. Mona and Katie could pretend to dislike each other all they wanted to. She'd just seen proof that they loved one another.

"What do we do first?" Jack asked as he joined Fenella.

"I'm going to dig out my recipes, then we'll have to decide what we actually want to make."

A short time later they had a list of five cookies they wanted to make. "Now we need to see what ingredients we need," Fenella said. She had Jack read out the ingredients for each recipe while she checked her cupboards and refrigerator.

"We need to go to the store," she sighed when he was done. "We don't need a lot, though, just a few things. I think we'll try the convenience store next door rather than fight the crowds at ShopFast."

"You'll pay more at a convenience store," Jack warned her.

"I can afford a small splurge. It is Christmas."

Fenella was delighted to find everything she needed at the store that was just a few steps away from her apartment building. A couple of the items were even on sale, making them only a few cents more expensive than what she'd have paid in ShopFast for the exact same thing.

"Let's mix up the chocolate chip cookies first," she told Jack when they were back in her kitchen. "That recipe makes the most, so they'll take the longest to get through the oven. We can mix up the next lot while the chocolate chip ones are baking."

Jack measured and mixed and took trays in and out of the oven with an enthusiasm that Fenella had never seen before.

"This is actually fun," he said as another batch of hot cookies came out of the oven. "I should have been helping you for the last ten years."

Fenella bit her tongue before she could start an argument. In the early years of their relationship, she'd always invited Jack to bake with her, but he'd always found an excuse not to help. After a while, she'd simply stopped asking and done all the baking herself, delivering a box of cookies to him on Christmas morning.

Someone knocked on the apartment's door as Jack was taking one of the last trays out of the oven.

"Shelly, come in," Fenella said as she hugged her neighbor.

"It smells wonderful in here," Shelly said. "Like butter and vanilla and chocolate."

"It's all of that," Fenella laughed. "We've been baking Christmas cookies."

"I want to try them all," Shelly replied.

Fenella took her into the kitchen and handed her a plate. "Help yourself," she said. "We've far too many for just Jack and me."

True to her word, Shelly took one of each cookie. "Tell me what I'm eating," she said before she took her first bite.

"That's a traditional chocolate chip cookie," Fenella began. "I suspect just about every household in America makes those for Christmas every year. The next one I call chocolate ecstasies. They're not much more than lots of melted chocolate and chocolate chips held together by a tiny bit of flour."

Shelly took a bite and then moaned. "These are amazing. I want to eat them all, and I want the recipe."

"The ones covered in powdered sugar are snowball cookies. They're mostly butter and powdered sugar."

"Do you mean icing sugar?" Shelly asked.

"Yes, that is what it said on the bag in the store," Fenella agreed.

"Delicious," Shelly sighed. "What's next?"

"Spritz cookies. I make them with anise flavoring, as that was how my mother always made them."

"I thought your mother was Manx?"

"She was, but she was given the recipe for these by my father's mother. I've no idea where she got it from, but he remembered them fondly from his childhood, which means I remember them fondly from mine now."

"We'd call it aniseed over here," Shelly told her.

"The last ones are my favorites," Jack told her. "Peanut butter."

Shelly frowned and then took a small bite. "I don't really like peanut butter, but these are good," she said. "The flavor is subtle."

"I used to make dozens of different sorts," Fenella told her. "These are my favorites, though, and Jack's."

"I'd have been happy with chocolate chip and peanut butter," Jack said. "Although I'll eat all of the others, too."

Fenella and Shelly both laughed as Shelly reached for another cookie.

"They're very moreish," she said.

"Moreish?" Jack questioned.

"It means I want more," Shelly explained.

"What a wonderful word," Jack grinned. "I may have to start using that one myself."

"Did you just come for Christmas cookies or did you need something?" Fenella asked Shelly as the woman reached for another cookie.

"Oh, goodness," Shelly laughed. "I'd completely forgotten why I came. Tim is at my flat. He'll be wondering where I've gone. As you're making Christmas dinner tomorrow, we wanted to invite you and Jack to have dinner with us tonight. We thought we might go out for Chinese or Indian food, as that's about as far from Christmas dinner as you can get."

"I've already made dinner," Fenella said apologetically. "I put beef stew into my slow cooker this morning. There will be more than enough there for four, though, if you and Tim would like to join us."

Shelly thought for a minute and then shook her head. "No offense, but I think I'd rather go out with Tim, if you don't mind. Meet us at the pub later, though, won't you?"

"I suppose we could," Fenella said, glancing at Jack.

"That sounds like fun. I've never been in a traditional British pub," he said. "I'm told they're the centers of the local communities."

"The Tale and Tail isn't like any other pub in the world," Shelly replied. "We love it, and it's the center of our community, anyway."

"I can get a taxi back to Poppy Drive," he told Fenella. "That way we can both enjoy a few Christmas Eve drinks."

Fenella smiled at him. "That sounds like a wonderful plan."

They agreed to meet Shelly at the pub around seven before Fenella tucked a dozen assorted cookies into a bag for her and then let her out.

"See you later," Shelly said, clutching her treats tightly. "Now to sneak these in so that Tim doesn't see them."

Fenella laughed and then shut the door behind her friend. Jack had started washing the bowls and measuring cups when she got back to the kitchen.

"Wow. I wasn't expecting to find you doing the dishes," she exclaimed.

"A little voice in my head suggested it," Jack explained. "I don't mean to ignore such things, I just usually don't notice that they need to be done."

Fenella nodded and then looked around the room. Mona had to be there somewhere, somehow managing to whisper in Jack's ear. Wherever she was, she wasn't visible, though.

"Are you hungry?" Fenella asked when all the dishes had been washed, dried, and put away.

"I may have eaten a few too many cookies while we were baking," Jack admitted. "I'm not sure I'll ever be hungry again."

Fenella laughed. "The stew should be ready in about an hour. Maybe we should go for a brisk walk to build up our appetites."

The promenade was quiet as they made their way from one end to the other. Fenella told Jack all about the Summerland disaster at one end and the Tower of Refuge at the other.

"The island is a really unique place, isn't it?" Jack asked as they crossed the lobby of Fenella's apartment building.

"It is, yes. I don't think there's anywhere else in the world quite like it."

"I can see why you love it here. If I could find a way to move here, I'd be quite tempted."

"I should check my mail," Fenella changed the subject. She quickly checked her mailbox and was happy to find a few Christmas cards inside.

"I wasn't expecting one from Hazel," she said, frowning, as she and Jack boarded the elevator. "I didn't send her one."

"Send it now. She'll just think it took a long time since you're so far away," Jack advised.

Fenella shrugged. "I may not bother. It isn't like I plan to see the woman again."

Jack nodded. "Who is the other one from?"

Fenella opened the thick cream-colored envelope. The card had a beautiful picture of Castle Rushen on the front. The message inside appeared to have been handwritten by an expert in calligraphy. Under the standard "Merry Christmas and Happy New Year" message, a different hand had written another note. "Missing you. I'll ring you on Christmas. Love, DD."

Fenella flushed. "It's from a friend," she said, shoving the card into her bag. She should have guessed the sender's identity by how fancy the card was, she thought as she opened her apartment door. She couldn't imagine anyone else sending something that posh to her.

The stew was done cooking and it smelled delicious as Fenella spooned it into bowls. She sliced fresh, crusty bread and put that on the table with some butter before she joined Jack.

"It's wonderful," he said happily. "I wish I'd been here to watch you make it so that I could try copying it next year."

"I can give you the recipe," Fenella told him, "although mostly I just throw it together without measuring much. I can do that because I used to make it at least once a month when I lived in Buffalo."

"I'd like the recipe. I may even try my hand at making it one day."

Fenella laughed. "I'll write while we eat so I don't miss out any ingredients."

After dinner, they each had a handful of cookies. "I want all of these recipes, too," Jack said.

As she already had those written down, Fenella was able to quickly make copies of them on the printer in her bedroom.

Jack folded them carefully and put them in his pocket. "It's difficult to think that I won't be spending Christmas with you again next year," he said with a sigh.

"Perhaps you'll have someone new in your life by then."

He shrugged. "I'm not sure I want someone new. Maybe I'll try being on my own for a while. I've never really been on my own. My mother was always there until we started dating. Perhaps it would be good for me to learn how to look after myself."

Fenella stared at him, almost unable to believe what she was hearing. "That sounds like a good idea," she said eventually.

Jack nodded. "I've been telling myself all along that you and I were going to get back together. That's let me put off actually starting to do things for myself. It was easier, you see, but it was also lazy. It's high time I started living my life to the fullest and I can't do that if I'm sitting around waiting for you to come back to me."

If Mona had been in the room, Fenella would have demanded that the woman tell her exactly what she'd done to Jack. As it was, she could only smile at him and hope that his newfound enthusiasm for independence would continue once he was back in New York.

"What do you think of Colorado?" Jack asked.

"Colorado?" Fenella echoed, feeling confused.

"I've been thinking about moving out of Buffalo and making a new start somewhere else," Jack explained. "There's a university in Colorado that's looking for an expert in US military history. I might apply."

"Have you ever been to Colorado?"

"No, have you?"

Fenella shook her head. "I've never been anywhere near that far west."

"I'm tired of snow," Jack told her. "I know I said I didn't really mind it, but the more I think about going home, the more I dread flying back into winter."

"I'm pretty sure it snows in Colorado. Aren't there lots of ski resorts there?"

Jack shrugged. "Maybe. It doesn't snow in Nevada, does it? I'm not sure I'd like living in Las Vegas, but there was a school there looking for someone, too."

"Las Vegas? That would certainly be a major life change for you."

"You seem to be thriving since you've totally changed your life," he told her.

"Just think carefully before you do anything. Maybe try making small changes before you make any big ones. Moving to Las Vegas would be a huge change."

"Maybe I could move to Vegas and become a professional gambler," Jack said. "I could learn to play poker or blackjack."

"I think you need to slow down," Fenella said, starting to worry that Mona was putting crazy ideas into Jack's head. While she wanted him to move on and be happy, she didn't want him to go crazy and possibly ruin his life. "See how you feel when you get back to Buffalo before you start making any serious plans."

"You don't have any regrets about selling everything and moving halfway around the world."

"I was very fortunate in that I inherited a home, a car, and sufficient funds to support me so that I don't have to work. You'd be leaving behind everything you know to take a new job in a new city where you don't know anyone. If you hated the job or you hated the city, you'd have to move again."

Jack nodded. "I won't do anything hasty, but I am going to start looking at options. This trip has been eye opening. I feel as if I've missed out on a lot of things because I've always been afraid to do anything. Coming here by myself was a huge step, though, and now I want to spread my wings and do a lot more."

"I'm happy to hear that. After all our years together, I really do want to see you happy."

"Will it be okay if I still call you once in a while? I'd really like to run some of my plans past you as I make them."

"I'd like very much for us to stay friends once you return home."

Jack smiled. "What about that pub, then?" he asked.

Fenella changed into a dark green dress that she thought was suitable for the pub on Christmas Eve. As it was one of Mona's, it fit perfectly and there were shoes that matched exactly. Fenella found the handbag that went with the outfit in the drawer in the bottom of the wardrobe and quickly moved everything she thought she would need from her usual bag into the small green one.

"I'm ready," she told Jack, who was busy playing with Katie when she emerged from the bedroom.

Katie quickly dashed away, jumping up on the couch.

"I saw you playing with Jack," Fenella told her. "It's no good pretending you weren't."

Katie curled up in a ball and shut her eyes tightly while Fenella laughed. "I'll put your dinner and some fresh water out in the kitchen. When you wake up from your nap, you can eat," she told the animal. After filling the bowls, Fenella added a few small treats to the top of the food bowl. Katie deserved them for being nice to both Jack and Mona recently.

On the short walk to the Tale and Tail, Fenella told Jack all about the pub's history. While she'd mentioned all of the books, Jack still stopped right inside the pub's door, his mouth open.

"So many books," he said eventually.

"There are more upstairs," Fenella told him with a grin.

❧ 14 ❧

Shelly and Tim were already settled in at a table on the upper level when Fenella and Jack arrived with their drinks. Shelly waved at them as they made their way through the crowded room. There were four empty chairs around the table, and from the looks of it they were the only available seats in the room.

"Merry Christmas," Shelly said happily.

Fenella smiled. "Merry Christmas."

Shelly laughed. "I may have had a few drinks already," she said. "It is Christmas, though."

"Merry Christmas," Fenella said to Tim as she sat down next to Shelly.

"Yes, Merry Christmas," he replied. "I think this is the first Christmas Eve in years where I haven't been working. It doesn't really feel as if it's Christmas Eve."

"I'm surprised no one wanted the band at their party or event tonight," Fenella said.

"Oh, lots of people wanted us, but Paul wanted to take the night off, and Todd is away. Henry still hasn't come back to play since, well, since the events during Hop-tu-Naa, which means were couldn't put together much of a band. In the end, we all decided it would be nice to take Christmas Eve off this year."

"Lucky me," Shelly giggled.

Tim put his arm around her. "Lucky me, too."

"Did you see the T-shirts?" Shelly asked.

Fenella shook her head. "What T-shirts?"

"The pub had some T-shirts and sweatshirts printed with the pub's name on them. The L in Tale is an open book and there's a cat sitting on top of the word Tail," Shelly explained. "All the staff are wearing them and they're for sale if you want one."

"How did I miss that?" Fenella asked. "Of course I want one, maybe two."

A pair of new arrivals at the top of the stairs caught Fenella's eye.

"They look familiar," Jack said.

"That's because you met them both at Dr. Grady's house," Fenella told him. As the women looked around, Fenella waved.

"My goodness, it is such a small island," Diane said as she and Hannah crossed the room to the table where Fenella and her friends were sitting. "I just saw you last night."

"I saw her last night, too," Hannah laughed.

"Where did you see her?" Diane asked.

"Christmas at the Castle," Hannah replied.

"Oh, I wanted to go to that, but I forgot to get tickets, and then it was sold out," Diane sighed. "Of course, I was on the worst blind date of my life last night."

"It didn't go well?" Fenella asked sympathetically.

"Is anyone sitting with you?" Hannah asked. "We should sit down if Diane is going to start telling stories."

Shelly waved at the empty chairs. "You're more than welcome," she said. "We got here early and grabbed the table, and then suddenly the rest of the room filled up with people. I'm surprised no one has come over and asked to take the empty chairs, really."

As Hannah and Diane sat down, Fenella introduced them to Tim and Shelly. She couldn't help but notice that they both had drinks in both hands. Diane drained one of hers before she sat back in her seat.

"Remember when we had drinks that day, before Peter's body was found?" she asked Fenella.

Fenella nodded.

"Well, Hannah and I have become best friends since then, haven't we?"

Hannah laughed. "We both have terrible luck when it comes to men," she said. "So we drink together and commiserate."

"At least you have each other," Shelly said, raising her glass. "A toast to girlfriends, who are more reliable than boyfriends."

The four women clinked their glasses together and drank. Jack and Tim both frowned. Shelly leaned over and whispered something into Tim's ear that made him smile.

"You saw the man who met me last night," Diane said to Fenella. "He looked so nice and normal, didn't he? I should know better than to trust anyone."

"He did look nice and normal," Fenella agreed. "I assume he wasn't either?"

"His name is Stuart, and he probably is fairly normal," Diane sighed. "I mean, aren't most men in their early forties married with children?"

"He was married?" Hannah exclaimed. "You should have seen that coming."

"The thing is, we talked online for weeks, maybe even months. The first thing I asked him was whether he was married or not. After that, I asked him again about a dozen times, to the point where he told me I was paranoid."

"How did you find out?" Fenella was intrigued.

"It was just dumb luck, really. Things were going well and I thought we were really hitting it off, and then one of his work colleagues happened to walk in. We were talking happily about our plans for Christmas and he was telling me all about how he was going to be working for a lot of the day because he always volunteered so that other people with families could be at home, when all of the color drained from his face and he jumped up and nearly ran out of the room."

Hannah leaned across the table and patted her hand. "Drink up. You'll feel better when you can't feel anything."

Diane shrugged. "I'll feel better when I meet a nice, single man who is ready to commit and not hung up on his mother."

"What happened after he ran away?" Shelly asked.

"Oh, he came back eventually and told me some story about how he'd suddenly felt ill. I was suspicious, though, and I'd noted where the manager had seated the couple who had walked in just as Stuart had rushed away. As we got up to leave, I pretended to recognize someone at the table next to theirs."

"That was smart," Fenella said.

"It was even funny," Diane told her. "I dragged Stuart along with me and then stopped and got all pretend flustered when I realized the woman wasn't who I'd thought she was. Meanwhile, the man at the next table stood up and said a big hello to Jason."

"Jason?" Shelly asked.

"Turns out my dinner companion, who called himself Stuart Douglas, was really a man called Jason Kane," Diane explained. "He introduced me to the other guy and his wife as a distant cousin, but I wasn't having any of that. I just looked as confused as I could and said something like 'but Stuart, we've been having so much fun on this blind date. I was hoping we could go out again one day soon. You said maybe we could spend some time together on Christmas, remember?' That's when the work colleague's wife jumped in to inform me that not only was Jason married, but he and his wife have two little girls and a third one on the way."

"Goodness me," Shelly exclaimed. "The poor woman."

Diane nodded. "I suppose I should be thankful I'm not that unfortunate woman. Anyway, I told Stuart-slash-Jason exactly what I thought about men who cheat on their wives and especially on their children and then I stormed out while he was busy begging the other couple not to tell his wife anything."

"I hope they rang her immediately," Shelly said.

"Me, too," Diane agreed. "If I ever run into them anywhere, I'm going to say something, that's for sure."

"Why do men behave so badly?" Shelly asked Tim.

He blinked like a deer caught in headlights. "I'm not going to try to explain other men to you. I've never cheated in a relationship and I've been cheated on, so I'm very much on the wife's side in this one."

Jack nodded. "Me, too. If I had ever been lucky enough to marry and have children, I would never have even looked at another woman. I didn't look at other women when I was with Fenella, and we weren't even married."

Hannah sighed. "There is such a thing as being too attached, though," she said softly.

"Are you okay?" Fenella asked.

"I'm going to sound horrible, but I'm very afraid that George is getting ready to propose," she replied.

"And you don't want to marry him?" Diane asked. "I'd love to get married."

"I'll introduce you to George," Hannah offered. "He's a wonderful guy, really. He has his own business, makes lots of money, and he's very generous with it, too. I shouldn't complain, but I'm simply not in love with him."

"You should end things with him if that's how you feel," Fenella told her, mindful of what George had said about proposing.

"It isn't that easy. Every time I try to bring it up, he gets upset and emotional and I can't bring myself to do it. I only started seeing him to try to make Peter jealous, which was an impossible notion, but I didn't know that at the time."

"You'll be hurting him more by continuing to see him and giving him hope," Fenella said.

Hannah nodded. "I feel guilty about using him, you see, and I feel guilty when he buys me expensive presents. Then I start to feel guilty about hurting him and I end up staying." She sighed. "I've made a huge mess of it, really."

"Break up with him tonight," Diane suggested.

"It's Christmas Eve," Hannah replied. "I can't break his heart on Christmas Eve. That would ruin Christmas for him forever."

"What if he gives you an engagement ring for Christmas?" Fenella asked. "When you say no, that will break his heart."

Hannah finished her drink with a single swallow. "Maybe I'll say yes, just for a few days," she said thoughtfully. "Then I can break up with him in the middle of January."

"That's a horrible idea," Shelly said. "The poor man deserves to know how you feel. You should tell him right now."

Hannah nodded. "I probably should, but I can't stand the thought of hurting him."

"You need another drink," Diane told her. "That will build up your courage."

"I don't think that's a good idea," Fenella said. "George might just think she's drunk and not believe anything she says."

"Fenella makes a good point," Hannah said. "The two times I have broken up with him were both times when I was drunk. He simply ignores me now when I've been drinking."

"If you broke up with him twice, why would you get back with him?" Shelly asked.

"He came to my flat and cried on my doorstep," Hannah told her, "and, yes, I'll admit it, he came to my flat with expensive presents after both fights. I'm a struggling working girl. Diamond bracelets aren't in my budget, but that doesn't mean I don't want them."

Fenella pressed her lips together before she could say something rude. Shelly wasn't as kind.

"You're using the poor man for his money," she said loudly.

Hannah flushed and then looked down at the table. "As much as I hate to admit it, you're right," she said. "The thing is, he's a really nice man. He helps me pay my bills and he buys me things I can't afford. I've really tried to fall in love with him, but I just can't do it. I thought once Peter was out of the way that I'd finally be able to fall for George, but that hasn't happened."

"Did George know about Peter?" Diane asked.

"He knew I was seeing other people, but we both were when we first met. He knows Peter was murdered because the police kept calling me and I had to explain why. We've never actually discussed Peter, though," Hannah told her.

"I'm going to get another round in," Tim said, getting to his feet.

"I'll come and help carry everything," Jack said, jumping up.

Tim took everyone's drink requests and then he and Jack headed for the elevator at the back of the room.

"I think we've scared them away," Shelly giggled.

"I don't suppose either of them know any good men," Hannah said.

"Jack might, but they'd all be in Buffalo, New York," Fenella told her.

"I'd love to met an American," Hannah said. "America might be just far enough away from George."

"Just end things," Diane told her. "The faster you do that, the easier it is. It's like ripping off a plaster. Just tell him you don't want to see him again and then block his calls."

Hannah nodded. "I should just block his calls and not say anything. He'd get the hint eventually, right?"

Shelly chuckled. "I know you're just kidding, but that must be tempting. We didn't have that option in my day. I wanted to end things with John at one point, early in our relationship, but when he rang my house my mother answered and invited him for Sunday lunch. She thought he was wonderful."

"Didn't you?" Fenella asked, intrigued to hear something unexpected about Shelly's former husband.

"I did eventually, but not at first," Shelly explained. "I thought he was too nice when we first started seeing one another. He never gave up, though, and we were happy together for a very long time." She wiped away a tear and then shrugged. "Holidays are difficult without him," she admitted. "I'm probably drinking too much to compensate."

"He never gave up? I think that's George's strategy. Maybe I should give him another chance. How long were you married?" Hannah asked.

"Over thirty years," Shelly replied. "The thing is, there's a very fine line between being crazily in love and being crazy. If you're obsessed with another person, you'll call it love, but that other person might call it stalking."

Hannah nodded. "I think that's where I'm at with George. He's obsessed and it bothers me."

"Then you need to end things now, before it gets any worse," Shelly told her firmly.

"I tried to persuade Peter to pretend to get engaged so that I could get rid of George, but Peter even hated the idea of pretend commitment," Hannah said.

"I thought you said you took up with George to make Peter jealous," Diane remarked.

"Yeah, that was the initial idea, but things didn't work out at all as I'd planned," Hannah sighed. "In the end, Peter started avoiding me, not answering my texts, and I sort of fell into George's arms to make me feel better about the rejection. Seeing all those cars on Peter's drive that day was horrible. It looked as if Peter was having some sort of party and he hadn't invited me."

"But it turned out to just be a bunch of his girlfriends trying to find him," Diane said. "I've told the police, so I may as well tell you, Peter texted me that he was back on the island. That's why I went to his house."

Fenella gasped. Surely that was a vital clue in the murder investigation. She just wasn't sure why.

"Here we are," Tim said as he handed Shelly a drink. "It took ages down there. It's really busy."

Jack slid back into his seat and passed around the drinks he'd been carrying to Hannah and Diane. Tim gave Fenella hers and then looked around the group.

"What did we miss?" he asked.

"Nothing," Diane said. "We were just bashing men in general and bemoaning being single on Christmas yet again."

"I'd rather be single," Hannah said. "Instead, I'm going to be spending Christmas with George."

"Cancel," Shelly advised her. "Tell him you're sick or something, but don't spend Christmas with him. Otherwise, you'll end up engaged and then married before you know it."

"Even if I do agree to an engagement, I'll never marry George," Hannah said.

"I'm sure you mean that now, but I've seen other women get manipulated into all manner of things by men like George," Shelly said. "You need to get out while you still can."

"He's a good person," Hannah retorted, "and he treats me much better than Peter Grady ever did."

"You can't compare the two," Fenella said. "Peter Grady was a player who was only looking for fun. George wants to marry you. If you don't love him enough to marry him, you should let him go so that he can find someone else."

"Maybe I'll learn to love him. Shelly learned to love John," Hannah replied.

"Because he was patient and kind and never pushed me," Shelly said. "Can you say the same about George?"

Hannah shook her head. "I don't want to talk about George anymore."

"Let's talk about Peter," Diane suggested with an evil grin. "He was too charming and too smart and far too good at getting what he wanted."

"All of that is, sadly, true," Hannah replied. "I'm sure I was dangerously close to stalking Peter, which is probably why he stopped returning my calls and texts."

"That doesn't sound like Peter," Diane laughed. "He loved it when women were obsessed with him. I went through a short spell where I texted him almost hourly, and he always replied. We both knew he was seeing other women, but he was kind enough to pretend that I was the only one that truly mattered, at least when we were together."

"Well, he stopped replying to me," Hannah told her. "He texted me from Liverpool about a fortnight ago to invite me over for the weekend, but when I texted back with the details for which ferry I would be on, he never answered."

Diane flushed. "What weekend was that?" she asked.

"I don't remember the dates. I only remember that it was the last time I heard from him," Hannah told her.

"I believe I may have received the same text," Diane said softly. "I was even dumb enough to go over to see him."

Fenella had to bite her tongue to stop herself from mentioning Bev and her fruitless trip to Liverpool. She took a sip of her drink and then looked at Diane. "Did you see him, then?" she asked.

"Oh, yes, we spent a day and a night together, and then he made some excuse about a seminar and abandoned me," Diane replied.

"Maybe he invited all of his women for the weekend and then split his time between them," Shelly suggested.

Diane nodded. "That's probably exactly what happened. I made a huge mistake after that, though, when I was still angry at Peter."

"What did you do?" Hannah asked.

"I'd met this guy on a dating site who lived in Liverpool. When I agreed to go across to see Peter, I let him know I was coming, but we didn't make any firm plans. After Peter disappeared, I met the man for drinks and dinner. The next day, when I turned up for the ferry back to the island, there he was, my new boyfriend, ready to come and spend a fortnight on the island so that he could get to know me better."

"Awkward," Hannah said.

Diane laughed. "It was horrible. We had a huge fight in the middle of the crowded ferry before I finally took myself off to the quiet deck to get away from him. He followed, of course, and spent the rest of the journey apologizing and begging for another chance."

"Love or stalking, it all depends on your perspective," Shelly said.

Diane nodded. "After last night's experience, I've decided to stay away from the dating websites for a while. There must be other ways to meet men."

"I have a cousin who's single," Tim offered. "He's actually a really nice guy who got his heart broken last month."

"Last month? It might be better if he has more time to recover," Diane told him.

Tim nodded. "You're probably right. You're a beautiful woman, though. I'm sure I must know someone who would love to meet you." He pulled out his phone and began to scroll through it.

"What about me?" Hannah asked. "I mean, once I get rid of George, I'll be looking for someone, too."

Tim shrugged. "You both need to come to the band's gigs. There are always lots of single guys there."

"What gigs?" Hannah asked.

"I play with The Islanders," Tim replied.

"Can you hook me up with the lead singer?" Hannah asked. "He's gorgeous and so talented."

"He's not really looking right now," Tim told her. "He wants to move across, anyway. He's focused on his career at the moment."

"It's okay for him," Diane sighed. "He doesn't have to worry about running out of time to have kids."

Hannah dug her phone out of her bag. "When is your next gig?" she asked Tim. "I'm going to be there."

Tim gave her the date and location and she added them to her phone. "You should come with me," she told Diane. "It'll be fun."

"Sure," the other woman agreed. "Why not?"

Diane added the date to her own phone.

Hannah was staring at her screen. "I can't seem to stop looking at this every time I open my phone," she told Diane, holding the device toward the other woman.

Diane read the screen. "That is word for word the exact same message he sent me," she exclaimed. "Wait, let me find it." A moment later she showed Hannah her phone.

"What are you comparing?" Shelly asked.

"My final message from Peter is the exact same message that he sent to Diane," Hannah said. "I keep looking at it and wishing he'd replied to me."

"At least you've changed his contact on your phone," Diane said. "I still have him as an active contact, which he clearly isn't."

"What do you mean?" Hannah asked.

"His name is greyed out," Diane told her, pointing the top of the screen. "That's what happens when you change a contact to inactive or block the number."

Hannah stared at her for a minute. "Block the number?"

Diane nodded. "Or make it inactive."

Hannah clicked through a few screens and then looked back at Diane. "Peter's number is blocked," she said tightly.

"So he may well have replied to you, but you never got the message," Diane told her.

Hannah nodded slowly. "I never noticed that his name was in grey."

"You must have blocked him accidentally," Jack said. "I do things like that all the time. I once blocked my mother's number from calling my house. She was very upset."

Fenella wondered just how much of an accident it had been, but she didn't say anything. She was too busy watching Hannah, who was looking increasingly angry.

"I didn't do it," she said. "I'm pretty sure I know who did, though."

"George?" Diane asked.

"I lose my phone all the time," Hannah told her. "More often than not, he finds it and keeps it safe for me."

"If George blocked Peter after seeing that message, he may have unblocked Peter when he had your phone at other times," Diane said. "You should check deleted messages to see if there's anything there from Peter."

Hannah nodded and then scrolled through another set of screens. "He replied to me," she said slowly. "There are several messages, actually, all asking when I'm arriving so he can meet the ferry. Then it goes quiet for a while, but there's another message telling me he was back on the island. It was sent on the day he died."

"So George knew he was back, even if you didn't," Fenella said.

Hannah looked startled and then shook her head. "That almost sounds as if you're accusing George of killing Peter," she said. "He wouldn't have done that."

"You still need to tell the police what you've found," Fenella told her.

"I'll think about it," Hannah said. "For now, I need to go home. I'm not feeling very well."

"Ring George and tell him you can't see him tomorrow," Diane urged her. "Even if all he's done is block Peter from your phone, that's still out of order."

Hannah nodded. "Yes, I think I'll tell him I have a migraine and need to sleep it off. I'll ring you," she told Diane.

"Keep your phone with you at all times," Diane said. "I don't want George blocking my number."

"Now that I know what to look for, I'll make sure that doesn't happen," she told her. "In fact, I'm going to change the password now so that he can't get access anymore. I never should have given it to him in the first place, but I never dreamed..." she trailed off and then spent a minute on her phone.

"All set?" Diane asked.

"Yeah, I'm set," Hannah replied. "There were other deleted messages in there. Messages from friends and from my mother. I can't believe I never suspected anything."

"Stay away from him," Fenella said. "Call the police and tell them everything. You can probably press charges against him for what he's done."

"I don't want him to go to prison or anything, I just want him out of my life," Hannah replied. "For tonight, I just want to be alone to think."

"Ring me tomorrow," Diane told her. "Better yet, come and spend Christmas with me. I won't be doing anything special."

Fenella thought about inviting both women to dinner at her apartment, but cooking for Shelly, Tim, Jack, and Daniel was enough worry.

"I'll ring you," Hannah said. "Beyond that, I won't promise anything at this point."

Diane nodded and then they all watched as Hannah walked unsteadily toward the elevator.

"I'm going to make sure she gets into a taxi," Tim said, getting to his feet. Everyone sat in silence until Tim returned. "I put her in a taxi and paid the fare," he said.

"I need to call Daniel," Fenella said. "She might be in danger."

"George won't hurt her. He loves her," Diane argued.

"I think he killed Peter. If he realizes that Hannah suspects him, he might kill her, too," Fenella replied. "I'm going home to call Daniel."

Shelly nodded. "I think you're right to be worried. I'll sleep better knowing that Daniel knows everything that Hannah told us tonight."

Fenella stood up. "Sorry to break up the party," she said.

"I'm coming with you." Jack got to his feet. "I can get a taxi home from your apartment once you've spoken to the police."

"Don't be surprised if they want to talk to you," Fenella told Diane. "They may want to talk to all of you," she added, glancing at Tim and Shelly.

Shelly nodded. "I'll stop drinking now, just in case. In fact, we'll go back with you and start drinking coffee."

Everyone stood up and headed for the elevators. They'd only gone a few steps when a swarm of young people descended on their table with shouts of joy.

"We've made someone happy tonight, anyway," Fenella remarked as they rode down to the ground floor.

Diane got into a taxi of her own after giving Fenella her contact details. "I'm going home, but I won't go to bed, not if you think the police will want to talk to me."

"I expect they will, even if it is Christmas Eve," Fenella replied.

"Tell them to send a good-looking single officer," Diane told her.

Fenella laughed, and then she and the others headed back to Promenade View. While Shelly started a pot of coffee, Fenella dialed Daniel's mobile number. She never used it, but she felt a sense of urgency tonight.

"Hello?" Daniel sounded half-asleep.

"I hope I didn't wake you," Fenella said, glancing at the clock. It was after ten, so it was possible that he'd been in bed.

"What's wrong?" Daniel asked.

"We ran into Hannah and Diane at the pub," Fenella replied. "I'm afraid that George killed Peter Grady and I think Hannah could be in danger."

"Tell me everything," Daniel said.

He listened as Fenella recounted the evening's conversation, stopping her when she told him the bit about George blocking calls on Hannah's phone. "Wait a minute," he said.

She could hear him talking to someone in the background. "Sorry about that," he said when he came back. "I just rang into the station and asked that a car be sent to perform a welfare check on Hannah. Once they're sure she's okay, they're going to go and pick up George for me. Tell me the rest."

Fenella did as he'd asked, sharing everything she could remember from the conversation. When she was done, Daniel sighed.

"We were looking very closely at George already," he said. "There are issues with his alibi and I spent the whole day trying to pin that down, but I had a terrible time finding people. It's Christmas Eve, apparently."

"It will be Christmas in a few more hours."

"Yeah, and it looks as if I'll be working all day."

"I can push dinner back if you want," Fenella offered.

"No, leave it for half five. I'll do my best to be there."

"Come whenever you can, no matter the time," Fenella told him. "I don't want you to spend your first Christmas on the island at work for the whole day."

"Thank you," Daniel said softly. "That means a lot to me."

"I have Shelly and Tim and Jack here with me. Did you want to talk to them? They all heard the same conversation that I've just repeated to you."

"Ordinarily, I would, but for tonight I'm going to focus on talking to Hannah and George. I may need to get statements from them tomorrow, though, so warn them."

"I will. If you talk to them here you can have Christmas cookies while you talk."

"I don't know what Christmas cookies are, but I'd rather interview them there than anywhere else. We'll have to see how tonight goes. I need to ring Mark and bring him up to date on what's happening. Officially, it is his case."

"Good luck," Fenella told him.

"Thanks. I'll see you tomorrow. I'll ring first if I need to do formal interviews with anyone. Otherwise I hope to be there to celebrate Christmas at some point." He put the phone down before Fenella could reply.

"Is he coming to talk to us?" Shelly asked.

"No, he's going to talk to Mark and then to Hannah and George. He may need statements from everyone tomorrow, though," Fenella replied.

"I hope Hannah is okay," Shelly said. "She seemed really upset when she left."

"I can't imagine how she must have felt, learning that George had hidden those messages from her," Fenella said.

"She was feeling guilty because she'd just realized that she was playing games with two men and one of them killed the other," Mona said.

Fenella swallowed her reply with a sip of hot coffee. The others didn't stay for long. Tim offered to drive Jack home, and since Tim hadn't actually been drinking, Jack was happy to accept.

"What time should we be here tomorrow?" Shelly asked at the door.

"Whenever you like," Fenella shrugged. "I don't have any plans, really."

"I'll collect Jack on my way," Tim offered. "Midday, maybe?"

Fenella was happy to agree. That would give her time to relax on her own before her guests arrived, but not leave her alone for too long.

"I'll pop over when I get up," Shelly said. "Maybe we can take a walk on the promenade before the men arrive."

"Perfect," Fenella replied. She let everyone out and headed to bed. Her last conscious thought was to wonder what Jack had bought her for Christmas.

❧ 15 ❧

Katie kindly let Fenella sleep until eight the next morning. She was rewarded with a pile of new toys and several boxes of treats. "I didn't wrap them," Fenella said apologetically. "I know you'd have loved to get your paws on a pile of wrapping paper, but having seen what you can do with toilet paper and tissues, I decided against it."

Katie was happily playing with a fabric mouse when Shelly knocked on the door a short while later.

"Any word from Daniel?" she asked as Fenella opened the door.

"Merry Christmas to you, too," Fenella laughed.

Shelly flushed. "Merry Christmas. I'm sorry, but I woke up worried about Hannah."

"I know what you mean, but no, I haven't heard from Daniel."

Shelly nodded and then shook her head. "Merry Christmas," she said excitedly. "I have presents for you." She held out a large bag that was bulging with wrapped items.

"I'll get yours," Fenella said. "I was afraid if I put them under the tree that Katie would unwrap them."

Shelly laughed. "Smokey had a go at the ones under my tree, but they were all for her, so that was okay."

"Thank you so much," Fenella said after opening and admiring the gifts that Shelly had obviously carefully selected for her.

"Thank you. I love everything," Shelly replied.

"How about a nice brisk walk?" Fenella asked. "We're going to eat a lot later, after all."

"I hope so," Shelly giggled.

Fenella picked up the bag that had gifts for Harvey, Winston, and Fiona, just in case they bumped into them, and then she and Shelly headed out for their walk. They were nearly home again when Fenella heard Winston's familiar bark.

Both Shelly and Fenella found themselves carrying presents, officially from the dogs, back to their respective apartments.

"I'll be back in a few minutes," Shelly said at Fenella's door. "I'm covered in dog hair, so I'm going to change. Then I'll help you start Christmas dinner."

Fenella opened her apartment door. "Merry Christmas," she said to Mona, who was inspecting the pile of gifts from Shelly.

"Shelly has good taste," Mona said.

"I hope Harvey does, too," Fenella replied, opening the package he'd given her. She found a small electronic photo display unit. When she plugged it in she found that it was already loaded with dozens of photos of Winston and Fiona.

Mona clapped her hands. "What a clever idea. It will be nice to see the dogs regularly."

"I wasn't sure what to get you," Fenella said hesitantly. "I thought you might appreciate this."

She pulled the small, neatly wrapped package out of a drawer.

Mona looked surprised and then shook her head. "You'll have to unwrap it for me."

Fenella unwrapped the picture frame and held it up so that Mona could see the photo inside.

"It's Max and me," Mona said softly. "Where did it come from?"

"The *Isle of Man Times* archives," Fenella explained. "They had a thick file on both you and Max."

Mona stared at the picture. "They never printed photos of us together. Max, well, he insisted that they respect our privacy. It was complicated."

"You don't have any photos here. I wasn't sure why."

Mona glanced around the room. "Max bought me art to cover my walls. He didn't like being photographed and he never let me take any pictures of him myself, either. I never had a single photo of him, not even after all of our years together."

"Does that mean you don't want this one?"

"I want that one very much," Mona told her. "I wish it were from when we were younger, but as it's all that I have, it will have to do. It's perfect, really."

Fenella glanced at the picture. Max was helping Mona out of a fancy car and it was obvious that neither of them were aware of the camera. They were looking at each other, seemingly unaware of anything else.

"I'll put it on the mantle," Fenella offered. "Unless you'd rather I put it somewhere else?"

"That mantle is fine," Mona replied, still staring that photo that had captured something many years earlier.

Mindful of what Shelly had said about dog hair, Fenella changed her clothes. She was heading for the kitchen when someone knocked on the door. Assuming it was Shelly, Fenella pulled it open without a thought. The woman standing on the doorstep was a stranger.

"Fenella Woods?" she asked.

"Yes?"

"Mr. Donaldson asked me to deliver this today," the woman replied. She handed Fenella a beautifully wrapped box. "Merry Christmas."

"Oh, yes, Merry Christmas," Fenella replied, feeling flustered. The woman walked away before Fenella could say anything further.

"Open it," Mona said eagerly.

"I hope it wasn't expensive."

"Of course it was expensive. It's from Donald. I can't imagine how much of a bonus he'll have had to give that woman to deliver it on Christmas morning."

Fenella frowned. "He didn't have to do that. I sent his gift weeks ago."

Mona nodded. "Yes, after much debate about what to get him," she said dryly.

The wrapping paper was thick and difficult to tear. Mona looked as if she wanted to grab the package and rip it open herself as she waited. The box inside had clearly come from a jewelry store. Fenella opened it and then gasped.

The long gold chain was a lot like the one she'd bid on at Christmas at the Castle, but the links were both heavier and much more intricate.

"There's only one jeweler in the world who makes pieces like that," Mona told her. "Donald will have had that made especially for you."

"And it probably cost a fortune."

Mona named a figure that made Fenella feel slightly dizzy. "Try it on," Mona suggested.

"I can't keep it, not if it cost that much."

"You can't return it. It was custom made. Besides, you love it too much."

Fenella bit her lip and then slid the chain over her head. Mona was right; she loved it too much to even consider returning it. The phone rang as she stared at her reflection in the mirror.

"Merry Christmas," Donald's voice boomed.

"Merry Christmas," she replied. "It's gorgeous, but it must have cost a fortune."

"It was worth every penny if you like it," he replied.

"I love it," Fenella said honestly.

"Good. I'm hoping you'll be able to thank me in person soon. Phoebe has recovered enough to want to get out of here. We're looking at moving to London early in the new year. That makes a quick day trip to the island a possibility."

"I'm glad she's doing better."

"Yes, I am, too. She has a long way to go, but she's already exceeded her doctor's initial expectations. They don't expect a full recovery, but they're far more optimistic about the quality of life she'll be able to have regardless."

"That's great."

"And on that note, I have to go and spend Christmas with my baby girl. I'll ring you soon," Donald said.

Shelly was knocking almost before Fenella had hung up the phone. She admired Fenella's new necklace, and then the pair got busy with preparations for dinner. Jack and Tim arrived a short while later and they all ate sandwiches and Christmas cookies for lunch.

Fenella gave Jack the small pile of gifts she'd bought for him, and he handed her a small box. Her heart skipped a beat as she took it from him. It looked very much like a ring box.

He smiled at her. "I know what you're thinking," he said. "It's not an engagement ring, although I did consider that while I was in Buffalo. I'd have exchanged it for something else by now if I had bought you an engagement ring, though. As hard as it's been to accept, I know we're better off apart."

Fenella nodded, feeling unexpected tears welling up as she realized that Jack meant what he was saying. They were really finished, and as much as that was what she wanted, it made her feel sad, too.

She unwrapped the box and found that it was, indeed, a ring box. The ring inside was quite unlike anything she'd ever seen before. The thick gold band had several things inscribed into it. She laughed as she recognized the Buffalo Bills football team logo. Next was the Buffalo Sabres hockey team logo, and that was followed by the logo of the university where she and Jack had met and worked together. The last symbol on the ring was a tiny outline of New York State, with a small heart marking Buffalo's location.

"I hope that a little bit of your heart will always be in Buffalo," he said softly.

Fenella found herself crying almost uncontrollably as she slid the ring onto her finger. "It's beautiful," she said. "It even fits."

"I bought you a ring once before," Jack reminded her. "I wrote down your ring size then."

He'd bought her a thin diamond band on the first anniversary of their first date. It had been about five sizes too big, and getting it sized to fit had proven almost impossible. Fenella was hugely impressed that he'd not only made note of her ring size, but that he still had the note all these years later.

"I hope you really like it," he said. "I had it made especially for you and I can't return it."

"I really love it and you can't have it back, even if you want it," she told him. "I hope it wasn't too expensive."

"I can afford it," Jack replied.

The foursome played some cards and drank some wine together as dinner cooked. Fenella was just starting to pile things onto plates when Daniel arrived.

"I wasn't sure you'd make it," she said as she greeted him with a hug.

"George made it easy for us, really," he replied. "I'll tell you all about it after dinner."

"That isn't fair," Shelly said. "Tell us now."

Daniel compromised by sharing what he could while they filled their plates and then ate.

"When our patrol got to Hannah's house, they interrupted an argument," Daniel told them.

"George was there?" Shelly asked.

"Yes, George was there. One of the neighbors works for the local paper, so I'm not telling you anything you won't read in tomorrow's paper, by the way. He was taking notes from the house's front garden when the constables arrived."

"He should have rung the police," Fenella said.

"His wife was on the phone with 999 when the constables got there, actually. Anyway, they separated Hannah and George and brought them both in for questioning."

Daniel stopped for a bite of his dinner. "Take his plate away," Mona hissed. "He can tell us everything and then eat. Food is overrated anyway."

Fenella hid a laugh behind her glass of wine as Mona paced back and forth behind her.

"To keep the story as short as possible, Hannah confirmed everything you'd already told me, and then George confessed," Daniel said.

"Confessed to Peter's murder?" Jack asked.

"Yes. Apparently he intercepted the message announcing Peter's return to the island and went over to confront him. He had Hannah's keys as well as her phone, so he let himself in. He claims he didn't go planning to kill Peter, but he did take a knife with him. George's story is that when he found Dr. Grady in bed, he was enraged by the idea that the man was planning to take Hannah to bed. He claims he just lost his temper and lashed out."

"Poor Peter," Jack said.

"George had already told Hannah all of this before we arrived at her house," Daniel added, "and the neighbor already had it all for his story."

"They'll sell a lot of papers tomorrow," Fenella said.

"They sell the same number no matter what the headline," Shelly laughed. "No matter how lurid the story, the island's population remains the same."

The others asked Daniel a few questions, but after a minute or two the conversation turned to other things. Shelly had brought a Christmas cake for dessert, and Fenella even tried a bite, but it wasn't really to her taste. She filled a plate with Christmas cookies and then refilled it when everyone dug into them happily.

Tim and Jack insisted on cleaning up the kitchen and washing all of the dishes, jobs Fenella and Shelly were happy to get out of doing. With the chores out of the way, the little group took a walk on the promenade and then played more cards and drank more wine. Tim and Jack finally left not long before midnight.

"We're going to the pantomime tomorrow," Fenella told Jack. "I'm not sure what to expect, but I'm told it will be fun."

"Pantomime?" Jack repeated.

"Imagine the retelling of a fairy tale," Shelly explained. "With songs and dances, a man in drag, audience participation, and ice cream in the middle."

Jack looked confused. "I don't have that much imagination," he said.

Shelly laughed. "Tim and I are sitting with you and Fenella. We'll explain anything you don't understand."

Fenella let the two men out. Shelly was standing right behind her as she shut the door.

"I'm going to go, too," she said. "I'll see you tomorrow."

Fenella let her out and then realized she was alone with Daniel.

The little gift she'd bought him was in the spare bedroom, but she felt weird about offering it to him.

"I didn't want to do this in front of everyone, but here," he said, handing her a small box.

"I have something for you, too," Fenella said. She raced into the bedroom and grabbed the box. "It's just a little something," she told him as she handed it to him.

"Likewise," he said nodding at the box in her hand. "You can buy anything you want or need, so I got you something I hope you'll simply like."

As he unwrapped his gift, Fenella opened hers. Inside the small box was a small round enameled box. Fenella lifted it out and studied it. The picture on the top of the box was of Castle Rushen. She opened the lid and found words in Manx printed there.

"It's says Merry Christmas and Happy New Year," Daniel told her.

"It's exquisite," she said.

"I thought you'd like it. The castle is beautiful."

"Thank you," Fenella said.

Daniel nodded and then opened the box she'd given him. The leather driving gloves inside didn't look anywhere near as expensive as they had been. Fenella had ordered them from the US in the hopes that Daniel wouldn't realize how costly they'd been.

"They're really nice," he said, trying one on. "Warm and incredibly soft."

"I'm glad you like them," she replied.

"I should go. It's late."

Fenella nodded and then walked him to the door. He reached for the knob and then turned around. "What's the story with you and Jack, then? Are you thinking about getting back together?"

"No," Fenella told him. "Even he's realized we're finished."

Daniel smiled. "That might be the best Christmas present I've had this year," he told her. He pulled her into a kiss that made her forget about Jack, Donald, Christmas, and her own name. When he lifted his head, he winked at her. "Merry Christmas."

"Merry Christmas," she echoed as he let himself out.

ACKNOWLEDGMENTS

I truly appreciate my beta readers who help make each book better.

I'm always grateful to my editor, Denise, who corrects my mistakes.

Linda at Tell-Tale Book Covers designs the wonderful covers for these stories and I appreciate all of her hard work and dedication.

I'm especially grateful to my readers – you are why I keep doing this.

KITTENS AND KILLERS

AN ISLE OF MAN GHOSTLY COZY

Release date: June 14, 2019

Police inspector Daniel Robinson wants help with another cold case, and Fenella Woods is always happy to assist. This time, it's a fifty-year-old murder case that has captured Daniel's attention.

With witnesses and suspects well into their seventies, working out what happened to Mabel Gross all those years ago is going to be a real challenge. When Winston, the neighbor's dog, starts barking at a storage shed on the promenade, Fenella can't help but fear that he's uncovered a more modern murder mystery. Instead, she finds herself looking after an injured mother cat and a foursome of extremely active kittens.

Things are still somewhat awkward between Fenella and Daniel, but helping him with the case seems a good way to work toward a new beginning. Between looking after kittens and taking a class in reading old records, Fenella doesn't have much time for investigating the murder.

Can Fenella help Daniel solve such an old case? It feels as if nearly everyone is keeping secrets. How can she persuade Mabel's family and friends that now is the time to reveal all? And can she find good homes for the kittens and their mother before their antics drive her crazy?

BY THE SAME AUTHOR

BY THE SAME AUTHOR

Aunt Bessie Solves
Aunt Bessie Tries
Aunt Bessie Understands

The Isle of Man Ghostly Cozy Mysteries
Arrivals and Arrests
Boats and Bad Guys
Cars and Cold Cases
Dogs and Danger
Encounters and Enemies
Friends and Frauds
Guests and Guilt
Hop-tu-Naa and Homicide
Invitations and Investigations
Joy and Jealousy
Kittens and Killers

The Markham Sisters Cozy Mystery Novellas
The Appleton Case
The Bennett Case
The Chalmers Case
The Donaldson Case
The Ellsworth Case
The Fenton Case
The Green Case
The Hampton Case
The Irwin Case
The Jackson Case
The Kingston Case
The Lawley Case
The Moody Case
The Norman Case
The Osborne Case
The Patrone Case
The Quinton Case

The Isle of Man Romance Series
Island Escape
Island Inheritance
Island Heritage
Island Christmas

ABOUT THE AUTHOR

Diana grew up in Northwestern Pennsylvania and moved to Washington, DC after college. There she met a wonderful Englishman who was visiting the city. After a whirlwind romance, they got married and Diana moved to the Chesterfield area of Derbyshire to begin a new life with her husband. A short time later, they relocated to the Isle of Man.

After over ten years on the island, it was time for a change. With their two children in tow, Diana and her husband moved to suburbs of Buffalo, New York. Diana now spends her days writing about the island she loves.

She also writes mystery/thrillers set in the not-too-distant future as Diana X. Dunn and middle grade and Young Adult books as D.X. Dunn.

Diana is always happy to hear from readers. You can write to her at:

Diana Xarissa Dunn
PO Box 72
Clarence, NY 14031.

Find Diana at: DianaXarissa.com
E-mail: Diana@dianaxarissa.com